THE ELBERG
COLLECTION

THE ELBERG COLLECTION

Anthony Oliver

HEINEMANN : LONDON

William Heinemann Ltd
10 Upper Grosvenor Street, London W1X 9PA

LONDON MELBOURNE TORONTO
JOHANNESBURG AUCKLAND

First published 1985
© by Anthony Oliver 1985
434 54394 2

Phototypeset in Great Britain by
WILMASET, Birkenhead, Merseyside
Printed in Great Britain by
REDWOOD BURN LIMITED
Trowbridge, Wiltshire

❧ ONE ❧

"THERE WOULD BE a surviving widow," Webber said. "There always is."

"No, she went with him – a nasty accident – bizarre, one of the newspapers said at the time, and it was all of that. They were burnt to death on the beach at Le Bosquet. It's a small seaside resort in Northern France."

Webber drank some of his beer and waited. In the old days when they had worked together as a team, before Webber's premature retirement from the police, the pattern would have been the same. They had respect for each other and when one of them talked the other listened.

"It was Easter," Snow said, "Easter Monday. Apparently the sands stretch for miles there and they were in the habit of taking an early morning walk along them before breakfast. There was a witness, maybe more than one, but she was the one who gave evidence at the inquest or whatever the French equivalent is. A maid carrying a breakfast tray looked out of a window of the hotel where they were staying. It was a good day for Easter, she said, bright early sunshine, no clouds but a stiff fresh wind off the sea. She recognized Madame's white dress, lots of skirts with lace and a pretty blouse, very chic. They were a long way away, walking together arm in arm and leaning against the wind. Madame's dress blowing out behind her and Monsieur holding on to his hat with his free hand. The theory is that the wind caught up the glowing tobacco from his pipe and slammed the shower of blazing sparks into her dress. They tested what was left of it later. It should have been flame-resistant but it wasn't; highly inflammable, the police analyst said. She'd bought it cheap in Hong Kong or Singapore, somewhere like that; women can't resist a bargain. She was a flaming torch within seconds. He must have tried to smother the flames but in that wind there

1

wasn't a hope. Their arms were still round each other when the first people got to them. They were both quite dead, thank God."

"Accidental death."

"That's what the French verdict was. Burns and shock."

"Difficult to question, isn't it?"

"Nobody wants to—officially that is. The Foreign Office is satisfied and without them the Yard can't touch it, even if we thought the verdict was wrong."

The pub was in Strutton Ground, only a few hundred yards away from Snow's office in Scotland Yard. The back room was empty, small and dark with Britannia tables. A gas fire with imitation logs flickered on the walls and ceiling, both of which had been painted white thirty years ago; now they were stained dark brown with tobacco smoke. A wall clock with Roman numerals swung its pendulum with soft muffled thuds. Webber collected two fresh pints of bitter from the hatch in the corner and carried them back to the table near the fire. A ginger tom-cat sat stolidly in the hearth blinking at the flames. Webber had to step over it to sit down.

"So, unofficially, who's complaining—family?"

"The daughter, yes, she lives in Kensington. She sent a letter to the Commissioner and complained of poor service, not my department but I happened to get a read of it. I imagine she would have written much the same sort of thing to Harrods. She probably got much the same sort of reply too."

Snow looked older than Webber had remembered him. As Webber's sergeant when they had served together he had been full-faced with a straight back and thick brown hair. Now a detective inspector himself and in charge of his own squad in Scotland Yard, the hours of desk work had bowed him, his face looked tired and drawn and he was losing his hair.

A man with tattooed forearms whom Webber rightly took to be the landlord brought in a plate of ham sandwiches, the thick meat pink and succulent. Webber noted with approval that Snow made a point of paying for them, politely refusing the man's offer to have them on the house. Quite right; only a fool of a policeman would think of mumping on his own ground and Snow, thank God, wasn't a fool.

"As it happened I had a bit of routine in Kensington that same day," Snow said, selecting a sandwich with care. "A meet

2

with someone who didn't turn up so I had a bit of free on my hands."

"You went to see her," Webber said. It was a statement.

He had worked for so many years with Snow that he could guess the form before he was told. His ex-sergeant had never been afraid of sticking his nose in where, strictly speaking, he had no official business. Sometimes it had paid handsome dividends. Once or twice it had gone wrong.

"I've been thinking about something like this for some time. Yes, sure I went to see her. I could smell the money a mile off, John. I'd done a bit of homework and I was dead right. Real money. Rich rich. I played it safe. An unofficial visit, sort of courtesy call really."

"And you told her that if she really wanted the matter investigated her only hope was to employ someone privately."

"That's it. Because if she was up against the Foreign Office it *was* her only hope."

"And then you phoned me."

"And then I phoned you. Everything seemed to fit in for once. There have been other chances, things I couldn't touch officially, but there was no one I felt like trusting. If I'd known you were fit again I'd have spoken before."

"You haven't approached anyone else then?"

"No, there were one or two good detectives who got combed out in the old Countryman purge but I wouldn't risk working with them, too much grief. I couldn't believe my luck when your lady – Mrs Thomas is it?"

"Lizzie Thomas, yes."

"When she came in and chatted in my office."

"Chat much, did she?"

"Enough for me to see she wasn't a nutter. She didn't muck about. She thinks you retired too soon, said you ought to be working again and if I could ever put you on to a good thing she'd be grateful." Without malice, and only stating something they both accepted, he added, "Said you could be a bit lazy sometimes. Anyone who knew you as well as that I reckoned had to be safe. Bright too."

"Lizzie is very active," Webber conceded. "Didn't make an appointment I suppose."

"No, phoned up from the desk and said she was a friend of yours. Had to see her, didn't I?"

Busy with a mouthful of food, Webber nodded.

3

Snow wondered about the exact relationship between the little Welsh woman in her odd-looking clothes and his old boss. When they had first worked together Webber had been married to Lilian. The divorce must have been a blessing for him.

Without having to look at him Webber felt the question in the air.

"She came up from Cardiff to look after Doreen, her widowed daughter," he said.

Snow nodded and they both drank the beer slowly.

Then Webber did look at him and added, "Doreen, that's the daughter, married again and Lizzie stayed on in the village to look after me."

"A nice woman," Snow said, after some thought.

"She needs calming down sometimes," Webber said, "but yes, she's nice. She's a good cook—quality stuff."

"Make a good policeman's wife?" Snow ventured daringly.

The pause was long enough to make him wonder if he had trespassed too far on an old friendship.

Webber's answer was evasive.

"She'd make a bloody good policeman," he said.

From the saloon bar crowded with the street-traders of Strutton Ground came the muted hum of conversation, the sudden shouts of laughter and above that the sound of an old Beatles recording, 'Lucy in the Sky with Diamonds'.

"Goes back a bit?" Webber said.

"The governor here is very conservative, an old chum, he likes the old-fashioned tunes. He owes me a few favours; that's why no one will come in the back here, he keeps it cosy for me when he can."

"Handy for a chat with a snout."

"Yes, where would we be without informants." Snow checked his watch with the clock on the wall.

Webber knew he was disappointed in him. What Snow would have liked was a quick decision. The disappointment had taken away the expression from his face. Like all detectives he had learned the trick of disconnecting the muscles around his mouth. Without them the face is a blank. It is the mouth more than the eyes that reveal the thoughts and feelings, unless of course you knew someone as well as he knew Snow. Webber was sorry to see the barrier come down between them.

"If any of your top boys get on to it," he said at last, "you'd be out on your arse without a pension and you know it."

4

"Why should they? I run my own squad and I run it my way. You taught me that."

"A county force. It's not the same as the Yard."

Snow pushed his beer aside and leaned forward over the table. "Of course it's not the same! Jesus, John, we can't miss! God knows they don't come better than you. All these sod-awful little firms calling themselves investigators couldn't touch you on your own, let alone with the back-up I can give you. Criminal Record Office, computers, laboratories, the lot. Worth considering?"

"If they get a sniff of it," Webber said quietly, "they'll put a rubber heel on to you. One of your own men most likely. He'll watch you closer than a dirty film, and who'll pay for your kids' private schools then?"

"Who's paying for them now? I am, that's who, and we can't afford it, not without crippling ourselves we can't. Betty's a good girl, John, she deserves a few perks. I'll tell you this, matey, that posting from south of the river just about saved her sanity; mine too I think."

"Bad was it? Brixton?"

"Like a bloody war," Snow said. "Perhaps we could have coped, Betty and I, but not with the two kids. I'm too old for all that lark. Black power, white fascists, I thought we were supposed to be living in England. If I'd wanted that I could have emigrated to Africa."

There was silence between them and they watched the ginger cat make a pillow with its paws and rest its head near the fire.

"One day," Snow said, "I found half a joint in Alan's pocket. He said he'd accepted it to prove he wasn't a copper's nark. He's twelve; bright too. I felt sick."

He stood and shrugged himself into a creased raincoat.

Webber said, "And do people really pay that much for investigators?"

He watched while Snow connected all the muscles up around his mouth so that his smile was real again.

"They do if they are as rich as she is and if they want the best."

"But you admit it's a risk? For you I mean."

"What isn't? I might stop a bullet or some joker could plant a bomb under the car. It's not impossible. Against that? No, this is nothing. It's acceptable. I must go. Listen, think on't eh? Speak to . . ."

"Lizzie, is the name."

5

"Yes, speak to her. Here, this is my home number and address. If I'm not there Betty will take a message. Better still come and see us."

In the car as he drove home to Suffolk it was difficult to analyse his feelings or even to sort them into some sense or order. "Speak to Lizzie." Yes, he'd do that. Snow's phone call and summons to London must have come sooner than she had expected or she would have said something to prepare him for the shock. She had a shock coming herself.

"For God's sake, Lizzie, I'm supposed to be retired!"

"It might turn out to be a lovely murder and then you'd be sorry."

Mrs Thomas finished the washing-up and stored everything away tidily in its appointed place. She knew John Webber's kitchen as well as she knew her own and she knew John Webber too. Normally a mild and gentle man, when he appealed to God it wasn't seriously disturbing. It was merely an indication that she would perhaps have to work a little harder to make him do what was best for him.

He sat at the table and glared at her. There were times, and this was one of them, when he wished very much that she wouldn't interfere, that she would confine herself to her allotted duties of two hours' housework in the mornings and the occasional meal cooked and shared in friendship in the evenings. It had crossed his mind that he could have kept quiet about his visit to London and Snow's story, but you didn't lie to Lizzie even by omission. No, judging by the controlled energy with which she had washed up she was bent on a confrontation. She would probably win but it was worth a fight. She dried her hands and sat facing him, a plump Welsh widow dressed in an unsuitable dirndl dress and elastic stockings.

"Retirement is it?" The dark intelligent eyes regarded him thoughtfully. "Well, fair play, it's a tidy little village, Flaxfield. You could do worse."

"I was born here, you know that," he said defensively.

Experience had taught him that the more amiable her tone of voice and the stronger her Welsh accent the more reason there was to treat her with caution and respect.

6

Now she was smiling too and he waited with genuine apprehension. She nodded at him happily.

"Yes John bach, I do know that. So – give it, what? Six years? Ten if you're lucky, and then you'll die here too and that will round things off nicely, won't it?"

"I don't frighten that easily, Lizzie."

"Yes you do, you've gone pale."

"The village is full of old men, really old."

"Cabbages. Be sensible, John, you can't chase villains for thirty-five years and then settle down to grow roses, not at your age, you're too young."

"In five years' time I shall be sixty."

"We are both," she said delicately, "in the prime of life."

"I'm not fit."

"Arthritis never killed anyone, if you can dig a garden you're fit."

It was like playing tennis against a concrete wall.

"I was pensioned off early with a suspect heart."

"Nerves, overwork after a rotten divorce. That police medical board panicked. Dr Collins says you're fit for work."

Sarah Collins was his nice village doctor.

"You put that to her, did you?"

"Certainly."

"I see. What makes you think I would enjoy life any more than I do now?"

"You need pushing, you get bored but you won't admit it and you need money. That pension is a joke."

"I manage."

"So they do on the dole. If I didn't shop for you you'd soon see the difference. You wouldn't know a cheap cut of meat if you saw one, let alone know how to cook it."

"Am I ungrateful?"

"No, but you are lazy. It's a waste. I hate waste. I told you – you need pushing."

"You are quite serious?"

Why did he bother to ask. She never joked about things like this.

His first anger had gone, lost in what he was forced to admit was unmistakably a quickening sense of excitement.

Outside the evening light clung to the tops of the apple trees. Soon it would be April and then with the warmth of summer

7

would come the old man's garden chores he pretended to enjoy. They would contain his entire life. At the window she slipped her arm through his, sharing his view of the winter wilderness.

"What makes you think it was murder?" he said.

✌TWO ✌

"I DIDN'T SAY IT was murder. I said it might turn out to be."

"Why?"

From the hall where she was putting on her duffel coat and what she honestly considered was a matching hat, Lizzie called out "Come on! Time for a drink before they close."

Webber switched off the electric kettle with which she had earlier threatened to make tea for him.

The Bull was conveniently situated midway between Webber's cottage and her own. They sat in their own corner under the water-colour of the unnamed racing pigeon whose past triumphs had been long forgotten by even the oldest of the old men who lived in Flaxfield. The bird's head was cocked attentively, fixing a beady pink eye on the two old friends in the prime of life while Lizzie Thomas talked and ex-Detective Inspector Webber listened.

"Because it doesn't make sense, that's why."

"Go on."

She considered carefully, lips pursed, eyes brighter than the pigeon's.

"I don't believe it, that's all. I don't care how cheap and inflammable her dress material was, I can't see sparks from a pipe doing that. Can you?"

"It made more sense when Snow told it."

"Pipe sparks! All right, now listen. Even suppose she did truly burst into flames poor thing, right? So what did he do? He did the most sensible thing, he grabbed her, grabbed her fiercely and crushed her to him within seconds, and you're telling me that she went on blazing until they were both dead! What was she supposed to be dressed in, for mercy's sake? Celluloid?"

"Something must have satisfied the French inquiry. On the whole I don't approve of dismissing all foreign verdicts as unsafe."

9

"Did Mr Snow—"

"Ted."

"Did Ted have any transcripts of that inquiry over there?"

"He had a report of some kind certainly, but we didn't discuss it in detail. I haven't even said I'll take the job yet."

"But you will?"

They both knew that he had decided and so as a courtesy he answered at once.

"Yes—yes I will."

"What about money?"

"I'll go up and see her—I'll see Ted too."

"What does he get out of it?"

It was a curious thing about women, he thought, they had no scruples at all about discussing money. Lilian had been the same.

"We didn't mention it. We didn't have to really," he added evasively. "We never got that far—I told you—besides, he's an old friend."

She had no doubt of Webber's ability as a policeman, but if his weekly housekeeping accounts were anything to go by she intended to oversee the business side of any agreement. She wondered what Detective Inspector Snow's wife was like. A money-grabber perhaps.

"You'll stay in London?"

He would like to have afforded himself the luxury of a grin. This was something she hadn't considered until now. She wouldn't like being on her own.

"I expect so. I'd better see what's involved. Flaxfield is hardly a convenient centre for international inquiries, is it?"

It seemed the right moment to fetch some more drinks from the bar. On his return he found it odd that she was composed and amiable. Her face indeed reflected nothing but what he could only describe as controlled enthusiasm. She smiled at him with genuine love and happiness and for a quick moment he felt his breath catch with pleasure. She appeared not to notice, being too busy adjusting the fierce apple-green skirt.

"Now let's see, I'll have to get Doreen to keep an eye on things down here for us. She's not ideal but she'll have to do unless I can work out something better. Anyway I'm not so sure you're right about Flaxfield. We might find later on that we can work from home."

"You thought about coming up to London with me then?"

10

"Certainly. Why? Had you thought about gallivanting off on your own?"

That's what she had to let him do in the end. It took longer than she had realized to organize the safeguarding of their homes. Newspapers and milk to be cancelled, someone to look after Bunter her cat. The plumber coaxed and bribed to repair a leaking tank. In books, she grumbled to her daughter and son-in-law, things were arranged better. In books detectives jumped into trains or aeroplanes without a thought for the expense, or for who would look after the cat.

Webber arranged a room for himself in the Glockemara Hotel in Notting Hill Gate. Both he and Mrs Thomas were well known there, it was a cheap if slightly grubby haven for their occasional shopping trips to London. On his first morning he phoned Snow at home and got his wife. When he had still been married to Lilian the four of them were much in each other's company. Betty's voice took him back over the years, reminding him of her niceness. He'd always liked her. A no-nonsense face with red hair and freckles, a snub nose and plump pink cheeks, like a farmer's wife. Ted had worked late, she told him. God alone knew what time he had got home. She was going to let him sleep on until lunchtime. Why didn't he come out to Finchley and eat with them? He accepted before he remembered what a terrible cook she was.

It didn't matter, it was a good bright morning with the promise of spring in the cool air. He left the tube at Finchley Central and following Betty's directions walked the short distance down Ballards Lane to Berrywood Gardens. The sun came out and pulled his back up straight like the tulips standing alert in the council flowerbeds. The house was semi-detached, standing in a gentle curve of Thirties villas whose bow windows swelled out proudly over minute front gardens.

Like Snow she had aged. The cheeks were no longer round and the fresh colour had gone. The green eyes and the smile were the same.

"John! How lovely!" She kissed his cheek and the hug she gave him was warm and spontaneous. She chatted to him happily through the narrow hallway cluttered with the children's clothes. She saw him looking at the football boots and hockey stick and he remembered her laugh.

11

"Yes you're right, they're growing up! Alan is twelve and Alice nearly ten although she's not much bigger than her hockey stick. Come through to the back, the kitchen gets the morning sun."

In the kitchen she held him at arm's length. "Here, let me look at you — yes, a great improvement. Poor Lilian, she did give you a rotten time didn't she? All of us come to think of it. Sit, do. I'll make some coffee. There was a divorce wasn't there? Yes, we heard. I should have written I know, but we've had so many moves."

He thought, Ted's told her about Lizzie's visit, soon she'll ask me about her. She remembers Lilian as an impossible wife, sad, not responsible, a born hysteric. She'll wonder if I've found someone to replace her. She won't say so, but she'll try and find out.

"Ted told me about Brixton," he said. "No place for copper's kids."

"No —" She seemed about to enlarge on it but plunged slapdash into the coffee-making instead.

It was like old times to see her banging cups into saucers. She would know why he was there. Ted shared things with her.

"You've decided then?"

"Yes."

"Good! I hope you don't think we're counting on you to pay the children's school fees?"

He smiled, remembering her trick of coming at once to the point she wanted to make.

"Don't worry. I understood what Ted was saying. A bit extra on the side wouldn't be out of place. Well that's the same for me too, you know."

"That's what we thought. It all seemed to fit for once. Everything coming together at the right time. It's wildly unofficial isn't it?"

"Ted's very discreet."

"Oh John how can you say that! After all the things you've known him do."

"All right — he is, or he will be, careful."

She smiled her relief. "Yes I know, at least I hope I do — oh good that's the lavatory, he'll be down soon. I must tell you he was very impressed with your friend, very sane indeed he thought. Mrs Thomas isn't it?" 'Sane' was a slip, not a probing of old wounds, she was too kind for that.

12

"Lizzie Thomas – yes."

She brought the coffee to the table, slopping it into the saucers.

"You know, considering that he is supposed to be such a clever policeman, I've always thought that Ted never seems to ask the right questions."

He poured the coffee from his saucer into his cup. He correctly surmised that she wouldn't need any prompting. She would want to fill in the gaps in Ted's information quickly before he came down to join them. He sipped his coffee and waited.

She said, "I mean not what *I* call the right questions. Like for instance . . . housekeeper. What sort of housekeeper? Live in or out? Oh damn! Isn't that just like Ted, keeps you waiting for hours and then barges in at exactly the wrong moment. You are a beast Ted, I was just about to quiz him gently about his love life."

The three of them sat drinking coffee in the early spring sunlight and the years slipped away in the gentle teasing, the memories of old cases, the talk about the children. They had found decent schools for them both, private and near enough for them to live at home.

"You knew Daddy died?" Betty asked. "No? No I suppose not. Heart and quick thank goodness. He didn't leave very much bless him, but there'll be enough to cover the school fees. Well, almost enough, we could just do with a bit of topping up from time to time. I've forgotten, do you eat curry?"

Webber watched apprehensively as Betty produced a cold shoulder of fatty mutton from the fridge and began to cut it into rough cubes. He was grateful when Snow suggested a stroll in the garden. The last owners of the house had built a glass conservatory out beyond the kitchen and at the bottom of the long narrow garden there was a dumpy summerhouse crying out for paint.

The summerhouse was meant to revolve so that it could be pushed round to capture the suburban sunshine. It had long since seized up for lack of lubrication. Snow tried his shoulder against the door frame.

"One day," he said, "when I've got time, I'll have a go at that."

"That maid's evidence," said Webber, "the maid who saw it from their hotel, where did you get that from?"

"The Foreign Office. I know someone there, we help each other from time to time. Not official of course and nothing on paper, we chat on the phone sometimes or meet for a drink, a useful lad. I knew they were bound to have a report from the French police.

Webber wondered what kind of favour Snow's informant in such exalted circles might have owed him.

"What did the daughter's letter to the Commissioner say?" he asked.

"She wasn't satisfied with the official explanation of her mother's and father's deaths. She wanted a full investigation."

Webber sat carefully on the edge of an old wickerwork chair that smelled of mould and damp earth.

"I'm impressed Ted, the Foreign Office I mean. I like a bit of class, most of my snouts were old lags."

"This one nearly was."

"Ah!"

"Been a silly boy in a lavatory. I was able to keep it out of court."

Webber nodded approvingly.

"Very useful. Did he perhaps say something to suggest that the daughter might be right? I mean, was that why you went to see her?"

For a moment Snow had the grace to look discomforted but with Webber he had always been honest.

"No, that wasn't the reason. The address was the thing. Holland Crescent is millionaire land. I checked her out. Does the name Elberg ring a bell?"

"There's a chain of supermarkets," said Webber, "but apart from that . . ."

"Well done John, that's the one, bull's-eye, she married him."

In the kitchen they could see Betty moving between the sink and the stove. Webber wondered if even at this late hour he could avoid lunch with a courteous excuse but abandoned the thought with a feeling of shame. Lizzie's food had spoiled him.

"What did he do, the poor old sod on the beach at Le Bosquet?"

"He ran a small pottery in Staffordshire. Nothing grand, mugs and jugs, cheap tea sets, that sort of thing. He wasn't all that old either, fifty-three, she was eight years older. I've dug out a bit of background for you, routine stuff but it'll save you some slog. I'll give it to you before you go."

The chair pushed a splintered dagger of cane into Webber's buttock.

"There was a time, Ted, when you used to look over the notes of a case and then lay bets with me."

14

"I had more money than sense in those days."

"No bets on this one?"

"No – no bets. All the same . . ."

"Yes?"

"All the same – it was a funny old way to go wasn't it? Foreign jobs are right sods aren't they John, especially our froggy friends, they don't half like to tie a case up quickly."

"Different on a beach at Bournemouth?"

"Oh yes. I'd have liked a go at it in England."

"You do get a sniff then?"

At the kitchen window Betty held up the fingers of both hands to promise her meal would be ready in ten minutes. Snow waved acknowledgement.

"I've got a drop of whisky," he said, "I think it might be an idea before the curry. Nothing personal, she's a good girl. How do you think she looks?"

"Fine – a bit tired perhaps. Not surprising after Brixton. The kids don't come home for lunch?"

"Too far, they get collected and delivered by private mini-bus, very grand. They feed them well too."

Webber envied them. "Do you want to discuss money?" he asked as he grunted himself out of the wicker chair.

"Not unless you do. No problem – not with us is it?"

"No, not with us thank God."

They walked slowly down the sad winter lawn towards the house. Snow stopped and looked at him.

"Remember all those letters we used to get from the nutters? Poor sad dafties being bombarded by wireless waves, and the rich old girl who said Jesus had killed her sister? Well we get them at the Yard too. This woman's not one of those, she may be rich but she's not a nutter. I wouldn't play that game on you, not just for the money I wouldn't."

Snow had answered his question. Webber knew he'd got a sniff.

He took Snow's elbow kindly and led him into their slow walk again, a gesture he had used in the past to convey approval without words.

"I'll go and see her. Should I quote that fee you mentioned?"

"Why not. It's what she offered – for the right man, as recommended by Scotland Yard itself don't forget!"

"Five hundred pounds a week plus expenses. It sounds a lot of money."

15

"Nothing to her I promise. Wait till you see the house."

Ten yards from the open door of the conservatory a smell of unbelievable pungency hit them.

Snow said wonderingly, "You'd think Brixton would have put her off curry for life wouldn't you?"

৶ THREE ৩

WEBBER READ THE notes on his way back in the tube. He smiled to see that Snow had typed them on what looked like pages torn from a school exercise book. The smile was because Snow's typing was as instantly recognizable as his handwriting. The frequent crossings out and handwritten notes in the margin had not changed with the years.

'David Walton, born 1930, Stoke-on-Trent, Staffordshire. Son of a bus driver. Left school at 15 to work as an apprentice decorator for Smith and Lakin, one of the oldest established pottery firms. They encouraged him to attend art classes at night school. At 20 married one of his teachers there, Jane Bennett, 28; small inheritance of £4000 from her father's will.'

A note in the margin said, 'Appears to have been a genuine love match though.'

'With this money she encouraged him to set up in business as a potter on his own account. She acted as secretary and they took Arnold Swan, a clever working potter, away from Smith and Lakin. Swan had no capital but they made him a partner to keep his talent and experience. The firm became therefore Walton and Swan. Seems to have been a reasonably successful venture. Both the Waltons and Swan lived in houses of some style and drove good cars. (A Rover and a Jaguar).'

At this point Snow had marked a red star with a felt pen which directed Webber to a handwritten note on a separate page, presumably because he suspected the margin wasn't going to be big enough.

'I've had this information from two or three sources in Staffordshire, not of course from Swan because he seemed a bit too close to it all and you will probably want to chat him up yourself. (You see how sure I am of you! Not really. I'm just keeping my fingers crossed.) The thing is I don't quite get the

17

picture with Walton and Swan Ltd. It was never a big set-up–just a medium-sized factory in Hanley. Work-force of twelve, small warehouse, modest, all of it. Swan took it over and still runs it under the same title. You'll remember how difficult it is to get co-operation from the Inland Revenue and now there's the Customs and Excise lot as well in charge of the Value Added Tax. However I cashed in a few favours and it amounts to a clean bill on both scores. All the same I get a sniff–Jags, Rovers, the houses, all that lark–plus a few grand holidays. Walton and his wife went on a world cruise for instance. That is my only break for you. I managed to check that one out. Walton paid for it in cash. I could be wrong but that seems a bit more than the average tax fiddle? With a bit of leaning I got the local tax people to chat, and that might interest you. There were no fiddles–the books were clean, every entry double-checked, no way wrong, receipts, bills, invoices, the lot. After that the VAT was easy to calculate and that was the same–clean. Funny?'

The typewritten notes continued.

'There were two children of the Walton marriage (Swan is a childless widower). Jessica Walton, born 1952 (married Hans Elberg), and Donald a late child born in 1960 when Jane was 38. He had an address in London but now lives in his parents' house in Solihull, a wealthy residential area about 45 miles south of the factory in Hanley. There isn't much background on Donald yet but I've got some lines out and I should be able to fill him in for you soon.'

The rest of the notes gave an account of the Le Bosquet deaths more or less as Snow had already told it. A few more details–the name of the hotel on the sea front and a cutting from a local French newspaper. Webber's French was very poor but he could manage enough to see that it was a report on 'The Horror on The Beach'. With Gallic delight in the macabre there was a photograph of the beach with the caption 'Scene of the tragedy'. The bodies had been removed but the stark area of roped-off blackened sand in the foreground was more horrible than if they had been allowed to remain in the photograph.

After the French judicial inquiry, and the verdict of what in England would have been called accidental death, the bodies had been sent to Folkestone by sea. After the usual formalities they had been released into the care of the Walton family. There was no account of the funeral and what few cuttings there were from the English newspapers added very little to what Webber already knew. One or two of the tabloids had made the most of the gruesome details but the verdict had killed the story and it had obviously been a one-day wonder. The Waltons were not famous and accidents, Webber thought, don't sell newspapers unless they happen to be nuclear.

At Tottenham Court Road he changed on to the Central Line and by the time he got off at Notting Hill Gate it was nearly five o'clock. At the Glockemara he ran a bath and wondered how he could pass the evening alone. He had a choice, he could watch television and eat in, but the thought of the gloomy hotel restaurant and the poor food depressed him; he could go out and pay for a decent meal but that would be expensive in London. The thought of money reminded him that after his bath he must telephone the ex-directory number Snow had given him and make an appointment to see Jessica Elberg. The water was hard and only just hot enough, it didn't encourage him to linger. He changed and considered a drink in the bar. It didn't attract him any more than the restaurant and he poured himself a whisky in his tooth glass before dialling the Elberg number. The voice that answered was foreign and difficult to understand, he was grateful when Jessica Elberg took over at the other end.

"I'm sorry, he doesn't speak English very well yet, he's Filipino and learning. Who is that please?"

Snow was right. She wasn't a nutter, very sensible and with it. She was, thank goodness, going to be easy and intelligent to talk to. It was a pleasant voice with only a trace of the Potteries left in it. She would see him at 16 Holland Crescent at eleven o'clock the next morning.

He gathered Snow's notes, which he had intended to read again with his whisky, and tidied them into his briefcase. The French newspaper cutting lay on top. Lizzie would translate it for him when she came up. During the war her mother had billeted a long succession of boys from the Free French Airforce. Lizzie Thomas's French, if not of the purest, was virile, colloquial and fluent. "When you're as young as I was," she had explained, "you learn quickly and you don't forget." He didn't doubt it. She had long since ceased to surprise him, but even as the thought crossed his mind she did just that by knocking on his door, pushing past him and collapsing on the bed.

19

"My God I'm whacked! Tried to phone you but you were out. You'd think those lazy devils downstairs would carry the luggage up wouldn't you? I'm in number 38, two doors away, nearest I could get." She used the spring in the mattress to heave herself to her feet. "Give us a kiss, there's a love. Ughh! Curry! Turn my back for two seconds and you're eating rubbish. Why curry? You hate it."

Webber explained, pouring her a drink and trying not to show her how delighted he was.

"Stop pretending to be blasé, doesn't suit you." She eyed herself doubtfully in his wardrobe mirror. She had allowed Doreen her daughter and her son-in-law to persuade her into a plain brown woollen dress, without what she liked to call accessories, and she regretted it.

Webber stopped trying to pretend and gave himself up to honest enthusiasm as he brought her up to date. This entailed following her down the corridor and helping her to unpack. When she pinned a large artificial rose constructed of green feathers to her shoulder he professed himself pleased with the effect. And so he was, it was more like the Lizzie he knew. Their meal did not, after all, cost them a lot of money, she knew of a fish-and-chip restaurant where the food was superb and served at civilized gingham tables with respectable wine.

It was give and take. He listened and approved her arrangements with their homes in the village. Then she listened, and after the food read through Snow's notes and the newspaper cuttings while they finished the wine. From time to time she fed a cold chip to a solemn dog whose feathered tail gently swept the tiled floor at her feet. When she'd finished she remained silent and thoughtful. Webber and the dog regarded her with interest.

"Questions?" Webber said gently at last.

"What is Ted Snow's wife like?"

It wasn't what he had expected but she seldom asked impertinent questions.

"Betty? She's good, very sound, a nice girl."

"Not a money-grabber?"

"No."

The dog gave up and transferred his hopes to another table.

"Detective Inspector at the Yard is a good job," Webber said. "It's overworked and underpaid but it's good. If you're bright and active, and Ted is all that, you might finish up one day a good bit higher up, and with a lot more money, but that's only one day, and only perhaps. In the meantime he's got kids and a mortgage and he's comparatively poor. He is also," he said carefully, "a straight copper," adding with unconscious irony, "There is more honesty in the police force than most people realize."

It was what she had wanted to hear. She herself had approved of Ted Snow but she liked to have a full picture. A man was only half a picture, she liked to know about wives or lovers, a selfish rider could ruin a good horse.

"As far as they go," she nodded at Snow's notes, "they are good. And you say he'll give you more when he can – technical help?"

"The deal comes with a back-up service no private detective could match. Not outside of TV filmland anyway."

"A risk?"

He considered. "Some – not much, and for Ted, not for me. There are technically two senior officers above him but he virtually runs his own squad."

"And money?"

"I'll see Mrs Elberg first – we'll talk then."

"You and Ted?"

"No – you and I first. Then Ted."

She tidied Snow's papers together, tapping them into symmetry on the red gingham tablecloth. For a moment he was tempted to tell her what Snow had said about the fee but he held back. He felt a natural reluctance to say anything until it was settled. He reached under the table for his briefcase to take the papers she had tidied into a neat pile. She pointed to the photograph in the French newspaper cutting.

"When do you reckon that was taken?"

He put his glasses on and studied it carefully.

"Quite soon after it happened I think."

"Why is that?"

"They died on April the 12th, Easter Monday, this paper was published on the same day, you can see the date at the top of the cutting. I can check but my guess is that it comes from a local paper; an evening edition."

She nodded. "It reads like a local paper – go on."

"The shadows of those stakes holding the tapes are long, early morning then, not evening because it would have been too late for the paper to print and the sand around about would be much more

21

churned up with the usual ghouls crowding round during the day. There's another point too. The maid said they were a long way away. If that meant towards the sea then the police and photographer would have to move quickly to beat the tide."

Webber filled and lit his pipe to avoid any expression of smugness in his face. All the same it was pleasant to know that he still had the ability to look carefully and analyse accurately. He blew a cloud of smoke politely away from the table and signalled to the waitress for their bill.

Mrs Thomas nodded with interest. He was right, the photograph could only have been taken in the morning. She looked at it again. Around them the restaurant was filling up. Two teenagers, a boy and his girl, smiled shyly and asked if they could share the table. The waitress hovered behind them with their plates piled high with steaming chips and one piece of fish which, after they were seated, the boy cut in two for them to share. The dog appeared from nowhere and sat silent and patient between them. They were nice-looking youngsters she thought, bright and loving and hungry, with eyes and ears only for each other. She wanted to catch the waitress's eye and order more fish for them. She felt suddenly shy, not liking to intrude. It was not only because they were young and poor, she told herself, but it would have been a pleasant way for her to celebrate. She decided to order the fish for them at the desk on the way out as they paid the bill. It would be a fitting end to a most satisfactory evening. She caught Webber's eye.

"So according to this," she said quietly, tapping the photograph, "if they'd gone for their walk a bit later they'd still be alive."

Webber took the cutting from her.

"Look at the tapes," she said, "and look at the flags on the promenade in the distance. No wind, dead calm, not even a breeze. It might have dropped of course. All the same it's interesting isn't it?"

❧ FOUR ❧

IN THE MORNING they decided that Webber would see Jessica Elberg on his own. The idea of starting off with Lizzie Thomas and working openly as a team had much to commend it in his eyes. She persuaded him against it. She would keep her cover she said. You never knew how things would develop, the time might come when they would be grateful that their connection was unknown. When he left the hotel at 10.30 am she was happily sorting out the problem of the lukewarm water with the management. Webber felt sorry for them.

The back streets of Notting Hill Gate where the Glockemara struggled for respectability are a dull desert of sad buildings crammed with Thomas Cubitt's pretentious Victorian porticoes, the pillars cracked and flaking. Sometimes Webber passed houses where the window-boxes nursed tired geraniums which had survived the winter. Once he had crossed over the Bayswater Road and was walking down Kensington Church Street he could have been in a different city. Specialist antique shops lined the road until he turned right at the Carmelite Church towards Holland Park, where it was not only a different city but a different world.

Holland Crescent overlooked the park; the houses stood in their own grounds, as solid and uncompromising as the city merchants who had built them as rural retreats when Victoria was a young girl and a near neighbour in her palace across the way in Kensington Gardens. Some of the houses in the crescent were now embassies of new and obscure Third-World states, some had been divided into flats. Number 16 had remained intact. It was smaller than some of its neighbours but still impressive; at the turn of the century a fashionable painter of Edwardian society had added French château towers to the roof. Beyond the wrought-iron gates the red tarmac drive curved round a lawn to the imposing entrance. A gardener was digging over a flowerbed ready for the bedding-out plants when the weather was safe enough. Webber's garden in Suffolk was always two or three weeks behind London. It wouldn't be safe to risk the frosts there much before the middle of May. Perhaps, he thought, he would be too busy for his garden this year. He watched the man straighten up slowly, the palm of his hand pressed into the small of his back. If Snow was right he would be able to afford a gardener of his own; someone to do the digging anyway.

The car under the trees further down the drive was a dark green Bentley. Like the house and the garden it looked cared for and groomed. Snow was right, the Elbergs were rich. Everything said it, the gleaming coachwork of the car, the fresh-painted wood around the windows of the house.

The Filipino opened the door in answer to his ring, white-jacketed and silent but smiling that he knew Webber was expected. He followed the little man across the marble floor of the entrance hall and on up the great curving staircase. For an instant he wondered if in some previous life he had been born rich, so vivid was the feeling that he had seen it all before. Before he was shown into the big drawing-room he knew that what he remembered were the Hollywood films of the Thirties. Vast well-lit mansions with butlers and elegant society heroines embroiled in unlikely plots. At home in Flaxfield he had sat and watched them on late-night television with Mrs Thomas. It was she who later pointed out to him that in none of them could she remember two characters burning to death on a beach in broad daylight.

The room was big, with a high ceiling and tall windows in sets of three giving on to Holland Park. The room smelled of beeswax and hyacinths. At first he couldn't see anyone and then Jessica Elberg rose from a high-backed chair and came to greet him. For some reason he had imagined she would be taller. She barely came up to his shoulder when she shook his hand. She had a generous open face, wide eyes and a good nose over a large mouth. She could easily have looked plain, unattractive even, but she didn't, perhaps because there was a look of frailty about her. The eyes and the mouth smiled and her brown hair fell naturally about her face, framing it and softening the features. He wondered how long she had been married to Elberg, some time, he guessed, for she moved with ease and assurance amid the

24

wealth of the room around her. She was used to servants too, dismissing the Filipino with none of the awkwardness of the newly-rich. With Webber she showed no trace of superiority, if anything he thought she seemed hesitant and shy. It wasn't unusual and he was used to putting people at their ease.

One of Snow's favourite stories was about Webber arresting a murderess in the street. She had shot her husband dead, and his mistress, and a taxi driver who had tried to disarm her. Snow had suggested bringing her down with a rugby tackle from behind but Webber had walked up to her and politely raised his hat; later they found the loaded gun in her handbag. She still sent him Christmas cards from Broadmoor.

Jessica Elberg waved him to a chair. They sat in front of the fire and discussed smokeless fuel and the problems of central heating in such a large house. She ordered coffee and smoked cigarettes, encouraging him to smoke his pipe. It was no effort to break down the shyness. She told him she had been married to Hans Elberg for five years. They had met at a trade exhibition in London when Hans was looking for cheap pottery to sell in his supermarkets. Both her parents had approved of her marriage even though it meant that she saw less of them afterwards.

"Why was that?" Webber asked.

"Oh, there was no row or conflict, nothing like that. No, being married to Hans is a full-time occupation." Her smile, Webber thought, made her look very young. "For one thing," she went on, "there was a great deal more travel and entertaining than I had bargained for! You see Hans has business interests apart from the stores themselves. There are some factories in Holland—his grandparents were Dutch, they settled in Scotland, and there are suppliers in America and in Hong Kong. We were in America, on our way to Uruguay in fact, when we eventually heard about —when we heard about Le Bosquet."

"That was last Easter wasn't it?"

"Yes." She stubbed out a cigarette and found Webber's eyes on her when she looked up after the silence.

One of the first things people noticed about Webber was the colour of his eyes. Many people had blue eyes but for all his gentle mildness of expression his eyes shone with an intelligence that in his youth had made girls think of periwinkles and in latter years had encouraged both sexes to tell him the truth.

25

"You mean, why did I leave it so long before I asked for an inquiry?" When she looked at him he was interested to see in her face nothing except an eagerness to explain. "I was ill when Hans heard. I'd picked up a tropical bug of some sort in an awful town called Carmelo. The doctors got me into hospital in Montevideo and for a long time, nearly three months, I was too ill to be told anything. They were afraid the shock would bring on a relapse. When we finally got back here it was all over and done with."

"Your husband told you before you came back?"

She nodded thoughtfully. "I'd been convalescent for about three weeks. We had a villa, some friends of Hans's who were in Europe lent it to him. I was reading a magazine in a chair with wooden arms. It was an old copy of *Country Life*, 1965 I think. I remember listening to Hans's voice and keeping my eyes on a photograph. I'd been reading an article about Chartwell, it was going to be opened as a museum to Winston Churchill. There was a photograph at the top of the left-hand page. The caption said, 'The library, looking through into the studio'. I can still remember the photograph quite clearly. The walls lined with books, an armchair with a loose cover and comfortable-looking arms, not wooden arms, a heavy oak door, oriental rugs on the polished floor and a wastepaper basket with brass rings round it. I kept thinking how sensible and calm I was. I wanted to say something when Hans finished telling me, something to show him that I had understood what he was saying. Instead I kept looking at the photograph. It was so English, nothing to do with South America or with France. I started to laugh because it seemed so ludicrous. I wanted to tell him that people were murdered in English libraries not on the beach at Le Bosquet."

She took a cigarette and Webber lit it for her.

"Why did you think your mother and father were murdered, Mrs Elberg?"

She considered, anxious to please, to explain as fully and accurately as she could.

"It seems silly now but at the time it seemed the only possible explanation. I heard Hans say the word accident – dreadful accident, he said, and I knew that meant that he was telling me they were dead. After that I heard the word fire, but I thought he was telling me that someone had fired at them, that they had been shot. I realize now of course that I was in a state of shock."

Webber said, "When you wrote to the Commissioner of Scotland Yard, you no longer believed them to have been murdered – you simply wanted an inquiry?"

"Yes – yes I suppose so. I felt – I don't know, it's difficult to explain."

"Try," Webber said gently.

At once he wondered if she had taken his manner to be too paternal, as if she suddenly resented being treated with over-consideration. Like an invalid or someone only recently bereaved.

She answered quickly, almost angrily. Webber remembered Snow's description of her letter to the Commissioner, 'The sort of thing she could have written to Harrods'.

"I felt I wanted to do something, that there was something . . . unfinished. A bit like losing a book when you've just started to read it. Everyone was kind of course, all our friends and my family – my younger brother Donald, he'd had to do everything. The funeral, all the letters, coping with the newspapers, it was all *done* you see. I suppose everyone was trying to spare my feelings because I'd been so ill. I resented it, I still do. I take after my father, he disliked being patronized."

A less intelligent man than Webber might have taken that as an attack on his gentleness; a rebuke. He knew now it wasn't meant for him. She was simply explaining her feelings of frustration. His instinct told him that it was the right time to be business-like and practical.

"Mrs Elberg, we have been talking for a little while now. Do you wish to engage me as a private investigator to inquire into the circumstances of your parents' death?"

She said, "Inspector Snow has warned me that I can expect no further help from official sources. As you know he gave me your name. He spoke very well of you."

"We are old colleagues," Webber said.

In the pause that followed she got up and fetched a photograph in a silver frame from a small desk near a window.

"I don't know if you know what they looked like " She didn't wait for his answer but left it in his hands while she went on. "It was taken about the time they were married, in 1950, I was born in '52. Why do you smile?"

"I'm out of touch with ladies. In my day they weren't so forthcoming about their age."

27

"It's never worried me, perhaps because Hans is so much older than I am. I don't think it matters, I think some of Hans's friends did at first." She nodded at the photograph in his hands. "She was older than my father, it doesn't show so much there but it did later."

The photograph was a posed studio composition in the rather artificial style favoured by the glossy magazines of the Fifties. David Walton's face peered out over his wife's shoulder. He had passed his features on to his daughter, the small nose and the large mouth, only they had suited him better. His wife was not unpleasing to look at but curiously without character, in spite of the lipstick and unhelpful eye-shadow, the hair was untouched since the hairdresser's dryer. It was too severely back-lit by the photographer's lamps, giving her a fierce hot halo. Webber thought of the beach and suppressed a shudder. If she noticed it she gave no sign of having done so as she took the photograph from him and crossed with it to the desk. When she spoke she still had her back to him but the voice was not coloured with any hint of emotion, it was flat, almost casual.

"I'm sorry, you must think me rude. Of course the answer is yes. I want you to try and find out what happened. I hope you will accept."

The small ashtray on the table by the side of his chair was adequate for cigarettes but not for his pipe. Webber went to the fire and tapped it out on the palm of his hand.

"I'd like to make three points, Mrs Elberg, there are probably more but these seem to be the most important. The first is that however unlikely it might appear, your mother and father may have died in exactly the way the French inquiry said they did." He was pleasantly surprised when she didn't comment. His first assessment of her character when he'd spoken to her on the telephone had been right; she was intelligent. "The second point is that I have never yet inquired deeply into the circumstances of sudden death without upsetting someone. There is always the possibility," he said, "that it might be you."

"And the third?" she asked.

"The third point I would like to make is that although I have spent many years in the police force I have never conducted a private case before."

Webber hadn't heard the heavy door open but followed Jessica Elberg's look over his shoulder.

"Mr Webber, this is my husband, Hans," she said.

28

✑ FIVE ✑

It came as something of a shock to Webber to see that Hans Elberg was probably about his own age. He'd kept his figure better too. Webber tried not to feel pleased that the man had lost most of his hair. He had to admit that his baldness hadn't aged him. It suited his personality, the frank open face like one of Rembrandt's Dutch burghers was straight out of a painting in the Hague, contrasting oddly with the Scots accent. Some people when they smile a lot give cause for concern, mistrust even; Elberg gave the impression that he genuinely enjoyed life, that he liked people. Webber could imagine him inspiring trust and affection in those who worked for him but without ever losing authority.

"You'll forgive me if I don't stay just this minute, Mr Webber?" The handshake was firm and friendly. "As always, I seem to have left myself short of time but I didn't wish to appear rude." When he looked at his wife it seemed to Webber as though he was saying, "This is my wife, am I not a lucky man?"

"Have you discussed Mr Webber's fee yet, Jess?"

"No Hans, he hasn't been here very long."

"That's all right then, perhaps you'll look into my office downstairs before you go? Maybe I'm a wee bit premature? I'm assuming you have accepted the assignment. Am I jumping the gun?"

"Hans, Mr Webber says he accepts."

Elberg smiled happily at her. "You looked so relieved that I guessed so. My dear, forgive me, you too Mr Webber. I'm sure my wife can tell you all you want to know."

He couldn't have been in the room more than three minutes Webber knew that his whole day would be like that, some of the night too probably. That was the way you built up an empire of chain stores or rose to be a chief superintendent. Elberg probably

29

attacked his leisure with the same intensity, skiing or tennis or swimming; most likely all three to have kept his stomach as flat as that.

Webber didn't use a notebook, sometimes as she talked he jotted down a few words on the back of an envelope. He caught himself hoping that she would be impressed by his power of memory. Well, it was good, always had been, he could still produce Christian names from the past, not only of villains but their wives and children – lovers sometimes. He could do it with faces too. His performance now, he had to admit to himself, was a bit of a cheat. Snow had done his work well. The background was good and most of the facts she was giving him he already knew.

"Do you know what they were doing in France?"

"They liked it. Le Bosquet had been a happy place for them, they often went back for a few days when they could."

"So it was a happy marriage you would say?" He wasn't going to apologize. She was employing him and these were things he had to know.

"Yes – at least as far as I know, but then as I told you I saw less of them after my own marriage." She paused, not out of embarrassment but only to choose the right words. "I suppose it could seem odd, but Hans saw more of my father than I did."

"Why was that?"

"Mostly business, the pottery had quite big contracts from Hans, inexpensive kitchenware. It wasn't because he was my father, Hans is far too shrewd a businessman for that. I think – no, I am certain – that if my father and mother had been unhappy together Daddy would have said something to Hans. It wasn't just a business relationship, they got on very well together and of course my father advised him about his collection."

This was something Snow hadn't covered.

"A collection?"

"Antique English pottery, my father was very knowledgeable."

"Your husband has always been interested in pottery has he?"

This time he thought the pause did hold some embarrassment. It was the second time and on both occasions it had been when her husband had been involved in his inquiry.

"No – no, not always. Hans is a great enthusiast, Mr Webber. In some ways he is rather like a schoolboy trying to find the right hobby." She smiled, he thought a little ruefully. "A rather rich schoolboy so he has been able to indulge himself. In a way I

30

suppose it's part of his nature, all his passions have made money for him. Schoolboys collect stamps but they couldn't afford to do it like Hans did. He works his hobbies as hard as his business. The pottery seems to have held him longer than most of the others."

It was Webber's gift that he could draw people out when he sensed that they would rather have not discussed something. It was odd too the way he would pursue a line of inquiry when he couldn't have explained the reason why it interested him. It was an instinct. Sometimes in the past he had pressed on with questions which at the time he could not have given a logical reason for asking. Like a man in a dark room probing with the beam of a flashlight. Often he had lit up odd corners which in the end had had no bearing on the case at all, but a surprising number of times he could look back and wonder if it had been instinct or luck which had shown him some small corner of the truth which had been the beginning. And then there were the cases he had never solved at all. He tried not to think of them, that way you lost faith in yourself. In the early days of his retirement he had taken to reading detective stories and they had depressed him, with their neat cleverness, until he learned to enjoy them like crossword puzzles and nothing to do with the real world of crime in which he had earned his living and been sometimes quite astonishingly successful. Meanwhile he was far removed from the fictional world of neat problems, he couldn't even be sure that he had a real problem at all. Yet he trusted Snow and Snow had thought the case was worth a go, and it wasn't only for the money either. Supposing it had indeed been on the beach at Bournemouth and that he and Snow had had the case to themselves? Ah! But that was making a story out of it, right down to a lurid paperback cover with flames licking the letters of the title *The Bodies on the Beach*. Well, it wasn't simple, and there were no longer any bodies because one of the notes on his envelope said 'Quiet service, few mourners – cremated'.

He kept his eye on the time. For the first interview he wanted as many facts as he could but he wanted to leave before there could be any suggestion of encroaching upon a meal-time. Business was best unencumbered by the social formalities of food. She may not have asked him but he wanted to avoid the possibility if he could. He had arranged to meet Mrs Thomas at the British Home Stores restaurant at one o'clock and there was still Elberg to see before he left.

31

Now that she had become accustomed to him scribbling on scraps of paper he produced a notebook and wrote down her brother's address in Chelsea and that of her parents' house in Solihull. He asked for the address of the factory and of Arnold Swan, her father's partner, and at his suggestion she wrote him a few lines of introduction saying that he was acting on her behalf and that she would be grateful for any help they could give him.

Webber stood and she rang for the Filipino to show him down to Hans Elberg's office. The sun shone through the great bank of windows, making the oriental pattern of the carpet leap into bright colour.

When she rose to say goodbye he was impressed again by the small neat figure. She knew how to dress too, the soft cashmere and the single row of pearls hadn't come from one of her husband's stores.

"I've no idea what happens now," she said. "I mean, will you submit a report, or come and see me or – what?"

Webber produced one of his very best smiles. It was not part of his usual run of facial expressions but came quite spontaneously to inspire confidence and trust. When accompanied by a most unexpected chuckle as it was now it succeeded very well.

"Neither have I! You forget this is my first private job. Let's see how it goes shall we? I imagine Mr Elberg will want to arrange the business side. I suggest you try and relax for a while and let me get on with it as best I can."

The Filipino knocked and stood politely holding open the door. Webber took her hand in a formal handshake but before he turned to leave her she said quietly so that her voice wouldn't carry across to the door.

"Mr Webber, I trust you. I think you must know that. If this had come to you when you were a policeman – you know what I mean. Would you – that is . . ."

"Would I be taking the case without a very generous fee?"

"Yes."

For a moment he saw the photograph in the French newspaper with the tapes and the flags hanging limp and considered telling her. It was too soon, and there was too much to be done, in any case he was disinclined to discuss the case in front of the servant, however poor his English might be.

32

"I have friends who tell me that I am a lazy man." Webber's eyes were very blue and bright but his face was serious. "I can only tell you that it would take more than money to get me out of my village retirement."

He knew it was what she wanted to hear; and it was true.

Downstairs the manservant delivered him to a door at the end of a long gallery. Webber's knowledge of tapestries, paintings and furniture was not great but you didn't need to be an expert to recognize that the style of the gallery was consistent and Elizabethan throughout. The woman who was about to greet him, a secretary of some kind he guessed, was suddenly replaced by Elberg himself.

"All right Miss Evans, I'll take care of the Inspector."

He took Webber's arm solicitously guiding him through outer offices, empty except for banks of machinery clicking away to themselves. Webber was no better informed on technology than he was on Elizabethan antiques but he recognized his old enemy the computers and liked them no better than he had in the past. There was something sinister and unnatural in their lack of any human quality.

All the time they walked Elberg chatted and chuckled at his own jokes. What had she said? "Like a schoolboy – a rich schoolboy." It wasn't bad, he was very like that as he gave Webber a brisk guided tour as they walked past the muttering machines.

"Toys! Just toys, Mr Webber. I see from your face that you don't care for them. Aye, well they work well enough if you know the tricks. I call them my Meccano set. My wife says it reminds her of a James Bond film, and to be honest I don't think she meant it as a compliment!"

At the mention of his wife Webber thought he detected a slower, more thoughtful tone to Elberg's voice but if so the mood passed quickly. He even tapped the dialled front of one of the machines as he passed. It was almost, Webber thought, a gesture of affection, as in the old days one patted a secretary's bottom.

"This lot here are just children," Elberg said, "but very bright children for all that. There are some grown-up creatures at my headquarters that frighten even me, but then we live in a frightening world do we not?" Without apparently expecting an answer he paused at a door marked simply 'OFFICE' and ushered Webber in.

33

The contrast with the clinical rooms through which they had just passed was astonishing. Elberg's office was furnished quietly but luxuriously. Indeed the only thing which established its function as an office was the large desk which dominated the centre of the room. Most of the wall space was fitted with glass display cabinets. They were cleverly lit to show his pottery collection to its best advantage and it was some moments before Webber realized that all the lighting in the room was artificial. There were no windows but the atmosphere was air-conditioned and fresh.

Elberg didn't play the tycoon by sitting at his desk, he waved Webber to a comfortable armchair and sat near him on the arm of another.

"I don't believe in prevarication," he said. "Indeed I don't have time for the luxury of beating about the bush. What I shall tell you may surprise you."

❧ SIX ❧

Hans Elberg was as good as his word. He didn't beat about the bush and he did surprise Webber. He talked simply and sincerely but always with that authority which comes as second nature to men with power.

"It was the disease as well as the shock of course. Her doctors tell me that, so I accept it. I have to because they are top men."

"You never considered the possibility that she could be right?"

"Mr Webber, my wife is not mad, you might judge that yourself from your own observations. She has an obsession, against all the evidence I must say, that her parents' death has a sinister element to it. However I did not dismiss her fears without trying in every way to see if there could be any basis in fact for them."

Jessica Elberg had said nothing about any inquiries her husband had made. Elberg saw the surprise on Webber's face.

"May I ask where you inquired?" he asked with genuine interest.

"She didn't mention it?"

"No."

"We had tried the British police and got nowhere – not really in their domain they said, but you would know about that. The French police simply repeated the bare facts. Accidental death, unusual, but beyond doubt. They said they had submitted the relevant facts through the usual channels; in effect to the Foreign Office here in London."

"And you made your inquiries there?"

"I did."

A low buzz summoned him to the desk where he spoke briefly into a telephone. It sounded as though he was being reminded of an appointment. If so he showed no sign of bringing their conversation to a close. Back on the arm of the chair he looked at

35

Webber as though, for the first time, he was assessing his character.

"I did my best to stop my wife seeing you," he said. There was no emotion in his voice, it was a statement of fact.

Webber decided it was better to let him take his time and left it unanswered.

"Do you think her beautiful, Mr Webber?" It was asked not as a jealous husband but as a proud one who already knew the answer.

"Your wife is a fine-looking woman, Mr Elberg."

"Aye, but for me she's more than that. You'll have noticed a difference in age no doubt. Well, marriage came late with me. It takes time to build a business like mine. It's a question of values, I don't grumble, but it comes hard to me now to see her so distressed when I thought it would be a time to give her everything to make her happy."

"Did you find the Foreign Office helpful, sir?"

"I did. Too damned helpful in a way. I'm not without contacts of course so there was no sort of difficulty that perhaps some people might have had."

"Too helpful?"

"They opened the files for me. I saw the French police report and I saw the report of their pathologist. She had burns over an area of 70 per cent of her body, David over 40 per cent, he probably died of a heart attack. They had photographs of them as they were found on the beach. I saw those too. I gave Jessica a simple account, I never told her the details. How could I? That bloody bug she caught in Uruguay had left her in a delicate state. Have you heard of a man called Humper, Sir Michael Humper?"

Webber shook his head.

"He's a specialist, a nerve man. He's one of the people we got in for advice. I had a feeling that perhaps I'd got the wrong approach, that I'd been over-protecting her. I thought that if I gave her a complete and detailed account of the report she would accept it. Humper wouldn't allow it, wouldn't take the responsibility."

"Does he know that she has initiated a private investigation?"

"He is most strongly against such a move and he has advised her against it on medical grounds."

Webber thought, it's a stopper – I can't fight that. In law she is perfectly within her rights, but if Elberg's against it what can she do? Why didn't he come out with it just now when they were all three together? He looked at the man on the arm of the chair and thought he saw the answer in his face. Elberg would pay him to confirm the French report, he was buying an expensive rubber stamp. A month's salary, perhaps six weeks. A golden handshake and then back to the garden. Unless he refused.

"You want me to make a token inquiry."

He was surprised and a little angry with himself that he had allowed his voice to betray his distaste of the whole business. It was a new experience for Webber and he didn't like it. Would Elberg change his mind if he told him about his own doubts? That would mean explaining them, giving his reasons, and he didn't work that way. You didn't display your cards as early as this. Raw young coppers did that. The less you said at the beginning the less of a fool you looked if you were wrong. Suppose he politely told him to go to hell, and that as far as he was concerned his client, sick or well, was still Jessica Elberg? He caught himself wondering if she had any money of her own.

Elberg had risen from the chair and seated himself at his desk. A desk suited him, it gave a natural setting for his authority. Webber remembered a time when he had been summoned to the office of a chief constable. He found himself now standing and waiting as he had then. Elberg didn't sound like the chief constable. He was writing and talking quickly and deliberately as a man does when he wishes no confusion in what he is saying.

"I told you I tried to stop her seeing you. Since I did not succeed we have a new situation." He paused in his writing and met Webber's gaze evenly. "Are you married Inspector?"

"I am divorced."

"I'm sorry. Do you have any financial commitments?"

"I have an assistant, a woman. I shall pay her a portion of my fee."

Webber couldn't see what Elberg was writing, his hands were obscured by the clutter of books on his desk.

"I see." He finished what he was doing before addressing Webber again. "A token inquiry is out of the question Mr Webber. I have no intention of insulting her intelligence – or yours. On the contrary I wish you to know that you have my full authority to make as searching and complete an investigation as you can. I hope you will still accept."

"Against your medical advice?"

"To hell with Humper. I know my wife better than he does. It might indeed be painful for her but she is not a child, she's tough

37

like her father. She would agree with that. I think the doctors have had their chance – and missed it."

He rose abruptly from the desk, not to dismiss Webber but to guide him back to the armchair. This time he seated himself comfortably in the other one, checked the time on his wrist and spoke as if a weight had been lifted from him, a decision made.

"It's half past twelve. You'll need to ask questions, how long do you want? Roughly."

"Say half an hour, twenty minutes if you have an appointment."

"They can wait."

Webber hoped Lizzie Thomas would be as accommodating in the British Home Stores restaurant.

Elberg was the ideal man to question. His answers were a model of concise information. He had a businessman's gift of listening and supplying facts. If he didn't know something he said so. When he felt that he could usefully elaborate he did. Within ten minutes he had outlined his early association with the Walton family.

"David Walton was a remarkable man, he owed his wife a good deal but he would have been exceptional even without her help. He wasn't a man who boasted about his ability. In a way his own business success, modest though it was, was unfortunate for him."

"Why was that?"

"It made money for him but it was a waste, a distraction. He could have made more."

Elberg expected Webber to ask him how, but Webber said, "What was your father-in-law like?"

"A quiet enough man not much formal education, not much of a head for business either. The pottery was more or less run by Jane, his wife. Swan, the partner, was brighter that way too; between them they ran it properly. Don't mistake me, David wasn't a business fool; but it wasn't his interest, the man was a potter, it was in his blood, even the name Walton is one of the most famous in Staffordshire history. I don't know if there was a connection but it wouldn't surprise me. I asked him that once but he didn't seem to know or indeed care and that was typical of him. My wife says she found her father secretive, but it wasn't that, I think. He was a much more sensitive man than most people guessed. Jessica says that I probably knew him better

38

than anyone. That might be so, but if I did it was because we had an interest in common."

Webber's eyes went to the pottery cabinets around the walls.

"Aye." Elberg rose and beckoned Webber to follow him. "Don't worry!" His face, Webber thought, even looked like a schoolboy's in the soft light reflected from the display cabinets. A bald schoolboy; it didn't seem impossible when you saw the pride of possession shining in his eyes.

"Don't worry, you're not in for a lecture man! I've more sense and we've neither of us the time, but just stand here and look. Now then: not a guided tour, but you are looking at the most comprehensive collection of antique English pottery in the world."

"I'm impressed."

"Good, I mean you to be! Do you like pottery Mr Webber? Don't answer, I'm not being rude, it's a question of time and I have a horror of boring people. You are, incidentally one of very few people to have seen it."

Webber found himself wondering what satisfaction a collector could have who was so reluctant to share and boast of his acquisitions to others. It was true, he was impressed, intrigued too. The buzz of the telephone took Elberg away to the desk again and out of politeness Webber concentrated on the display cases, moving slowly down the room. The cabinets were arranged as a progression by date and period. The exhibits had simple but effective labels, not handwritten but printed expensively, it all looked very professional. The glass sliding doors were safeguarded by what he recognized as burglar-alarmed locks. He could have been in a museum, he thought.

The early cases held mostly broken pieces of Roman and medieval pottery. They had little appeal for him and he moved on round the room and through the centuries. The later cases were more interesting and he found himself looking at them with genuine pleasure. Shelves with pottery figures of birds and animals in soft muted shades of brown and grey led on to primitive groups of miniature musicians, a mounted military band with, at the head, a little soldier puffed up with pride on a prancing horse as ridiculous as its rider.

He registered the names on the labels, Astbury, Whieldon, Wood, Tittensor, Pratt, Sherratt, Lloyd, but they meant nothing to him. He was aware of Elberg standing silently beside him.

39

"I sometimes wonder," he said, "if the collecting bug is a refuge from my work or a part of it. Do you collect anything Mr Webber?"

"Cigarette cards, but a long time ago."

Elberg didn't acknowledge it as the joke he'd intended.

"You should have persevered, the market for cartography is very bright just now."

"I wasn't in your league I'm afraid."

"It's a question of degree, that's all." He wandered ahead, his hands clasped behind his back. He nodded at the figures in the collection. "Some of this was cheap, some expensive – it evens out, you buy the best you can find and then the whole is more valuable than the parts."

"You make it sound simple."

"It isn't, it can be damned hard work. You need more than money, you need time and knowledge."

"You pay for expert advice?"

"Certainly I do and the best advice isn't cheap, but time is more expensive still."

"And David Walton was your expert?"

"Among others. Och, there was no real comparison with the others, they were just plodders next to him, journeymen, labellers, that sort of thing. D'you know of a man called Spavin?"

"No – at least I don't think so, the name is unusual."

"Art critic, pompous old fool but a good enough scribbler. I've had all my collections written up by him. Print a limited edition catalogue with colour photographs and you're ready for the market. You have to tell people what you've got. Do I shock you Inspector?"

"No, I have no strong feelings one way or the other. I told you – I'm not a collector."

"It shocks some people. I quite enjoy that."

The schoolboy was back again. Webber thought that women could find him attractive, here was a powerful personality that would charm without his money and in spite of his age.

'There's a lot of damned nonsense talked about art, they don't like the market-place. Well I do. If you want a yardstick you won't go far wrong with money. I did it with Etruscan bronzes, paintings – I had these rooms full of Bacon and Hockney once – then paperweights, then Victorian primitive paintings and now this."

40

"And David Walton advised you on pottery from the beginning?"

"No, I'd been collecting it for some time, Spavin had already started the catalogue. David transformed it. The man was a natural, he was wasted turning out pots and pans for peanuts. Oh, I paid him well enough, but he could have made a fortune as a dealer. He could spot a really fine piece in a saleroom full of rubbish, anywhere if it comes to that, village junk shops, Bond Street," he chuckled. "Oh yes, even Bond Street! A bargain doesn't have to be cheap Inspector. I don't fool myself. Self-deception is just as disastrous in collecting as in business. It's all the same. I've read all the books of course, you must do that, and if I'd given you that guided tour it would have been impressive, I promise you. But that's all, I'm not a true expert, not like Davey. He was, my lovely man."

"You'll miss him."

"I will."

There was a knock and the woman he'd called Miss Evans stood in the doorway.

"You asked me to remind you. Mr Spavin is still waiting."

"Tell him I'm busy. Make another appointment for him."

"Very good, sir."

For someone for whom time was expensive Elberg was according VIP treatment. Webber accepted it without a polite protest. He sensed that his reticence was intriguing Hans Elberg; often you learned more that way. When he was ready he would ask questions.

As if on a sudden impulse Elberg walked to some large doors at the far end of the room.

"You think you have seen the whole collection?"

He grinned delightedly as he pushed open the double doors to reveal another windowless gallery.

As Webber joined him the lights in the display cases burst through the blackness to reveal such a shout of colour and life that he held his breath.

The whole of the wall space was crowded with pottery figures as unlike the pieces he had already seen as dull brown moths were to blazing butterflies.

"I see you like them," Elberg said, watching him.

Without his realizing it Webber's face had creased into a happy smile.

41

"The right reaction," Elberg said, "in case you were about to play safe and look impressed."

"They don't look like antiques," Webber said.

"Victorian," Elberg gestured towards the figures massed on the shelves. "Fifty years ago you could have bought Staffordshire figures like these for pennies. People couldn't see them for what they were. They are still grossly undervalued I believe, the trick is to get in while the market is still comparatively low. It's fine modern art of course, naive, primitive, but quite superb. These Victorian boys – quite unknown most of them – were at it long before Rousseau and Picasso, just look at the colours! Makes that early stuff look pretty sick eh? It's Hockney too, the same passion and sheer love of life. Someone, I forget who, said that they were like a brass band on a sunny day. My Hockneys were like that. Maybe I should have kept them a wee bit longer."

"All his passions have made money for him," Elberg's wife had said.

The man fascinated Webber. His preoccupation with money and yet his obvious love for the things he had collected.

Elberg crossed to a table in the centre of the room.

"Will you take a glass of sherry or am I being selfish and keeping you from your luncheon? I don't eat at midday myself and it seems I have the luxury of a little extra time."

Webber pictured Lizzie Thomas patiently waiting for him in the restaurant of the British Home Stores. It was a lesson she would have to learn. There were still things he wanted to know.

"Thank you, dry if I may. I'm in no hurry."

✺ SEVEN ✺

LIZZIE WAS LATE herself. It had been a busier morning than she had planned for. She sat in the self-service restaurant and sipped a cup of tea until he came. Ten past one. It was unlikely that he wouldn't have waited ten minutes for her. No, he must have been delayed and she in her turn would wait for him, there would be no limit to her patience. It was her private fantasy that patience was one of her strongest virtues. Policemen were not as other men. They needed loyalty and loyalty was begat of patience.

She did not realize it at the time but later she would look back and see that it was there, during her long wait for him, that she had put herself on trial and found herself not guilty. The issue before her was simple. What right had she to uproot him from the pleasant comfort of his village retirement and push him protesting back into a way of life he swore he disliked. As a professional policeman, he told her, his successes had been merely the acceptable average, modest and largely unacclaimed by his superiors or indeed his equals.

She had not believed him. It was the reason she had taken courage and gone to see Snow, and Snow had told her what she had most wanted to hear.

"Average? It's not a word I'd choose for John," he had said. "I've worked with a lot of policemen in my time, Mrs Thomas. We don't work miracles – not like they do on the telly I'm afraid. You could call a lot of us average, John Webber was better than that. Faint praise?" She remembered his grin. "Better than average is very high in my book. I'll put it another way if you like. I think he was better at his job than any policeman I've ever worked with."

The memory of that conversation was dear to her. A justification.

43

Webber realized with a pang of conscience that it was nearly three o'clock. He thought he had got as much out of Elberg as he usefully could, slipping his questions into the lecture he had been promised he wouldn't get.

"It is literally," Elberg concluded, "a potted history of their Victorian world, it was their colour TV if you like, only silent thank God! They commented on everything around them, wars, theatre, the Royal Family, politicians – by the way 10 Downing Street has a good collection of those I'm told – sport, saints, sinners – they loved a good murder, some of their bloodiest villains fetch the highest prices I'm afraid! Bad taste to mention murder, Mr Webber?"

"No, sir, it has been a part of my life for a good many years. You get paid and you do your best." Well there it was, a bit crude perhaps, but after all the question of his fee had not been settled.

Elberg closed the doors on the Victorian collection and walked back to the desk.

"Quite right, you've been very patient, you must excuse a young man's enthusiasm."

Webber's face didn't change but Elberg explained it just the same.

"It's the great secret Inspector, enthusiasm is the key. Better than all the bran diets for keeping a man young."

In his shaving-mirror that very morning Webber had compared his own face to that of a sad spaniel. Perhaps Elberg was thinking the same.

"My wife tells me that your Scotland Yard colleague seemed to think that £500 a week and expenses would be acceptable."

He didn't wait for Webber to confirm or comment but handed him the cheque he had been writing earlier.

"Four weeks in advance. Obviously you can't put a time limit on your inquiry but after a month we should both have some idea."

The cheque was made out for the sum of £4000, payable to John Webber.

"It's all right, not a mistake. I've doubled it. I pay my experts well. I'm not a fool, I don't throw money away."

"It's very generous."

"Money doesn't go far today. I'd like some news of you when you're ready but I won't tie you too closely, a weekly report seems reasonable, would you say? You can send your expenses to me

44

here by letter. I don't want receipts, they're insulting I think, I'd like an indication that's all, just for interest, air fares and so on, that sort of thing."

Webber thought of his police diary in the old days. 'Entered King's Head public house to purchase refreshment for informant,' and then on the right-hand page, 'Seven shillings and sixpence'.

"I'll see that your bank account is credited, you can give Miss Evans the details when you go. A few more points and then I've done. First. The whole reason for this exercise is to put my wife's mind at peace."

"And if it doesn't?" Webber interjected.

"Then that's my problem, but I have no doubt that it will. The chance that her poor parents' death could be anything but an accident must be millions to one but if it exists then for God's sake find it. Then perhaps she can start living normally again. She can't go on as she is now, I'm damn sure of that." He said it quietly and Webber saw something of the strain the man must have been under for many months and felt sorry for him. "She will accept the truth from you, Inspector. That is why you're here." He pressed a button on his desk and walked with him to the door, opening it to the clinical smell of the new technology in the room outside.

Webber said, "And the other points?"

"I'm only interested in facts – the truth, speculation won't do. Right? Four weeks should be enough for that I think – I hope. You'll forgive me but a thousand pounds a week cannot be an open-ended commission. If you genuinely need longer that will be different, it's for you to work at your own pace, we can discuss it again then. The fee by the way includes VAT. I don't want to ask how you run the business side of your job, but your money has to be by cheque, cash is not possible I'm afraid."

It didn't annoy Webber; he liked Elberg better for it. He nodded his agreement, adding casually, "A happy marriage, would you say – the Waltons? Get on well did they?"

Only for a moment did Elberg hesitate.

"Nothing is perfect Mr Webber – they did better than most."

Miss Evans appeared at the end of the computer room, her shoes tapping a human defiance to the clicking robots around her.

45

"I don't know what these things do for you," Webber said, "but I could never get along with the computer age. We had them in the force. They scare the hell out of me."

"These are friendly wee things," Elberg smiled mischievously. "They're monitoring their big brothers at my headquarters for me, just to see they don't step out of line! A man needs friends Inspector. You might say I rather need you at this time. I'll help you in every way I can. I think I've made it clear that I like my experts to have a clear run. When I was a young man I found it difficult to believe that anyone could do anything better than I could myself. It's a stupidity I have learned to curb. You will, I imagine, go to France?"

"Yes, I shall have to cover it."

Elberg nodded. "In the old days I would have wanted to come with you and you wouldn't have enjoyed that at all. Now I'm too busy, and wiser. If I'm not here Miss Evans can usually contact me."

He shook Webber's hand and was gone.

She saw him first, across the restaurant, scanning the tables as though it was a duty but not expecting to find her still there. She allowed herself the pleasure of the moment until he should see her. His back was straight, that was good, and his head well up. Above average. A two-fingered whistle is not an accomplishment given to all women. She had learned it from a shepherd as a child in Wales, on a mountain called Plum Pudding. Every whistle was a specific instruction and at full blast could cross a valley with ease. She chose medium strength, "Come over by here and sit."

He did that, a light springy step, face beaming. It was going to be all right. No he hadn't eaten, but he wasn't hungry. She bought him sandwiches from the counter. Webber looked at her with such obvious pleasure that she was afraid she might forget herself and fling her arms around him.

"Had enough of this?"

She nodded.

"Come on then, fresh air."

They walked up Kensington High Street past the shell of the old Town Hall, sad and ravished by the demolition workers, the bright blue of the domed ceiling indecently exposed like an old woman showing her knickers. The rain which had threatened

46

earlier hadn't developed and in Kensington Gardens it was early spring again with white puffs of cloud in a blue sky. They sat on a bench at the Round Pond; children and grown men played with toy boats while she heard his account in silence. Instead of interrupting she made mental notes and waited.

A few yards away on the edge of the pond an old man was feeding stale crusts to a screaming flock of seagulls and water birds. A goose, bolder than its fellows, detached itself from the fracas and waddled up to inspect the packet of sandwiches on the bench between them. With neck extended and beak some seven inches from the paper bag it unwisely chose to glance up and received the full impact of Mrs Thomas's blazing stare. Webber watched the bird recoil as if struck and slink away. In the past he had observed others similarly affected. It was a gift. Some people could bend spoons.

His account of his visit to the house in Holland Crescent was factual, almost clinical, unadorned by any personal reaction of his own. He didn't refer to his notes, he had no need, it was all there in his head. He was aware of this as he completed his account and was pleased and relieved that his memory seemed unimpaired. He could have been reporting to a colleague, she thought, and adjusted the weight of her bottom on the bench with pride and pleasure. Best of all was his face. It was wide-eyed with something very like excitement.

A young man walked slowly past them holding a miniature transmitting radio set, the bright rigid aerial extended, his serious eyes fixed far out on the water where a red, speeding motor boat obeyed his every command on the surface of his private ocean. The sun was low in the sky, dipping down to the roof of Kensington Palace. The air lost its grip on early spring and resigned itself to late winter again.

"Getting nippy, too many questions for out here," she said, "best go back and talk in the warm. You haven't touched your sandwiches."

Webber looked at her with deep admiration. He had told her everything except the amount of money written on the cheque, and she hadn't asked. He took it from his wallet and held it in front of her to read.

"I think you'll find the water will be hot," she said, rising to her feet. "We can have a bath and then a good dinner somewhere, treat ourselves. Then work."

She took the sandwiches out of the wrapping. The goose had removed itself from its fellows and was convalescing thoughtfully at the edge of the pond. Mrs Thomas laid them temptingly on the ground before it.

"Come on my lovely. You're in luck, and God knows we all need luck isn't it?"

⚜ EIGHT ⚜

WEBBER WANTED TO eat English food but she wouldn't hear of it.
It was, she told him as she helped him button his braces, an art
only successfully achieved at home, it did not lend itself to
commercial interpretation. The choice of restaurant presented no
difficulties for her. She confronted the Italian head waiter in the
dining room of the Glockemara and asked him if he could
recommend somewhere where they could get a decent meal. Her
instinct was right, Mr Trissino not only thought the request
reasonable but was grateful that she would not be dining at the
Glockemara. On a previous visit she had invaded the kitchen to
settle a point of culinary interest. He had no wish to see her in
there again. The Irish chef had resented constructive advice and
had countered with some of his own. Mr Trissino liked a quiet
life and was happy to direct them to a small restaurant nearby.
They made their own pasta, he said, and he had eaten there with
Mrs Trissino; also, he assured them, it was not in the *Good Food
Guide*.
     She was well pleased. The Prodigo did not run to a fatted calf
but the pasta was indeed home-made and the wine cheap and
good. They ate and drank in silence by mutual consent. The
room was small but uncrowded. Over coffee she said, "It's a lot
of money John."
     "And four weeks isn't very long."
     "To find out what happened?"
     "That's a hell of a short sentence, isn't it? Yes, to find out what
happened. If anything did."
     "But you're going to try, aren't we?"
     "I've never been paid so much money in my life. I'd be a fool
to turn it down. I think he's a fool to pay it." He made a small
tower with the paper-covered sugar lumps and they watched in
silence until he over-reached himself and it collapsed. Then he

49

said, "I know it sounds cruel, but why didn't he make her go back to the Foreign Office with him – let her see the report for herself? A damn sight cheaper than paying me to convince her."

"That would be very cruel John, besides she knows what the report says. What good would it do if he made her look at those photographs? I can understand her. She wants an investigation and she chose you. He'll pay the price because he knows she will accept your report."

"I'm not even sure she believes that they were burnt to death. If she'd seen the photographs then she'd have to believe it. Is that more cruel than letting her imagine things for the rest of her life? Like murder say? When he first told her in South America, she was ill you remember. She couldn't take it in, she thought he was trying to tell her they'd been shot. Perhaps that's still in the back of her mind. There's not much of her but I'll give her this Lizzie, she's a very determined woman. And of course you're right, he knows that too."

She guarded the last of the wine in her glass and said nothing. Let him talk. It was his way of thinking. A stranger might have thought him despondent but he wasn't. The excitement was still there. He cleared a space in the middle of the white paper tablecloth and carefully placed two of the sugar lumps at the centre of it.

"Not another soul in sight," he said, "just the sea and the sky and miles of empty sand and two charred corpses."

"And a dead calm."

"Wind can drop. I have to tell you Lizzie, there have been stranger accidents. Anything is believable if it's possible."

"She doesn't believe it."

"Does she know something else? Then why not tell me?"

"Perhaps she wants you to tell her it isn't true. Something she won't face herself or even bring herself to discuss with her husband. What kind of a marriage was it, her mother and her father?"

"They did better than most. I'm quoting Elberg."

"Did you ask her?"

"Yes. Happy – as far as she knew."

"Suicide?"

He nodded, staring at the table. "Possible. It's a hell of a way to go. A pact – or one of them was going to make sure the other went too." He remembered Snow's words. "Their arms were still round each other when the first people got to them."

50

"They were walking on a beach–you'd need more than a bottle of lighter fuel for that," she said.

"Terrorists do better than lighter fuel. Incendiary bombs can be small enough to go in a parcel–even a letter. I suppose they can be bought somewhere if you're determined enough. Yes, they'd do it better than pipe sparks."

"Nasty."

"Yes."

"I saw a list on your chest of drawers. I don't suppose it had anything to do with shopping."

"It's not all that different." He produced a paper from his wallet and handed it to her, signalling to the waiter for more coffee. "Since we're a bit flush shall we treat ourselves to a brandy Lizzie?"

"Why not, but not Italian." She forced her eyes up from the paper. "Not brandy at all, come to think of it. Dr Collins says whisky is better for you. Ask him for a malt if he's got it."

She studied the neat, almost feminine handwriting on the page of ruled paper he had torn from his notebook. He had filled it down to the bottom line, the list carefully numbered.

1. Snow. Meet soon as possible at home. Take Lizzie.
2. Donald Walton–The son.
3. Arnold Swan–The partner.
4. James Spavin–The cataloguer.
5. Sir Michael Humper–The specialist.
6. Holland Crescent.
7. The Elbergs–more background–South America?
8. The Staff–numbers?

When she looked up he had built the sugar tower to a surprising height.

"Don't breathe too hard," he said amiably, "it might fall down again."

"Are these in order of priority?" she said.

"No, it's a check-list, it looks tidier than it is."

She sipped the malt whisky appreciatively. "I can help a little bit I think, with some of it anyway."

"That would be nice–go on."

"Staff at Holland Crescent. Only two living in the house. That's the Filipino couple, cook and butler, only she can't cook not as she should anyway. The woman you met, Miss Evans –she's not Welsh by the way–pity, I might have done well

51

there. The Elbergs own two of the cottages in the mews that runs along the back, behind that big garden. Miss Evans is his private secretary, she's got a degree in computer programming. A spinster, about forty or forty-five, lives in one of the cottages. The chauffeur lives in the other, he's about thirty, trained as a mechanic with Rolls-Royce at Derby, lost his job when they cut down their workforce, not married, lives with his girlfriend Lorraine, about twenty-five, she's his second, the first one, Trina, was a bit older, nearer his own age, they split up after a row. There are four cleaning ladies, not women – ladies, it's the new style of addressing them, it hasn't reached Suffolk yet. They do mornings only and they need them, it's a big place. They don't clean downstairs where you were, the Filipino woman does that with her husband."

Webber said, "I got a bit disorientated this morning – you're right it is a big place. Do you happen to know why the offices have no windows?"

"Because they're underneath the garden, that's why. He asked for planning permission to build out at the back and it was refused. He called in a firm who build underground car parks and they did it for him. Then they put the garden back on top, trees and all. They couldn't argue with that. I shouldn't worry about your fee, I don't think it will break him. Did you like him? I meant to ask."

"He's got style, I felt sorry for him. I don't think he's particularly happy. Admired him is better. You might as well ask someone if they liked Woolworth's."

"The staff like him, they're not so sure of her – a bit aloof. The malt's good isn't it?"

"Shall we try another?"

"You'll only have one in your bedroom if we don't. One more here and no more at the hotel, right?"

"A promise – this is pleasanter anyway and without wishing to seem pushy may I inquire where Madam got the information from?"

"Madam had a look at the place this morning. I spotted one of the cleaning ladies leaving and got chatting. Nice little woman, married unwisely in Wandsworth. The husband drinks but it gives her more time for the telly."

"You approached this informant and just said 'Excuse me but . . . '?"

52

"I wasn't looking where I was going and knocked her over – well, not *right* over, I was able to grab her. I was a television researcher getting information for a modern version of 'Upstairs, Downstairs'. The title," Mrs Thomas added delicately, in her best media jargon, "is not finalized at this moment in time."

The warmth of his hand covering her own brought a sudden flush of pleasure beneath the broderie anglaise fichu at her neck.

"How much will you give Ted Snow?" She asked so that he would see she was able to control her delight and he understood that.

"We've had good luck Lizzie. I'd have settled for half that. We can go back to square one. I'll give him two thousand pounds. We've still got expenses. It's enough. Nice to be able to do it."

She nodded. "Quite right – and then?"

"After a month? God knows. I'm not that far ahead. Wait and see. Ted doesn't know about the money yet. I rang earlier, we're seeing them tomorrow evening."

Snow was late. At five o'clock he phoned Betty from the vast reception hall of the Old Bailey where he had waited all day to give evidence in a stabbing case, a left-over from his days at Brixton. She took some time answering and mentally he followed her fluster in the kitchen. A bad time to phone, it couldn't be helped. On the walls inside the telephone box he read the graffiti of the courts. 'Sid's counsel is a fat wanker' and 'Public schoolboy, pretty face, cheap, daytime and school hols only, ring – –' At least someone had scratched the number out, Snow thought glumly. Perhaps the new school was a mistake after all. First pot and now sex, you couldn't win. He was half joking; fed up and tired. He pictured her hurriedly drying her hands in the hall and dead on cue she picked up the telephone. He delivered the message she had heard thousands of times over the years.

"It doesn't matter, well it does of course, tonight I mean. How long do you think?"

"Not long, the old man won't sit late. This is just in case. Hang on." Through the glass of the telephone box Snow saw his courtroom emptying, spilling out among the mosaic pillars and the plump-lady frescoes, counsel, witnesses, and detectives, like children out of school. "No panic, the gaiety's over for today, give me an hour and I might beat John and Lizzie to it. Kids back yet?"

"They're doing their homework."

"Good. Careful with that oven, it's hotter than the old one."

It was the oven that broke the ice. Webber and Mrs Thomas arrived before Snow. The blue haze of charred food in the hall took Betty and Mrs Thomas hurrying to the kitchen, leaving Webber with the children.

"Not disaster," she told Betty cheerfully, peering through the smoke billowing from the door of the open oven. "Only the baked potatoes. Good job you've only just put the chicken in. Got a pinny?"

Webber liked the children. He had never blamed Lilian for refusing to have a family. Even in the early days he could see that it wouldn't have been right for her. Perhaps he'd been wrong to give in, it might have steadied her. If there was any blame, it was his as much as hers.

The children were both fair, he could see Snow's face in them, Snow as he'd known him God knows how many years ago. Their fair skin and green flecked eyes were Betty's. Alice was shyer than her brother, tracing the pattern of the carpet with her toe; Alan bright, as his father had said, and already with the gawky assurance of adolescence on him. Webber remembered reading somewhere that you shouldn't ask children how they liked school. It showed a lack of conversational invention, stamped you as a Victorian uncle. Perhaps they were wrong; the boy seemed happy to talk, a bit solemn, careful choice of words.

"It's much better really sir. Science for instance. We had a computer at Brixton – actually it was rather better than ours at St Peter's but you couldn't really use it yourself. There were too many boys and the software was pretty dull, just library cassettes really. Now I can write my own programs – well, I try anyhow." He looked even younger when he smiled. "It's got 48 K RAM and a data transfer rate of 16 bytes a second. Of course you only get out of it what you can put in but it's awfully interesting."

"It sounds very exciting," Webber said. Computers, you couldn't escape them.

When Snow came they ate early to share it with the children. It was a happy evening, with Mrs Thomas disclaiming any credit for the food. No one believed her and it didn't matter. Webber tried to remember when he'd last eaten with the laughter of a family and failed. He was unexpectedly touched when Alice kissed her mother and father before going to bed and then shyly included Lizzie and himself. Alan claimed a later bedtime but behaved well.

"It's business son, and you know I don't get much time."

"If I go now and get ready for bed quickly, *really* quickly, can I show Mr Webber my print-outs? Oh please Dad! He's frightfully interested, aren't you sir?"

Betty tousled his hair on her way to the kitchen. "Yes let him Ted, he's been very fair. Only a few minutes Alan. No Mrs Thomas – sorry, Lizzie I mean – no honestly, you've shamed me enough, it won't take long. You've done most of it anyway, though God knows how."

In the kitchen she wondered why she hadn't resented the woman instead of liking her. John was a fool if he didn't marry her. He must see she's mad about him, perhaps not, he was never very bright with women. She would try and speak to him – not tonight – but when the right moment came. Any woman who could make rice taste like that and wash up at the same time was worth hanging on to. She wished she had asked her about the money. It didn't matter, Ted would tell her. At least she wasn't a gold digger, not with those clothes. That was something. Oh damn! She'd forgotten the coffee.

When she took it in, Alan, pink-faced with scrubbing and excitement, was sitting in his camel dressing-gown containing himself with difficulty and listening to his father.

Snow was smiling wryly at Webber and Mrs Thomas. "He would choose that one! Well why not? I give him projects – purely imaginary of course – for his programs. Chess held him for a while but you got a bit fed up with that, didn't you son? We had quite a good one on football riots, he fed in weather conditions, home win or loss, number of goals, police on terraces, that sort of thing. It had some merit but this one . . ."

"This one is jolly good," the boy said. "There's this man and his wife walking alone on a beach . . ."

55

❧NINE❧

THE BOY WAS old-fashioned, Mrs Thomas decided. The description wouldn't have meant the same to the others as it did to her but to anyone in the Welsh village where she was born the words would have conveyed an exact picture of Alan's character. Mentally advanced for his years, precise in his choice of words, quiet in Sunday chapel but given to questioning the sermon later – old-fashioned.

"Dad's quite right of course. It is unlikely that a husband and wife would have been strolling along on a beach in the Falklands but you see we already had a program on the task-force landings so I thought it might be quite fun to feed my data into that. Anyway it was miles better than chess, and you see Mrs Thomas, the more ridiculous the problem, the more fun it is seeing what comes out. My father's imagination is jolly sharp don't you think?"

"Like a knife," she agreed. "Can we borrow this? Mr Webber likes to read before he goes to sleep, he tells me."

In the car going back she sat quietly beside him, digesting the events of the evening and clicking them off with a soft snap of the catch on her handbag. She was restless. She might calm down with talk, he thought, or failing that he might find a pub on the way where she could unwind.

"Did you like her?" he said.

"Betty? Oh yes, yes I did – she must have the patience of a saint. All that waiting."

"They're a special breed, they have to be. The money went down well."

"She couldn't believe it. I'm glad. Did you know they had letters threatening his life in Brixton?"

"No, but it doesn't surprise me."

56

"She coped with that. When they started to write about the children she couldn't take it. She'd had enough."

"Poor Betty – the boy's bright, like Ted. Perhaps he'll go for a copper too."

"She doesn't think so, the Church perhaps. He finds it a challenge, seems the computer's very non-committal about God."

"They're not as stupid as I thought."

"It's only a list. You get out what you put in. Remember? I thought it was interesting."

He shot her a quick glance. "Fed up?"

She hauled herself by the seat-belt into a better position for attack. "Four weeks John. I don't begrudge Ted Snow his cut but if you're going to get anywhere you'll do it on your own. We won't get very far spending an evening with a happy family."

He risked teasing her. "Mr Plod the policeman. Mrs Plod the policeman's wife. Master Plod . . ."

". . . The partner, the specialist, the cataloguer and Walton's son. That's plod if you like, and what's the good of only fart-arsing around in England, why wasn't France on your list for God's sake?"

The traffic-lights at Swiss Cottage let him into Avenue Road and a turning into the car-park of a pub. The place was crowded with the audience from Hampstead Theatre Club anxious for a drink before closing time. They had to share a large table with a party of three people nursing small glasses of sweet sherry, a man in jeans, bald except for a defiant fringe of shoulder-length gossamer hair, and two women with wooden beads and earrings. Mrs Thomas sat at the end brooding, with their conversation pushing into her head while Webber fetched the drinks.

"Oh frightfully good, the commercial crowd won't touch it of course . . ."

"Good and Evil isolated in the gondolas of the separate balloons – brilliant – just drifting . . ."

"I loved the idea of using Bartok's music as a character, so moving, no actor could have done that."

"Von Sternberg did it with Bruckner of course, but somehow that missed."

"Glib."

"Yes, glib. With Bartok you just knew that the policeman was only part of a dream."

"Sinking back into the basket."

"Lovely."

"One gets so bored with reality."

At the crowded bar Webber fortified himself with a small whisky and carried beer and Guinness back to the table. It wasn't her fault: he knew her sense of frustration and it was time to let her off the leash. He checked his watch and sipped gratefully – twenty-five minutes; it was enough. The babble of the pub would make him raise his voice to get across to her. It was no problem, familiar ground for both of them, if she would let him make his points. Her silence and her slightly shamefaced look gave him encouragement.

"Two charred bodies on an open beach. Right? Now, you think that my approach to that gruesome little scene is pedestrian? Perhaps it is but I can't help it. Police work *is* plodding Lizzie."

She didn't interrupt. Good. He produced two pieces of paper from his wallet. His own list and the computer print-out Alan had been so proud of.

"You get cross easily so I'll start with an apology. My apparent lack of interest in this print-out was because I thought I hadn't got my spectacles with me. I've just found them in my overcoat so we can look at it together, I'll come to my list afterwards. Guinness all right?"

She nodded, silent, on her best behaviour.

"I did listen to the kid though and I knew there was something odd; see what you think. Interesting." He adjusted the half lenses on his nose and read clearly over the din.

"Double death – causes:

1. Landmine – anti-personnel.
2. Flame-thrower.
3. Incendiary bomb – letter-type or packet.
4. Exocet missile.
5. Meteor.
6. Satellite space debris.
7. Immolation – suicide pact – suicide and accidental death – suicide and murder.
8. Act of God – lightning – spontaneous combustion."

He took his spectacles off and said, "Come on then."

The three people at the other end of the table had fallen silent, the wooden earrings and the gossamer hair motionless.

"I'm sorry I swore. Fart-arse was indelicate."

58

"Forgiven, understandable. Forgotten. Now that we've plod-
ded through it together I want to know what you think."

She took the print-out and slowly read it again, wanting to
please him. "Allow for the Falklands and God and it comes down
to suicide. It's not very strong on murder is it?"

"No. And it ignores our logical French friends completely."

"No flaming tobacco sparks."

"That's the one, which brings me to my own list and I hope
another apology. We got rather side-tracked if you remember
with the last item on the page and your 'Upstairs, Downstairs'
research. If Madam will kindly turn it over she will see that I'd
written something else. I will refresh the glasses. I see we have
ten minutes left."

On the other side of his paper Webber had written:

'8. Lizzie – France.'

She became aware of the three faces at the table unashamedly
devouring her with curiosity.

Mrs Thomas beamed at them with genuine friendliness.
"Early days yet," she murmured confidentially, "but personally
I think it was murder."

She may have thought that her outburst of impatience had been the
sole reason for Webber's swift change of tempo but it wasn't that.
He knew his own way of working, and it would have been the same
whether she had been with him or not. Now that she had committed
him he knew that she had been right. He was surprised to find that
he was glad to get away from his comfortable retirement and noted
with interest that his arthritis troubled him less than it had done for
months. His respect for her had always been tinged with
apprehension, and he was too honest not to recognize that by
sending her to France he was not only making full use of her
linguistic talents in an environment in which he himself would have
been severely handicapped, but that it left him a welcome respite
when he could work – plod if she liked that better – at his own pace.
In France she would discover more than any official deputation
from the British authorities, of that he was certain.

On the station forecourt at Victoria in the morning he guarded
her suitcase and overcoat while she bought newspapers, a

magazine and a guide-book. She might, he thought, have been any ordinary housewife about to visit her grandchildren in the country. She gave no sign of having been up since dawn. She had organized herself with fearsome efficiency. She cancelled her room at the Glockemara, transferring most of her clothes to his wardrobe, collected travellers' cheques from the bank after a lively discussion on the current rate of exchange, and telephoned the Hôtel L'Aigle Royal at Le Bosquet. It was the hotel from which David and Jane Walton had taken their last walk.

The train was already at the platform and if it left on time they had only a few minutes. He listened patiently to a lecture on food and clean underwear and confirmed their arrangement for keeping in touch by telephone.

"Does it ever occur to you to wonder how I managed before I met you Lizzie?" he asked mildly.

"You didn't manage – you've forgotten. Keep warm, it's a funny old time of the year."

"You were going to phone Father Bernard at Calais, did you get him?"

"I left a message, he's an old man now, not fair to pester. I'll see how it goes. I did write but I haven't heard."

"You won't want that overcoat on for God's sake!"

The fur fabric garment reached from her ankles to the fringed parka hood framing her face. "I'll see what the heating's like first." She heaved herself into the first-class carriage and claimed a window seat with her suitcase. To their mutual relief the train shuddered and shook itself. She leaned out of the window and took his face in her hands. "Bye bye my lovely. Don't forget your All-Bran."

Ridiculously he found himself lumbering a few paces after the moving train, pulling up with a sheepish grin but watching until he could no longer see her.

Early that morning he had phoned Snow. A taxi took him to the Old Bailey where with luck he hoped to meet him. The arrangement was loose, Snow wasn't happy about a meet in a pub near the courts. Away from the stress and drama, eyes and ears became sharper, it would be safer to talk in the reception hall of the Old Bailey itself. Webber had never seen it, he was a provincial man, more at home with quarter sessions and crown courts. Climbing the steps to the main door with FIAT JUSTITA RUAT CAELUM carved over it he felt like a tourist.

Inside Snow claimed him and walked him briskly through the crowded hall. Black and white barristers, black and white witnesses, old women tired and frightened, young men frightened but defiant. They found a seat on a wooden bench and merged gratefully into anonymity.

"Lucky," Snow said, "I've done my first whack, that was the identification parade lark. Remember the drill? 'Inspector, was there not a gap in the parade in which Mr Hoozain was placed by the police officer?' In a bit I'll go back and explain that we didn't plant the knife on him either."

"Things don't change."

"The old man's no fool but it takes time." He produced a packet of papers from his jacket pocket. "I picked this lot up for you at the Yard this morning."

"Useful?"

"Could be, shove it away and look at it later. Lizzie got off all right?"

"I've just seen her on to the boat train."

"A bit sudden?"

"She likes to move. It makes sense, she tends to get a bit worked up. She'll be better off on her own for a while, and to be honest so will I."

"Who is this Father Bernard she mentioned last night?"

"One of Lizzie's lame ducks, she picked him up on a park bench in Calais once. He's old now, bright though, I liked him. Lives in a home for retired priests. She says she won't pester him but she will." Webber patted his coat where he had stowed Snow's packet of papers. "How useful Ted?"

"I don't know, it's mostly routine background stuff on the names you gave me. I was trying to get some sort of picture of Walton and his wife, put some flesh on them for you. They're not real people yet are they? It depends where you start. My job is to feed you some answers, all I want is the questions."

"I'm going up to see Arnold Swan, Walton's partner, and while I'm there I can have a chat with the son, young Donald. You said you had some lines out on him?"

"He's still living at his parents' house in Solihull as far as I know. His London address is in there, you've probably got it from his sister anyway. He shared a flat with a woman called Mrs Motherwell, she owns an antique shop, he worked for her in the shop as well."

61

"As well?"

Snow smiled. "Perhaps she was just living up to her name. What is he? About twenty-two? She might fill you in a bit before you blaze up the motorway." Webber had always been a bit of a joke as a cautious driver.

A voice at the other end of the hall was bellowing Snow's name.

He stood resignedly: "I must go and chat to his Lordship about cutlery." He paused before surrendering himself to the court. "Elberg's cheque go through all right?"

"How else would I find £2000 in cash for you. Why?"

"He might not be as stable as we thought. You'll find a whisper in there from C6 at the Yard. Nothing definite, but you'll see that the fraud boys have been nibbling at him. I shouldn't think it's anything he can't cope with, mind you. A couple of million one way or another – no sweat, not for him, he's too big. Interesting though."

"I'll read it," Webber said. "I think your usher is getting cross."

❧ TEN ❧

WEBBER HAD MISJUDGED her. Although she had considered visiting Father Bernard at the Hospice Ecclésiastique in Calais, out of kindness she had decided against it. When no reply had come to her long letter she pictured him perhaps frail and ailing after the cold winter. Whatever the outcome of her journey she would save her visit to Calais and the Hospice until she was ready to return. Flowers and delicacies, that's what she would take him, if the nuns would let him have them. He had never mentioned nuns, but in her imagination she had seen a grim-faced staff of scrubbed women in black. She must remember to wear something bright and cheerful for him.

The taxi she had hired at Boulogne deposited her on the promenade in front of the L'Aigle Royal at four o'clock in the afternoon, and on the pavement when it had driven away she made a careful note of the cost and the tip in the little book she had bought that morning to record her expenses.

The light was beginning to fade but she paused to look out over the smooth yellow sand. In the distance the waves of the grey sea made their own noise, like someone shaking rugs far away. She had expected to look on the beach and feel ... she wasn't sure which emotion would come to her first – horror, pity, revulsion, perhaps all of those. She was unprepared and slightly ashamed to find that the beach only took her back to her childhood. The red sun dipping down into the sea at Barry Island and she, the naughtiest child on the chapel outing, stubbornly paddling on the deserted beach with her back deaf to entreaties and commands. Her mother had fetched her and smacked her but on the bus her father had brushed the sand from her feet and stilled her tears with a piece of peppermint rock that had the words Barry Island printed right through it. Poor Mam, she had been sorely tried, the stubborn child had always been a Dadda's girl.

With the sun gone she felt the chill in the air and was grateful for the warmth of the hotel reception. Like all the hotels along the sea promenade the L'Aigle Royal was geared to supply the tourist traffic of the summer season. At this time of year there were few guests. The hotel was modest compared with the establishments at the more fashionable end of the seafront. In the Michelin guide it was listed as 'Comfortable', and in the chattier paperback guide she had bought that morning at the station bookstall she was informed that it had been owned and run by the same family since it was first built in 1904.

'My wife and I found this an unpretentious establishment catering mainly for French holiday-makers with whom, we were informed, it has remained popular for many years. Some rooms facing the sea have private bathrooms with interesting plumbing. We found the food adequate for the price, unambitious is a fair assessment perhaps. The proprietors, Monsieur and Madame Bouvier, do not speak English.'

The reception room was small with a curved desk in the corner of yellow oak, at one end of which stood a potted fern with tired fronds and a brass bell, at the other end a telephone and a switchboard. There were coloured posters around the walls and the black and white squares of the floor tiles were repeated on the steps of the steep staircase which curved down beside the desk. There was no sign of life, only a faint rumble from the great louvred hot-water radiator in the corner. The radiator reminded her of the wasteful monsters that had heated the classrooms of her schooldays. Her mother had warned her never to sit on them, sitting on hot radiators was an open invitation to piles. Everyone sat on them, if you were lucky enough to race the other children back from the bitter playground you were first on, otherwise you had to queue up until the teacher sent you all scuttling to the desks. Here at least there was no queue and pulling the fur fabric coat up round her waist she hand-tested the temperature and lowered herself gratefully on to the warmth and into the silence of the hotel.

She was, she decided, a mass of contradictions. Adoring John Webber as she did, and admiring him too, she had longed to get away to France and work on her own. And now within hours she missed him. Later it would be better. Then she could go back and tell him what it was like here and what, if anything, she had discovered. Perhaps nothing, but she would have been and seen for herself. The language, thank goodness, was no problem.

A foolish or conceited woman might have seen herself as a detective but she thought of herself in a less glamorous light. Sometimes if you talked and listened carefully then people told you things, sometimes they told you things that were not true and sometimes that was just as interesting. It was an instinct; something you felt and knew inside you. John Webber had smiled when she told him that, but John was a real policeman.

Over there. That was the staircase. Down those steps they had walked together on that Easter Monday morning and across these same black and white tiles. And who knew if there was hate or love in them? Could one or both of them have known that they would never come back? That they would walk out on to the sands and into a blaze of flames so fierce that they would die with the taste of their own burning flesh in their heads.

It wasn't possible.

"I'm sorry Madame, I didn't hear the bell."

The man who had entered through the door behind the desk was about thirty although his strong black hair brushed straight back over his head was already streaked with grey. Behind the thick glasses his eyes were bright and not unfriendly. The moustache, cut short and bristly on the round face, reminded her of a schoolmaster in a French film; not an English film.

Mrs Thomas detached herself from the radiator and advanced with an outstretched hand. It was very important to be open and friendly right from the beginning and in French.

"Monsieur Bouvier? I am Mrs Thomas. I telephoned you from London this morning."

"But certainly Madame." There was an open ledger on the desk but he didn't consult it. Not many guests then. He reached for a key from the rack behind him. "You have a very pleasant room facing the sea as my wife tells me you requested. Allow me to take your valise."

It was more than anyone did for her at the Glockemara.

It was also more than Monsier Bouvier was given to do for his guests. In the summer there were extra people employed for such menial work, a proprietor had to observe task barriers. But this woman with her curiously accented French, dressed as an Eskimo, intrigued him. Could she indeed be an Eskimo?

She saw the open inquiry in his face and was glad for it. Curiosity in others opened doors for satisfying it in oneself. Webber would have been surprised and impressed with her reasons for not opening up a congenial conversation with the hotelier. It was her way never to plan far in advance, she much preferred to assess situations as they arose. At this moment therefore she had not the slightest idea what she would say if anyone asked her the purpose of her visit.

The room did look out on to the beach and the distant sea. The light was nearly gone and she was grateful when he drew the curtains across the windows and she listened with a fair show of attention as he instructed her in the elementary precautions attendant upon the plumbing his grandfather had installed in the bathroom. He eyed the gleaming brass and flowered porcelain with pride.

"Roses and violets together one rarely finds Madame."

"They are indeed very fine."

She could not be English, one did not find such sensitivity with the Anglo-Saxons. He was touched by the childlike appreciation in her face. Was it perhaps possible that she was a comparative stranger to a bathroom? Was it indeed possible to accommodate one in an igloo? He was being ridiculous but one had a duty.

"Excuse me Madame," he edged past her delicately. "The porcelain in this bidet is quite sound. However the floorboards have a certain flexibility. It is only that which might give Madame a momentary sense of insecurity. Here, and here, one has attached handles in the wall. One may lower oneself with caution and in perfect safety. So! Eh?"

Mrs Thomas acknowledged the demonstration with gratitude.

"Will Madame be dining in the hotel?"

Why not? A little unambitious food would suit her well enough on her first evening. It might also serve to introduce her to Madame Bouvier. That indeed was the chief reason for her conversational reticence thus far. Certainly it was important to be open and friendly but it was also quite clear in her mind that such friendship should in the first instance be extended to the wife and not to the husband. She sank gratefully on to the edge of the bed and allowed herself a gentle smile, conveying, she hoped, gratitude, tiredness and a love of all things French.

"But certainly."

Monsieur Bouvier inclined his head and departed.

She wasn't really tired, she told herself, only a little travel-weary. Nothing a hot bath and some food wouldn't put right, and later she would telephone John. The arrangement was loose but practical, he would try and be available at the Glockemara each evening at ten o'clock. He had made a note of her number too as listed in the Michelin, one way or another they could talk and report. The telephone by her bedside looked encouragingly modern and she at once decided not to wait until ten o'clock but telephone him and report her safe arrival. Monsieur Bouvier proved to be efficient on his switchboard but at the Glockemara there was no answer from Webber's room.

In the bathroom she tried to recall the careful cautionary instructions she had been given and decided to leave the bath and settle for what she called a good wash-down. The water when it finally arrived in the floral handbasin was impressively hot and it was some time before she succeeded in conjuring cold out of the brasswork to calm it down. She found herself staring into the mirror above the basin, the towel held to her face with both hands, as if by holding the look in her eyes they would tell her what she was going to do.

They told her nothing, only that the light shining down from above the mirror was unflattering, it was cruel to the bags under her eyes. But it shone on her hair too, showing it strong and vibrant with the side parting she had worn since she was a child in the Thirties. Not dyed, only tinted to bring out the natural lights. Perhaps this had been their room and their faces had stared back at them as hers did now. With what thoughts?

It was too early for dinner. She dressed warmly in a woollen skirt and pullover, a bit bulky but the colours were cheerful and she would need to be warm if she was going to walk before she ate. She finished unpacking, hoping that perhaps a chambermaid would come in to turn down the bed. It occurred to her that apart from Monsieur Bouvier she had seen no one since she arrived. She would have liked a chance to talk to a chambermaid, it might even be that same one who had looked out of a window and seen them die, the breakfast tray still in her hands, coffee and croissants and bread fresh from the bakery. No one came to the room.

The corridor too was quiet and empty; if there were other guests they were remarkably quiet and it came as a relief when she heard voices coming up from reception as she walked down the stairs.

"Ah Madame! I was just ringing your room. You have a visitor."

The man standing with Bouvier in the hall was Father Bernard.

"Elizabeth! My dear daughter, how are you? I have been receiving apologies. You were not given my message."

Bouvier said, "I very much regret Madame, my wife spoke to Monsieur the priest earlier today and must have forgotten to tell me. See, here is the message she wrote down, I apologize. We are just the two of us and it is out of the season you understand?"

"Of course, it doesn't matter. Father!" She embraced him warmly. "How good to see you and how lucky! I was just about to take a walk before dinner."

"Excellent, then we shall take it together."

"Will you be dining sir?"

"Yes certainly he will." Mrs Thomas beamed at her old friend incredulous with the pleasure of seeing him.

"I will tell my wife. About eight o'clock, or earlier if you wish."

When they were alone together she hugged him again. The same white stubbly chin. He kept his razor blades far too long.

"You received my message?"

"Indeed, how else would I know where to find you? Come, let us go, it will be good to stretch the legs after that bus."

He seemed anxious to leave.

"Don't you want to pee or anything?"

"No, later will do. I have some excellent new medicine."

He took her arm and guided her firmly to the door, glancing over his shoulder to see the hotelier back behind his desk. Bouvier watched them go. She must after all be English, only the English could ask such intimate questions of a priest.

Outside only deference to his age modulated her pace to his and she released her enthusiasm in a burst of uninterruptible information and explanation.

The narrow streets of the little seaside town were neat and orderly, planned with French logic to cross each other with right-angled precision that was in contrast to her rambling account of the events which had brought them together in Le Bosquet Plage. Some he knew already from her letter but he listened attentively, seeing the picture more clearly with her there beside him.

The lights were on in the shop windows but the streets had little traffic in them and few people. Some of the small restaurants in the streets farthest away from the tourist promenade looked inviting and they smelled good too. He regretted that they were committed to the L'Aigle Royal for dinner, it was bound to be expensive and such reports as he had were not encouraging.

". . . I cannot plan like John," she was saying. "You know him Father, he thinks ahead and goes slowly step by step. I can't do that. I felt I must get here. To see, to talk and listen. I wanted to find the maid – the chambermaid who saw it happen."

Father Bernard paused and gazed into the lighted window of a charcuterie. She felt a quick pang of conscience. He was an old man and she had walked him too far, dragged him away from his peace and the companions of his refuge. She'd done it with John too, perhaps her daughter Doreen was right and she was a bossy old bitch. She hadn't been meant to overhear that but she had. She was not often at a loss for words but she stood silent at his side, the window bright with the butcher's artistry, pâtés, terrines, strange pale shapes of edible entrails, rare beef charred black and oozing blood.

"Elizabeth, have you talked to anyone yet in the hotel?"

"Only le patron, the one you saw."

"Does he know why you are here?"

"No, why?"

"The chambermaid," he said, "was called Julie Pichon, but we cannot talk to her because she is dead."

❧ ELEVEN ❧

MOLLY MOTHERWELL WASN'T drunk, Webber decided, just pleasantly sloshed. He sat talking to her in the tiny office at the back of her antique shop in a quiet side street behind Barkers department store. She sat amiably behind a desk on which were several broken pottery figures, some tubes of glue, and a litre bottle of white wine from which she occasionally refreshed her glass. The office was separated from the main body of the shop by a bead curtain through which from time to time she made sweeping entrances to deal with visitors.

She was easy to talk to, a pretty woman in her late thirties, perhaps a little more, not a bad figure and good clothes. The well-cut black woollen dress would have looked smarter without the hairs from her Old English sheepdog. Everything about her was slightly out of focus. There was nothing you could point to with certainty to account for it. It was a general effect achieved by small disasters, the slightly smudged make-up, the occasional careless consonant so trivial that you felt only a minor adjustment could have tuned her speech to perfect clarity. Webber guessed that it was her normal condition; not a retreat from reality but a reluctance to abandon the crutch which had helped her to accept it.

"I am a realist Mr Webber, all my friends – and I have many friends thank God – will tell you that. 'Molly may be a bad picker but she's not a moaner. Molly's a realist.' " As she talked she was conscientiously attempting to reassemble a broken pottery figure of Dick Turpin on his horse from the sticky pieces laid out on the blotting paper pad on the desk. "Legs can be very tricky," she murmured with professional concentration. "Get them the teeniest bit out of true and you've got a pantomime horse on your hands and that's not what we're here for, is it? No it is not. There! Come now, we're getting along nicely, only one more leg, and the tail, and then on with his head." She withdrew her tongue and beamed at Webber affectionately.

Her approval communicated itself to her dog who had been absorbed in the work of restoration, shaggy head resting on the desk at her side. Like her mistress she now sat up and transferred her attention to Webber. A chip of pottery had stuck to the fur under her chin.

"You look too young to retire," Molly Motherwell said. "Now let's see, where had I got to? Oh yes, the marriage, Molly's ghastly marriage."

"You don't have to," he said gently, "I told you I have no authority at all. It's a purely private inquiry."

"No, I don't have to; but I think I will." She disengaged the chip of pottery solicitously from the dog's fur. "Mummy quite likes a chat, doesn't she darling? Will you be staying for lunch Inspector? They do very good sandwiches across the road, it wouldn't take a minute to pop across. No? I expect you're wise. I don't really eat lunch myself. Let me top you up, you've hardly touched it, do you not like it?"

"It's very good, thank you."

"Marks and Spencer's, very reliable, I go early before the queues. I never really made much money as a dancer you know. It's such a short career, although dear Irving Davis said I'd got a good two years left in me. Then Mummy won the pools, didn't she darling? Yes! Not a fortune, although I thought so at the time. Sixty thousand pounds – and the first form I'd ever filled in! I'd done it all sensibly too, I put the little x in the square for 'no publicity', although of course I told some people, only friends, people I could trust. Harry for one."

"Harry?"

"He worked in my agent's office, a bit younger than I was, not too much, but a bit. It sort of brought us together – the money I mean."

Her laugh, thought Webber, wasn't bitter, she seemed genuinely amused.

"I suppose I should have guessed but I think I was a late developer."

"It didn't work?"

"No dear, of course it didn't, he went off to Rhodesia or Zimbabwe or whatever they call it, with a boy friend, to grow tobacco or wool or something."

71

"With the money."

"A joint account, silly Molly, but not all of it thank God. I still had this shop and the flat – quite a good lease too, so it could have been worse, although of course I couldn't buy the stock I'd hoped to. My own fault, the aftershave should have warned me, Dahlia hated it too, didn't you my petal? I suppose that's why Donald Walton was such a reassurance. Nothing like that about my Donald, he'll grow up into a lovely man one day. What's she like – the sister?"

"You never met her?"

"No, I knew his father, he used to come and see Don, he stayed sometimes, they were very close. I liked him. Don didn't talk about his sister much, she's very rich isn't she?"

"I believe so. She is very distressed about her parents' death."

She poured the last of the wine with elaborate care. "It wasn't the same for her, she was away, she never knew what it was like for Donald. They made him look at them, did you know that?"

Webber was thankful that she didn't appear to want an answer. She sipped the wine, leaving a trickle which escaped the brimming glass to run down her chin and not wiping it away. If he wasn't careful she would be too far gone to answer his questions sensibly.

"Tell me about Donald's father, what did you think of him as a person?"

Disconcertingly she looked into his eyes and started to giggle but controlled herself and recovered. "I'm sorry, old family joke. When I was young I went to see some terrible film or other with my sister. I can't remember what it was called, only the all-American hero telling the girl that her eyes were like two spoonfuls of the blue Pacific. We used to scream it at each other across the playground at school." With the laughter gone she appeared sober again. "I must tell her about your eyes, but she won't believe it. David Walton?" She concentrated, pushing back the hair which had fallen across her forehead. "He was very important, a great expert, I didn't know that. Did you know that? Excuse me."

Webber silently cursed the jangling doorbell. He noted with surprise that she could walk quite well. She steadied herself on the bead curtain until they had both stopped swaying and advanced with confidence into the shop where an old woman was unwrapping a brown paper parcel. He would have to be patient.

How reliable was she? 'In vino veritas' or 'Wine in, wits out'? She was lonely and unhappy and she seemed to have accepted him. He might be lucky. The dog looked at him solemnly while snatches of conversation filtered through to them from the shop.

"Well, you're quite right Hilda dear, it is Little Red Riding Hood and it is Staffordshire but it's not for me dear, not with the wolf missing and only half her basket, poor thing. No dear, it's ever so kind of you. Why don't you try Mrs Hamilton down the road? She's got one just like it, she could make up a lovely pair. I can't offer you a drinky today dear, I've got a visitor."

The old woman shuffled out with her parcel and Molly Motherwell settled at her desk again.

"That's when I miss the money. I used to be able to buy good things at auction. Now I have to rely on runners like poor old Hilda, lucky sometimes, but mostly rubbish like that. You have to be firm."

"Perhaps she'll sell it to Mrs Hamilton."

"Don't be silly dear, she bought it from her. It's been on her back shelf since Friday and she bought it in Portobello Road."

"You live in a small world."

"Yes, that's why Donald and his father gave me a bit of hope." She put the empty bottle in the waste-paper basket with a clink and replaced it without embarrassment from a drawer in the desk. "I met Donald at a party, he wasn't in the business, he worked for his father's firm, they had a small pottery in Staffordshire. Donald travelled round getting orders for them, Walton and Swan." She was having difficulty twisting the cap off the bottle and Webber did it for her.

"Thank you, how very kind, lovely strong wrists. Frankly I was surprised he noticed me. He was such a beautiful boy, I'm not a fool you know. I was so much older, even though I did knock a bit off and I wasn't drinking so much then. He seemed very interested in the shop and so I brought him back for a night-cap and that's how it started. We liked him didn't we Dahlia? Yes we did!" She made a conscious effort to concentrate. "He kept a bedsitting room in Chelsea for his London visits but after that he hardly ever used it, he came and lived here with me. I loved him," she said.

"How long before you met his father?"

"Oh almost at once, he was doing some research and working for what's-his-name."

"Elberg."

73

"That's it, Elberg, he married Don's sister. Frankly I was a bit scared of meeting Don's father, you know? Why are you sleeping with my son? Old enough to be his mother and all that. Mind you I wasn't, but still."

"But it wasn't like that?"

"No, he couldn't have been sweeter. I needn't have worried. It was on the first evening that I met him – quite soon anyway, and Don said: Well what do you think Dad? Will she do? Shall we adopt her?"

It seemed a curious phrase, Webber thought, for a son to introduce his lover to his father. To his dismay he saw that she had slumped lower into her chair and was beginning to tilt sideways.

"It sounds as though he was proud of you."

She righted herself slowly and concentrated. "I must spend a penny, keep an eye on the shop, don't take any cheques dear." There was a pause during which her distant voice floated through to him in an anxious afterthought: "Or any credit cards."

When she reappeared she had washed her face and combed her hair, the fresh lipstick was only slightly crooked. He felt sorry for her but had no intention of cutting the meeting short.

"You said research, what kind of research?"

"He was building up this collection of Staffordshire pottery for what's-his-name."

"For Mr Elberg, yes, I knew that."

"He found wonderful things for him – things I've only ever seen in books. You know?"

Webber nodded afraid of interrupting her flow. Now for the first time she was drunk, not entirely incapable yet, but the time was coming.

"You saw some of them?"

"Used to bring them in boxes – stored them up there." Her finger pointed to the ceiling.

"When he used to come and stay?"

She was trying hard to speak soberly, once or twice she cleared her throat and tried to do the same with her eyes as she stared hard at him.

"Mrs Motherwell, it's very important."

"Molly!" she said fiercely. "You call me Molly."

"Molly – did David Walton let you have things for the shop

74

sometimes? Things that were – " he thought carefully – "perhaps not quite . . . right for the collection?"

"What's your first name? I can't keep calling you Inspector."

"John."

He didn't try to stop her when she poured and drank. It seemed to clear her head. He'd seen it before. It wouldn't last long, but for the moment she was sensible. Over-solemn but sensible.

"My dear Inspector, that sort of stuff would be no good for me. Look at it," she nodded at the shop, "a crummy little hole full of tatty junk. No passing trade, no big collectors. You need a name to sell quality, not an ex-dancer in a back street."

"Do you still see Donald?"

She shook her head in tired resignation. "I tried to comfort him after they were dead but I couldn't. I think he must hate me. Even blame me."

"Why could that be?" He spoke softly, like a father with a difficult child. Her face was like a child's face too, daring herself to trust him in her misery.

"I told you, they gave me hope. I suppose I let them down. I've always talked too much. I like a chat, remember? And now you come pestering me to do it again. It doesn't matter any more anyway."

In the long pause that followed she made no attempt to pour more wine and he resisted the urge to do it for her.

"I used to take some of the best pieces and put them into auction for them. David said there was nothing illegal in it. Collectors like Elberg like a good provenance he said. Some of them fetched a fortune."

"And David paid you a commission for your help?"

"It made a big difference to me. I know it wasn't wrong because I asked people," she pointed a finger unwaveringly at him, steadying her elbow on the desk, "so don't you try and tell me it was illegal, Mr Cleverboots."

"Donald and his father found out that you'd been talking?"

"You said it yourself. I live in a small world, and a bloody awful world it is too." She withdrew from the desk and focused on the dog. "She won't touch tinned food, I have to walk all the way to Safeways for ox heart."

It was going to be a race against time, and he couldn't afford to lose her.

"And because of that they left you."

75

"Dear John—it is John isn't it? Johnny blue-eyes, and you don't know a bloody thing do you? No it wasn't only that. It was the book, that's what it was. The big beautiful book—big secret—type, type, type, I could hear them down here in the shop." She paused and made as if to adjust a scarf at her throat, frowning to find she wasn't wearing one, leaving her hands crossed at her throat like a dancer. "The big exposure, the lid off everything he knew, potteries, profits, dealers," the hands left her throat and she made an effort to count on her fingers, "collectors, critics, auction rooms, the lot—big deal."

"David Walton told you what he was writing?"

The hands pressed into her face and against the eyes filling with tears. He could scarcely hear her whisper.

"No, Donald did—he told me in bed. Told me never to tell a soul." She was crying freely now but silently. "I was proud of them, I didn't realize it was a real secret."

"Donald took it with him after David died—this book?"

She shook her head miserably. "It was stolen, we had a break-in, a burglary—that's when he left. Poor kid, you can't blame him for hating me can you?" She made an effort to control herself and succeeded, looking at him plaintively.

"I usually have a lie-down about now," she said.

❧ TWELVE ❧

SHORTLY AFTER TEN o'clock that night Mrs Thomas managed to telephone Webber, reversing the charges which he had previously instructed the switchboard at the Glockemara to accept and put down to his account.

"You first," he told her and then listened, wondering at her ability to convey her facts concisely. For someone who enjoyed nothing so much as a conversational ramble she adapted well to necessity and economy.

"Jay-walking, they said, she should have been on the pavement but the car must have hit her when she was walking in the road. That's where they found her in the early morning. She died in hospital about six hours later. A lonely road, not well-lit, she lived alone, not much more than a shack really. Usually she cycled to work and back but that night she found she had a puncture and had to walk."

"And the car didn't stop?"

"No, they just found her."

"It could be coincidence, hit-and-run, a drunk, it happens."

"I'm not phoning from the hotel."

"No?"

"Bernard is staying with the local priest. I'm phoning from the presbytery. I walked him back."

"A chum of his? Useful."

"No he hardly knows him, you just ring up and invite yourself, it's called Christianity."

"I can see Bernard is in good form."

"He sends his love. The priest here at Le Bosquet, Father Girard, he's quite young. He knew Julie Pichon, he was her confessor."

Webber wouldn't raise his hopes over that. He'd dealt with Roman Catholic priests in the past, mainly Irish it was true.

77

Irish or French, he doubted if even Lizzie Thomas had succeeded in breaking the silence of the confessional. On the other hand the priest was quite young. Webber felt a stab of pity for him and told her so.

"Nothing like that," she said with dignity, "I hope I know how to behave."

"Sorry – it just crossed my mind."

"Julie Pichon wasn't confessing anything, she was worried, confused, she went to him for advice. She couldn't understand why the newspaper had made her say things that weren't true. Things she'd never said."

"Like?"

"Like: 'They were leaning against the wind with Madame's dress blowing out behind her and Monsieur holding on to his hat!' She said it was quite calm."

Webber stared into the glass of whisky in his hand. "Why aren't you phoning from the hotel?"

"Bernard is an old fusser, he sees villains everywhere."

"Tapping your phone, you mean?"

"I suppose so, you know what he's like."

"He's not a fool, be careful. Do they know why you are there, the hotel people?"

"No, now don't you start fussing. There's no danger there except from the plumbing."

"I'm not fussing and neither is Bernard. No, Lizzie! Now listen to me. Be sensible, it might be all right but it might not, use a cover, if you can't invent something plausible no one can. I'll leave that to you but do it. I need you there. See if you can find out if the girl said anything before she died, and anything you can about the Waltons, what they were like together. They were well known there by the way. They spent their honeymoon there. They went back at Easter whenever they could. Doesn't sound very sinister does it, but you never know. I don't much care for the accident – the girl I mean. Had she complained to the newspaper?"

"She got Father Girard to speak to them. They told him she must be confused – a simple peasant girl, not very bright. They said they had taken her statement from the official inquiry. That was what she had said in her evidence and that was what they had printed."

"Surely to God other people in the town can remember what the weather was like that morning?"

78

"What was it like at Flaxfield last Easter Monday?"

Webber grunted.

"Where did you get the honeymoon bit from?" she asked.

He told her about his visit to Molly Motherwell. "She was pretty far gone by then but she was making sense – just about anyway. She told me. It confirmed something Jessica Elberg told me too. She said they'd been happy there, went back when they could. She didn't say they'd spent their honeymoon there, an Easter honeymoon."

"Is that important?"

"Well it means that someone could have made an educated guess they'd be there at that time. The book is the best bit though. It was important enough for someone to steal it."

"Important enough for someone to kill him too?"

"It depends what was in it – yes I should think so. I've known dafter reasons than that. It sounds as though quite a few people might not like it very much. Dealers, collectors, critics, auction rooms. How's that for a nice open field? Sorry, I'm a bit tired, you must be too."

"You'll go and see Donald?"

"It's the best bet. I'll get up there as soon as I can. Ted Snow is sorting out some bits and pieces for me, I'll see him first. I'll let you know where I am. You can phone me back if you don't trust your switchboard."

"Just a minute – what was she like?"

"Who?"

"This Motherwell woman."

Webber smiled delightedly. "Fair, fat, forty and drunk. She said my eyes were like two spoonfuls of the blue Pacific."

"Silly cat."

"Compassion, Lizzie, compassion."

"Goodnight John love."

"Goodnight dear old Lizzie. Take care."

"I will – and you!"

Webber's alarm clock woke him at 5 am. It was a terrible hour but he wanted to get out to Snow's house before he left for the day. He'd rather get up early than rush at the last moment. The days when he could have bathed, shaved and dressed in twenty minutes were gone. On a bad morning it could take nearly as

79

long as that just to get his clothes on. It depended mostly on the weather.

The day was bright and clear with a welcome hint of warmth to come. The breakfast room at the Glockemara had been empty with no sign of staff. He got to Finchley on the first tube of the day, grateful that Betty was a policeman's wife.

"Ted's in the summerhouse. If you stay indoors you'll have the children disturbing you. Alice gets in a state of near-hysteria before her bus comes. I have a nasty suspicion that Alan hides her things sometimes but I haven't got time to prove it. They're only just up, but from now I promise it'll be hell. Don't bother to give me any news, I'll get it from Ted later. Will tea and toast do or something more substantial?"

"Tea and toast would be very acceptable."

"So the Waltons died even before the book was stolen?" Snow said.

"Yes. It makes sense. If he's dead he can't write it again, can he? Steal it first and you put him on his guard, he might go to ground."

"So they go off on a sentimental journey to Le Bosquet. You don't do that if you're planning to kill your wife or husband do you?"

"You might if you wanted people to think that."

"On the other hand it was no secret, anyone might have known they'd be there."

"Just about everybody who knew them – or of them."

"Donald, the son, he took off because he blamed the Motherwell woman for blabbing about the book. Yet he doesn't seem to have connected it with his mother's and father's deaths. It was only when the book went that he dumped her."

"Perhaps it's not so strange. First the shock, then the official verdict, accepted, remember, by our Foreign Office as well as the frogs."

"But not by his sister."

"She was half-way across the world, she came late to it, she saw it from a distance."

"Like us."

"That's right, like us."

Betty brought a big tray out for them. He realized that she

must earlier have carried kitchen chairs and a picnic table down to the summerhouse. Anguished faces at the kitchen window and wails of despair from Alice took her back unhurriedly to the house.

Webber said, "She doesn't flap, does she – you did well there Ted."

"With Betty? Yes thank God, they don't come any nicer." He poured tea for them both, remembering how Webber liked it without asking. "I've got most of the stuff you wanted and a bit more – not much but some." He scowled resentfully at the early sunlight slanting past the door of the summerhouse. "If this damn thing would revolve properly we could be sitting in the sun." He reached down and pulled a manila envelope from his briefcase. "That's it – a routine search on the lot of them, everyone, all the staff at Holland Crescent, the doctor laddie, Humper, James Spavin, Elberg's art man and Arnold Swan the partner in Walton's pottery business. All clean, nothing sinister, nothing to interest Criminal Records anyway."

"Anything to interest us?"

'There might be, to be honest I haven't had a chance to go through it in detail. I picked it up from my office on the way back from court. The Elberg chauffeur is a bit of a Romeo, there was a row when he chucked his first girlfriend out to make room for the present one. They changed over about two o'clock one morning, not very quietly it seems, the neighbours complained and the local boys went up to calm things down. Domestic stuff, routine, no charges."

"Any address for the one who left?"

"I shouldn't think so, if you want it I'll see what I can do."

"Please – anything else?"

"Not much, the Filipino and his wife had some trouble with their entry visas, Elberg sorted it out. You'll find most of that bumph is about him. I don't know if it will make much sense. I got it from C6, the fraud boys. It looks impressive but if you try and sort it out I doubt if you'll be much wiser. I gave up on page three. Boardroom rows, take-over bids, holding companies, the lot. I spoke to someone I know in C6 last night. He doesn't think they can make anything stick, Elberg's too smart. Pin him down on a company's assets and you find he doesn't own it anymore. He's either a very successful tycoon or a thumping great crook, perhaps both. There could be another possibility. It could be

81

that he's hanging on and consolidating before the firm goes bust. It's what the fraud boys call an everyday story of city folk. You'll see that all his personal assets have been transferred to his wife's name. It's not a crime, but it's not without interest. It's often the first move."

"He can still make out a cheque for £4000 and sign it himself," Webber said, searching through the toast for the least burnt piece in the rack. "He's spent a lot on that pottery collection too."

"It could be a way of laundering the money. Walton seems to have done all the buying, most of it anyway, perhaps Elberg paid him in cash."

"He told me that cash was out of the question."

"He's not daft, you may be retired but you're still a copper in his eyes. Anyway I've never known one of those boys yet who couldn't sign a cheque when he wanted to." Webber sighed and buttered his toast. "You and Lizzie promised me a respectable murder case. You never threatened me with the Fraud Squad, now that's messy in my book, especially as they're not very happy about the punter who's paying me. Definitely messy."

"And definitely murder?"

"I reckon so Ted, yes." He told him about Lizzie's call and the death of the chambermaid who'd seen them burn. "So yes, I think it probably is – don't ask me why or how. But it's worth a go."

"And Elberg?"

"I can't see that it's relevant – not my pigeon anyway. At least we've been paid – well paid too and the cheque didn't bounce. I'll just have to try and go easy on the expenses that's all."

"Look John – if you think . . ."

"Don't be daft, I'm not short of a quid or two. Besides I quite liked the old sod. I expect him to pay up like a city gent. No sweat old son."

"So long as you're happy."

Webber dipped a paper napkin in the hot water jug and wiped his fingers. "Why does marmalade always get right in between your fingers? Yes I am happy. You didn't mention the French police report in the Foreign Office – your chum having difficulties getting a copy?"

"There's a purge on, mole-hunting, he'd have to take it out to get it photocopied and they've taken to checking briefcases. I could put in an official request but that always puts the barriers up. They're a funny lot, I'd probably stand more chance if I asked the Soviet Embassy to put a word in for me."

Webber said: "Still it's nice to have your own private mole — very classy."

"Yes — unless of course I'm sharing him with the Soviets. No, I'm getting cynical in my old age. Betty's fault, she's very keen on Le Carré."

"Elberg got access to it — no bother."

"A family request — and he's rich — as far as they knew, anyway money talks, even the FO respects money. I did the next best thing, I got my lad to jot down some bits and pieces for us, names, the inquiry officials, pathologist, anything useful, probably the best I can do. I'll try later when the panic's over."

Dressed in her school uniform Alice appeared at the kitchen door to wave them goodbye while her brother pulled faces behind her back at the window.

Snow glanced at his watch.

Webber stood and put the envelope in his own briefcase.

"How is the Bailey going?"

"Like a bloody snail John, waste of money, waste of time. I must check the office before I sit on my arse all day. Can I give you a lift?"

"Best not. I'll use the tube, probably quicker anyway." Snow hesitated. He was loth to interfere in what might be sensitive ground. He made it sound as casual as he could.

"Lizzie careful is she, over there? In case it gets naughty?"

"I have mentioned it," Webber said.

ঙ THIRTEEN ও

Mrs Thomas chose to take her breakfast in the dining-room. The other guests, if there were any, were either late risers or preferred to keep to their rooms. Her table in the window where she had dined alone with Father Bernard looked out over a cold deserted promenade, and beyond it the long stretch of sand and sea, and in the distance the smooth beach giving way to sand dunes anchored by coarse clumps of grass and scrub.

She gave her order for tea and boiled eggs to the woman she guessed must be the wife of le patron. Madame Bouvier was a neat woman in a fresh clean overall. She looked younger than her husband and the sallow complexion suggested Italian or Spanish blood. Both women studied each other with undisguised interest during their brief exchange on the boiling time most suitable for fresh eggs and the desirable strength of tea. Mrs Thomas was surprised but grateful when the woman left without asking any of the questions she had expected her to ask.

She had thought carefully about Webber's concern that she should invent a plausible reason for visiting a northern seaside resort, alone and at an unseasonable time of year. She saw the sense in his caution and it pleased her. Father Bernard and his younger colleague had accepted her plea that an invented reason for her visit would come perilously close to dishonesty and had contented themselves with advising her to keep her own counsel.

A thin drizzle of rain slanted across the window and the few people walking outside put up umbrellas. She had arranged to collect Father Bernard at the presbytery at ten o'clock. She thought back to the evening before, walking the old man back after dinner and sitting in the young priest's room with the two of them listening to her story. A cold, cheerless room, with a mean fire of sluggish coal smoking in the grate, and on the walls

84

garish paintings of the Virgin and obscure suffering saints, contrasting oddly with colour photographs of cyclists and football teams.

Father Girard looked more like a footballer than a priest. Indeed when they arrived he had been watching a rugby match on his small black-and-white television set. He had politely switched it off but she knew what men were like about sport on television and had cut that first meeting short deliberately. She wanted all the allies she could get and she had seen from the approval in Father Bernard's face that she was doing the right thing. There was a time and a place for long speculative discussions. Nevertheless, in the short time before she had made her excuses and left, she had listened to him with interest.

He had been called to the hospital shortly after nine o'clock in the morning. Julie Pichon had slipped into a coma and the doctor had seen no hope for her. She had been unconscious for some time before he got to her bedside.

"I gave her absolution but she showed no sign; one hopes, one always hopes. It was lucky that I knew her. She died, I am quite certain, in a state of grace. The nurses told me that she had been able to understand that I was coming to her."

"So at some time in the hospital she had been conscious?" Mrs Thomas said.

"She had extensive injuries, but yes, I understand that for some of the time at least she could speak. She hadn't been making very much sense poor woman, rambling talk, and nothing that helped to explain the accident."

She saw the young man's eyes glance for an instant at the television set. She rose to her feet to leave. "Father Girard you have been very kind, forgive me but it has been a long day." The boy, for she thought he was little more than that, jumped to his feet, only a shade too eagerly, to see his guest out. "Tell me," she said, "did you yourself ever think that Julie Pichon's death was connected in any way with the accident on the beach?"

"No Madame, truthfully no, I didn't."

Priests didn't tell lies so she knew it must have been his youth that made him blush so prettily.

For a modest family hotel in an unfashionable seaside resort the kitchen at the L'Aigle Royal was well equipped. Modern electric

85

ranges had replaced the old oil-fired cookers and the general air of well-planned efficiency would not have been out of place in a much grander establishment. Monsieur Bouvier timed the boiling of the eggs while his wife snipped open tea-bags and emptied the leaves into a pot. It was something she had learned to do for English visitors, barbaric, but they genuinely seemed to prefer it.

"Just the same," she said to her husband, "she is not typical."

"We have had other English visitors who spoke French as well as she does."

"School teachers and . . ." For a moment she hesitated, finding the word distasteful, ". . . journalists. And you are wrong, they may have spoken it more correctly but not as well. She has a knowledge that one."

Bouvier kept his eyes on the simmering water. "You must not become neurotic Maria. Does she look like a journalist? Most assuredly she does not, even less could she be anyone in authority." He removed the eggs and placed them on the tray she had prepared. "She is a housewife," he said, "that is what it says in her passport and that is what she is. Perhaps she married a French citizen. It would account for her friendship with the old priest."

"She stares at the beach. Every time I go into the room her eyes are on the beach."

"With an empty room with no other guests what else should she stare at?" He took her arm and turned her to face him. "It is all over," he said deliberately. "It is over and we have heard no more of it. It is finished. And we have done nothing illegal. Now take in her tray and let her see that you are a pleasant woman. Pleasant – and honest."

In the dining-room Mrs Thomas had decided on her course of action. She would reject both Webber's advice and that of the priests. She had come to Le Bosquet to find out what had happened, or as much of it as lay in her power to discover, and she wouldn't make her task any easier by pretending to be a lady novelist looking for atmosphere or a marine biologist studying the shore-line of northern France. She broke off a piece of fresh bread and buttered it.

Madame Bouvier, smiling, advanced with the breakfast tray. She was genuinely fond of her husband and was making an effort. "Ah good! You are hungry. I regret the delay Madame but the eggs and the tea are serious matters eh? I hope they will please you."

"I'm sure they will, you are very kind. I like a good breakfast." She toyed with attempting a translation of 'In England, we like to go to work on an egg,' but it sounded confusing and she rejected it, contenting herself with general pleasantries.

"Madame will allow me to congratulate her on her excellent command of the language. My husband," she ventured more boldly, "thinks that perhaps you must have married a French citizen."

Mrs Thomas beamed, both at the compliment and with satisfaction at the decapitated eggs, which were exactly as she liked them. She poured the tea and approved it.

"My husband is dead but he was Welsh, as I am." She chose her words carefully, remembering with affection the Free French airforce boys who had been billeted in her home during the war when she was still a teenaged girl. "For some years," she said, buttering her bread with concentration, "I was privileged to serve under the French forces of liberation, they taught me a great deal. But now it is I who must return your compliments. It is not everyone in France who could, if I may say so, produce such a breakfast to such a standard. You must have had many English visitors?"

"Thank you, but no, not so many. Le Bosquet is not a big resort as you see, we are a little . . . provincial? No golf, no casino, families, French families, they like it here with us, no excitements but the beach is safe. It is good for the children you understand."

Mrs Thomas nodded. "A safe beach is very important. The death of Mr and Mrs Walton, they were staying here with you were they not? That must have come as a great shock to you all."

Webber spent the morning in the residents' lounge of the Glockemara. It wasn't ideal but his bedroom would be even less suitable, no desk and open to invasion by armies of lethargic chambermaids. Luckily the clientele of the Glockemara were not given to lingering on the premises. Mostly foreigners on cheap package holidays, they tended to congregate in yawning groups in the entrance hall waiting to be funnelled into sightseeing coaches.

87

The writing-desk in the corner of the gloomy room was just adequate if you were bent on sending coloured postcards of the changing of the guard at Buckingham Palace. He made the best of it and went through Snow's notes in the manila envelope as methodically as he would have done in the days when he had an office of his own. When he had finished he ordered coffee and then went back to the beginning and read everything through again. Snow was right, a great deal of the contents of the envelope consisted of a lengthy photostat report from the Fraud Squad on Elberg's financial affairs. He read it carefully and with growing respect, both for the experts in that department, and for Elberg himself. With patience and perseverance he made more of it than Snow had had time for. There was no doubt in his mind that Elberg was fighting a fierce battle. What was more difficult, was understanding how the fight was going, or even identifying the protagonists. There were two facts of which he felt he could be reasonably sure. Elberg might still be an extremely wealthy man with large sums of money disguised and concealed in Geneva-based Panamanian-registered holding companies. Either that or his adversaries had been too clever for him and stripped those assets before he could move them on to yet another 'shelf' corporation refuge. If that were so, and it was a possibility that more than one opinion in C6 was inclined towards, then the alternative fact was that Elberg was a cardboard figure with no more resources at his command than the money and assets which he had transferred to his wife. Webber finished the coffee, which had grown cold, and turned again to the rest of the notes. From them he extracted the office telephone number of James Spavin.

He used the call box in the hall. When eventually his call was answered he knew that the girl on the other end would be difficult. She sounded as if she was eating and not enjoying it very much.

"Spavin? What extension?"

"I'm sorry, I don't know his extension."

"Well I can't connect you without the extension number, this is the switchboard."

"You must have an internal directory, could you look him up for me please?"

"Which publication is he?"

"I'm sorry, I don't know that, probably something to do with antiques."

She left him hanging on without saying anything more. At least he hadn't been disconnected for he could hear the background noises of the girl's lair. She might have been crackling through the leaves of a directory or possibly munching potato crisps, it was difficult to tell. It took another ten minutes and all his small change before he eventually found himself speaking to Spavin.

"Well I am, not to put too fine a point on it, actually rather busy today, who did you say you were?"

"I didn't, my name is Webber – Detective Inspector John Webber. I'd be grateful if you could spare me some of your time – over lunch perhaps?" The stick and the carrot. He could adjust his status later if necessary.

Spavin worked in a building in Bishop's Court, off Fleet Street. Webber arranged to meet him outside at half past twelve. He said he preferred not to go into details on the telephone. Spavin, he thought, sounded a little less pompous.

At the presbytery Father Girard had already left to attend to his parochial duties. Father Bernard was ready and waiting for her. She had hired a taxi and he sat beside her in the back, giving the man directions to the hospital on the outskirts of the town. True to his word the young priest had given them a note of introduction. They drove in silence, not wishing to discuss the purpose of their visit in front of the driver. He was a pleasant young man with an open face, a shock of carrot-coloured hair and freckles. She wondered if he was a legacy of the war, the son of an English soldier or a German perhaps. She smiled ruefully to herself, one forgot, more likely a grandson. In any case she had been lucky to find a taxi so easily on such a rain-drizzled day. They left the little streets of the town and almost at once the road entered a wooded landscape from which, presumably, Le Bosquet had derived its name.

The hospital lay in a clearing of the wood. An attractive building, it had once been the château home of minor nobility: the family had become impoverished after the First World War and were glad to sell it to the local Commune. At the back there were some ugly modern additions but the main entrance and facade still had dignity.

Telling the boy to wait they presented themselves at the reception desk with Father Girard's letter of introduction and were shown into a small room off the entrance hall. It had pale green walls and a few hard chairs, cotton curtains with a bright pattern of Van Gogh sunflowers. It made an effort to look cheerful and allay anxiety and yet, like similar rooms everywhere, it had soaked up the fears and doubts of the years.

She was glad when the receptionist appeared again and asked them to follow her. She led them through the main building and along a covered corridor to the office of the resident surgeon. Silver-haired with an aquiline nose, Doctor Masset waved them courteously to chairs facing his desk. He looked, she thought, like an elderly Sherlock Holmes. She hoped that his duties no longer involved active surgery for the hands that held Father Girard's letter had a pronounced tremor. On the desk lay what turned out to be the hospital record of Julie Pichon. He didn't question their right to interview him. He respected the Church and had frequent cause to be grateful to it. He himself, he said, had not seen the case, he was seldom disturbed at unsocial hours for accident casualties. He read them the casualty doctor's account of Julie Pichon's injuries.

"I would of course have seen the poor woman myself later in the day but as you may guess from this," he tapped the notes, "I could have done no more for her. These terrible injuries could only be terminal. They are entirely consistent with the effects of her being struck at great speed by a vehicle, an automobile, perhaps even a lorry. A familiar story I'm afraid. However, these notes contain no record of anything the patient may have said, only that she was indeed conscious for brief moments. Luckily the nurse who kept vigil that night is named here and I have sent for her, she might recall something for you."

When she came into the room the nurse looked tired but efficient and intelligent, she had kind eyes. A woman to trust. She listened quietly and attentively as the doctor explained the mission of his visitors, her large red hands folded in front of her uniform.

"Yes," she said, "she did speak. At the time I thought nothing of it. She was very ill – dying indeed. There was nothing to be done for her and afterwards there seemed little point in reporting it, and yet I have not forgotten her words. Looking back it seems such a strange thing to have said."

❧ FOURTEEN ☙

MRS THOMAS TOOK a firm grip on herself. It wasn't that she
didn't care about poor Julie Pichon's last words – the stranger
the better. It was simply that she didn't trust herself. At
moments of suspense and tension she had been known to
succumb to nervous giggles. Soap operas and even the most
solemn offerings of Hollywood often had the same effect on her,
she still felt ashamed of her reaction to the sight of Vanessa
Redgrave on crutches. She longed for one of Webber's steadying
scowls. It wasn't so bad in front of the television screen but
unnerving to find herself in the middle of it. She steeled herself
and hoped that the script would avoid bathos. A silver-haired
surgeon, a priest and a nurse keeping vigil at a death bed was
strong stuff for Mrs Thomas's nerves. At least the woman
wasn't a nun. There were limits.

"She was delirious," the nurse said, "wandering in her mind.
Yet I'm certain she understood when I told her that a priest
was coming to her. It seemed to give her peace. I have seen it
many times."

Mrs Thomas gave a warning nip inside her lower lip. Dr
Masset nodded and Father Bernard said gently, "What did she
say that you thought so strange?"

God bless him, down to the essence of it. The nurse was not
to be denied.

"For some time after that she seemed quieter – less agitated.
Sometimes she mumbled, but even with my ear close to her I
couldn't distinguish any words. She was still conscious but
sinking."

Mrs Thomas applied serious pressure.

"Just once, for a few moments, she rallied, she was quite
lucid, or at least I thought so. Certainly her eyes focused on
mine and she gripped my hand."

91

Mrs Thomas drew blood and steadied.

"Her voice was quite clear, weak but perfectly clear. Tell them, she said, tell them it was a Frelon."

This was decidedly better, not only an original line but a word Mrs Thomas didn't understand. She looked enquiringly at the nurse.

"A Frelon is the name of a motorbike," Dr Masset said, "only smaller. They make a terrible noise, like a frelon – a big wasp – in English I think you say hornet."

"After the war," Father Bernard said, "the Italians called them Vespas, these I think are made in Czechoslovakia, only with bigger wheels and noisier. They are very popular with the young men and I'm afraid a great trial to everyone else."

"They are scarcely heavier than an ordinary pedal cycle," the doctor said, looking down at his notes. "It is quite inconceivable that such a machine could have caused injuries like these."

"And she would surely have had ample warning, she would have heard it coming," Mrs Thomas said.

The nurse stood with her hands folded as she had done throughout the interview. She was not a fanciful woman, Mrs Thomas thought, as she watched her facing her superior.

"All this I knew," she said, "at the time I persuaded myself that the remark had been part of her delirium, because what she said could not be true. I dismissed it from my mind and said nothing – and yet . . ."

"And yet?" said Father Bernard.

"Yet, even so, as you see I have not forgotten," she turned to him. "You must have seen it many times yourself, Father. There is often a sudden rally before the final coma and death. It is a time for truth is it not?"

"Yes, I have found it so," he said, "but the truth is seldom simple. In this case, in the face of the evidence, we know that what poor Julie Pichon said could not be true. Such injuries, such an impact. And what would have happened to the young man, if such there was, or indeed to that wretched machine? No my child, your first instinct was right, it could only have been part of her delirium as you thought. It would not be the first time that it has been mistaken for the truth."

Outside the rain had stopped, the sky had cleared with only a few clouds scudding over a watery sun. The wind was cold and they were glad of the warmth in the taxi. The red-haired boy grinned a welcome at them and brushed aside Mrs Thomas's apologies for keeping him waiting.

"There is no hurry Madame," he said cheerfully. "Truthfully one is glad of the work out of season. Back to the hotel then?"

It was too early for lunch. "Are you warm enough?" she asked the old man. "We might go for a drive, if you would like that?"

"A moment!" the boy said, and running around to the boot he produced a travelling rug, which he arranged solicitously over the priest's knees. Madame, he thought, could have no need for it with a coat of that thickness.

"Anywhere you think pleasant," she said, "somewhere along the coast perhaps." She produced a paper bag of mint humbugs which she seldom travelled without and handed them to the men.

"Very good," the boy said, swinging the car expertly out of the gates of the hospital. "These I do not know, English sweets?"

She hesitated over the translation of humbugs and bull's-eyes but neither charlatan de menthe nor oeil de taureau sounded convincing. She settled for peppermint and concentrated on the scenery, the trees flashing past with only a hint of green in their branches.

"Disappointed?" said Father Bernard.

"Yes."

"One cannot bring back the dead. Perhaps it was indeed an accident."

"Perhaps, but I don't think so. I think Julie was murdered." She caught his quick glance of apprehension at the driver and smiled. "Don't worry. If people are not to know you are searching for something then how can they help you to find it?"

The taxi skirted the town and left the woodlands to strike across open fields coming out on the coast road to the east of Le Bosquet. Here the sand dunes and broad beach had given way to chalk cliffs topped with the brilliant green of spring turf. The boy pulled off the road on to a cliff-top lay-by with a view of the coast and the sea.

"Beautiful eh? Out there to the right you can see Cap Gris Nez and sometimes when it is more clear you can see right across the sea to England. Look, over there is one of the old German gun batteries. Blockhaus they called them. The walls are ten metres thick, imagine! They could fire shells right across the channel, over a ton every one, and over two metres high. You can still see some of them inside. It is a museum now, La Batterie Todt – The Museum of the Atlantic Wall – they call it."

93

The concrete blockhaus squatted on the green cliff-top, a grey misshapen obscenity, totally at variance with the land and sea around it. Mrs Thomas shuddered, it reminded her of the National Theatre in London.

"What have they put in there?" she asked the boy.

"Old uniforms, weapons, old posters from the occupation, it's all very old. We used to play there when I was a kid. The best time to go now they tell me is after the attendant has drunk his lunch, he's an old man, he can remember the war. When he's sleeping it off you can get in for free, he couldn't chase you anyway because he's got a wooden leg – an ex-soldier. I read in the paper that they want to close it down, not enough visitors and the Mayor and the Municipal say it costs too much. A pity, you should see it Madame, it would be of great interest for you."

She had seen his eyes rest on the bag of sweets on her lap and offered it to him.

"Thank you Madame, I like them very much." He leaned over the seat and took a sweet from the bag, smiling shyly at them. "Excuse me but I couldn't help overhearing, this Madamoiselle Julie you spoke of, was she the one from the hotel, the one who was run over on the road?"

"Julie Pichon, yes, why, did you know her?"

"It was in the paper, I read of it, and the police came to see us about it."

"Why should they do that?" asked Father Bernard.

"They came about a week afterwards, after they had been to all the garages. We have a small workshop, my mother and I have two taxis you know. She answers the telephone and she can drive too. I do all the servicing myself," he added proudly. "They wanted to know if anyone had asked for repairs to a car, but I told them no. It is a bad road where she died, no lights, there were letters in the paper but still they have done nothing." His freckled face looked solemn and yet excited. "Do you really believe she was murdered Madame?"

His face was such a comical mixture that she shocked the old priest by laughing.

"What's your name son?" she asked him.

"Paul Colbert, Madame."

"Well now Paul," she sensed Father Bernard's attempt to catch her eye and avoided it. "Yes, I think she was silenced because she knew something." With such an atmosphere of

94

disapproval from the seat beside her she reluctantly abandoned her decision to question the boy about his memories of the deaths on the beach. The priest's obvious concern at what he would consider her impetuous disregard of common caution made her hold her tongue. But only, she thought, only for the moment. Soon, over lunch, she was going to be firm with him.

The boy, wide-eyed with interest, said: "That would be a terrible thing, like one reads of the Mafia in the south, like one sees on television. What can *you* do Madame?"

"Probably nothing Paul, but it will not stop me trying. I shall ask questions. The people at the newspaper, the girl's relatives if I can find any, the police if necessary. Although they do not seem to have been very clever. No murderer would be so foolish as to have the car repaired locally. That would have been done miles away, in Paris probably. I can ask them but I don't think they will be pleased."

Father Bernard sighed with resignation.

The boy reached for his wallet and produced a brightly printed trade card, thrusting it at her eagerly. "But you will need a taxi Madame! You will allow me to drive you? Please Madame! We are not expensive. It is very quiet now in Le Bosquet," he smiled, "no excitements. I will ask my mother for a special rate, cheaper than all the others I promise!"

"And would you give me a receipt – an official receipt for all the journeys?"

"No difficulty, absolutely not."

She put the card into her handbag. "Why not, I shall certainly need someone and a special rate would be nice."

The clouds had thickened and covered the sky and it had begun to rain again. Here on the cliff-top there was no wind, not even a breeze, so that the flags of the Allies on the blockhaus hung wet and limp from their poles.

"You can take us back to the town now," she said.

The boy backed the taxi on to the coast road.

"It's funny," she said, as they left the massive bunker with its motionless flags behind them, "one would expect more breeze at the seaside. Is it often as calm as this?"

"It depends on the direction of the wind Madame, when it comes from the east like it does now we get the protection of Cap Gris Nez, then it is calm. Le Bosquet is lucky for that, but it can change quickly too, ask the visitors they will tell you! Back to the hotel?"

She told him to take them to one of the small streets where she had remembered the name of a pleasant-looking bistro. The boy dropped them there, holding the door and helping them out.

"You won't forget Madame?"

"I won't forget." She added the bag of sweets to his tip.

Webber took the tube to Chancery Lane and with the help of his London *A–Z* guide threaded his way through the maze of narrow streets until he found the Cursitor Building in Bishop's Court. James Spavin was a surprise.

From his voice on the telephone and from Elberg's description, Webber had expected someone much older. He was about fifty-five and khaki-coloured. He was all khaki, hair, skin, eyes, and he was dressed in the same dull shade of dust; raincoat, shoes, tie, and there was no relief from the tan briefcase and brown umbrella. In one particular Elberg had been quite accurate. He was certainly pompous and, Webber noted with relief, a chatterbox. A bit of an old woman; that might make it easier. The handshake was unexpectedly firm, perhaps he had more character than his appearance would suggest. Without preamble he placed his free hand on Webber's elbow and guided him through the pedestrian traffic of the pavement.

"Now I'm going to take a liberty if you won't mind, and I hope you won't, no I'm sure you won't. It was most kind of you to ask me to luncheon, most kind. But the fact is that there are very few restaurants that I can eat in with safety and pubs I'm afraid are quite out of the question, apart from all that the City is so very overcrowded at lunchtime. I am very lucky, I have an admirable arrangement with the editor of *Antiques for Pleasure and Profit*, a most charming woman, a shade lacking in some of the nicer points of judgement perhaps, but quite dedicated. She is the lucky owner of a flat in Red Lion Court; quite modest but a long lease which is a great blessing – do mind these cobblestones, so treacherous. The lady herself does not take luncheon and very kindly lets me have the use of the kitchen for my own simple déjeuner. In exchange I supply her with a few vegetables from my little garden in Kent, all macrobiotic, every one, I am a slave to my compost-heap. Now then, if we cross carefully, it is just over the other side of the road."

The kitchen was cramped, not so much because it was small but because it was crowded and everything in it was too big. Mr Spavin's friend had an eye for a second-hand bargain and size did not deter her. Two of the walls were only just big enough to contain a pair of Edwardian pine dressers, the shelves of which were completely filled with huge jars of pulses and pasta, interspersed with Spanish dolls and copper vessels which would not have disgraced the kitchens of the Royal Pavilion at Brighton. Webber thought Spanish holidays and second-hand furniture suggested a limited budget. *Antiques for Pleasure and Profit* couldn't be paying her very much. Spavin himself probably didn't earn much either. He was a freelance and wrote learned and erudite articles for any magazine he could persuade to accept them.

He seated his guest at an oak dining-table designed for suburbia in the Thirties and fluttered round the room like a brown moth, dispensing carrot juice and personal biography. He needed no prompting, only occasionally did Webber insert a question to divert the flow into more productive pastures as he dutifully consumed a plate of semolina with nut and spinach sauce. It looked like a cowpat on frog's spawn but he pronounced it delicious and waited for the caffeine-free coffee before asking:

"How did you get along with David Walton? I imagine you came into quite close contact with him?"

Almost for the first time Spavin paused. On the table in front of him lay the note in which Jessica Elberg had asked for help on Webber's behalf.

"When my wife was alive," he began unexpectedly, "I would have sought her advice in a delicate matter such as this. I miss her a great deal."

Snow's notes had covered Spavin's career pretty thoroughly but they had missed the wife. Somehow she was a surprise.

"I'm sorry," Webber said. "I didn't know your wife was dead."

Spavin's hand dismissed it gently. "It was a long time ago, she died far too young—of anaemia, she was eating all the wrong things, but of course we didn't know that at the time. She was a good woman." For a moment Webber thought that the man was going to cry and prepared himself but Spavin pulled himself together. "When you told me that your investigation was of a private nature and instigated at Mrs Elberg's behest, albeit with

97

Mr Elberg's full cooperation, I must admit that my first instinct was to say nothing." He paused. "My wife would not have approved of that. She would have said it was unworthy of me, and I agree with her. David Walton was a crude vulgar womanizer and I disliked him intensely."

⨍ FIFTEEN ⨍

HAVING DELIVERED HIMSELF of this minor bombshell Spavin's spirits revived considerably. Webber sensed a feeling of relief.

"There now, I've said it and I'm glad, one must have standards. Please don't move, finish your coffee and I'll just wash these few things up, I use an infusion of ivy leaves, it takes a little longer but it's kinder to the hands. I like to leave the place clean and tidy for Miss Musgrove. You see," he said, removing his coat and hanging it carefully over his chair, "you see how potentially embarrassing your question was. After all Mr Elberg has been extremely good to me. I don't mind admitting that without his patronage my earning capacity would have been considerably reduced, the catalogues you understand, he has been most generous, most generous. Of course he is not an easy man in some ways but one makes allowances for pressures of business. A closed book to me thank goodness, but I have often noted the syndrome in others with positions of power. There was an arts editor once on the *Daily* —"

"He has a temper?"

Spavin seemed delighted with Webber's candour, smiling with pleasure like a schoolgirl sharing a rude word. He raised his hands in mock horror so that the ivy water ran down to his elbows.

"A temper? Just so. Exactly! Cataclysmic!" he giggled. "One learns to avoid it if possible, which was why I most carefully refrained from discussing Walton with him, as a person I mean, naturally one had to talk about the collection but I never revealed my true feelings about the man himself."

"You could tell me perhaps? In the strictest confidence I can assure you." Webber looked supremely discreet and trustworthy.

"Yes – yes I believe I can." He checked the time by the hunter watch in his waistcoat. "I have some proofs to correct but nothing urgent that can't wait an hour. Shall we have some more coffee? Why not, it is so good isn't it, quite delicious after a good meal.

99

Well now, for some time my sole encounters with Walton were on the unavoidable occasions when I met him at Holland Crescent with Mr Elberg. I didn't like him from the first, there was – how shall I put it – an aura about the man. Nothing you could describe exactly, my wife always used to say that I could sense an aura but be that as it may, there it was. It wasn't his ability that I questioned, he was extremely good at his job, oh extremely! He had an eye, and yet he frequently sought to call my own judgement into question. My goodness didn't I have to bite my tongue? Didn't I just! You see Inspector, I may not have made a great deal of money but I am, if I may say so, extremely respected in the world of fine art. An acknowledged expert; I would go so far as to say a world authority. I have frequently been consulted by all the major salerooms, by the British Museum itself on one occasion, not to mention the Victoria and Albert. The study of nineteenth-century ceramics has been much neglected I have to say, and on that subject I will bow to no one, least of all to a tuppenny-ha'penny potter whose knowledge of aesthetics was abysmal."

"You mentioned women," Webber murmured.

"His private life, however reprehensible, was his own private business, or it should have been. I most certainly had no desire to be apprised of it, I was most terribly embarrassed." He finished the coffee in his cup seeking strength. "There was an occasion when he accompanied me to the studio to which I had entrusted the colour photography for the pottery catalogue. I always use Mr Bates, just off Bond Street, a man of great technical ability and impeccable taste, he and I had decided upon a most pleasant background colour, not exactly a dove grey, more subtle than that, more like the very palest grey feathers on a budgerigar's breast, absolutely right. Well judge for yourself." Spavin swooped on his briefcase and produced a large colour transparency protected by a clear plastic envelope. He held it triumphantly up to the light for Webber's inspection. "You see? Quite perfect!"

The photograph was of a Staffordshire figure which Webber remembered Elberg having given pride of place in his Victorian collection. A saddled stallion with wild flowing mane and tail, rearing up over the sprawling figure of its rider on the ground. It was titled in neatly printed letters on the base 'Sir Robert Peel. June 29th 1850'.

"Very nice," Webber said dutifully, adding quickly, "You'd need to have the right colour to set off a powerful piece like that."

"Exactly! And yet that awful man had seen fit to question it. He had the grace to admit he was wrong in the studio, I will say that, but the cheek of it!" He studied the photograph lovingly.

Webber waited. There were some people it was best not to push, you learned to wait for them.

"A wonderful thing," Spavin said. "Quite unique, no other example has ever been seen. Thomas Parr, a master potter at his superb best – his masterpiece without a shadow of doubt."

"Worth a bit then?"

"Oh yes, oh my goodness yes. How can you put a value on something like that? Think of it, Sir Robert Peel, a prime minister of England thrown from his horse on Constitution Hill in the very heart of London, and here Parr shows it all and dates it for the very day it happened! It should by right, I suppose, be in a national museum, but there it is. One of the great treasures of the Elberg collection. Actually I have just completed a monograph on it which *Dilettante* are to publish in the autumn, Mr Elberg has very kindly allowed me to reproduce the photograph."

"How could a rare thing like that turn up out of the blue?"

"Oh there's nothing strange about that, good gracious me no. In the world of fine art, Inspector, it happens more often than many people realize. One only reads of the more obvious things, headline-snatchers, Ming vases, Rembrandts and so on, some of them turn out to be fakes of course, nine-day wonders, you'd never believe people could be hoaxed so easily."

'But you have no doubts about Sir Robert?' Webber smiled.

Spavin chuckled delightedly. "I thought you might ask that. Quite right, a proper question, well done! No, absolutely not, but I do take your point, indeed I do."

"The point being that Walton was himself a potter."

"A working journeyman hack! We are talking of fine art, Inspector, not coronation mugs, we are also talking of antiques. In pottery, above all other art forms, it is impossible to simulate age convincingly. It has been tried but it fails utterly. No forger has ever succeeded in reproducing the authentic patina of true age on pottery. It is quite simply not possible."

"You said that he was extremely good at his job, that he had a good eye."

"He was clever when it came to finding things. I don't deny it, and he could recognize quality and rarity, he was a high-class runner, not an artist. He was never that."

"He seems to have been a very successful runner. Did it ever cross your mind that some of his lucky finds might have been stolen property?"

"No, never."

Webber nodded, Spavin was right, you couldn't hope to get away with it. It would be useful now to ease him back into an earlier channel of chatter. It was a question of finding the natural link.

"Yes, quite right, too hot to handle. So then, we are left with Mr Walton's good eye, good for the ladies too was it?"

"They weren't ladies, they were prostitutes." For the first time a smudge of colour came into his face. "That afternoon after we had left Mr Bates' studio we walked round the corner into Bond Street where I intended to hail a taxi-cab – Mr Elberg is very good about expenses. That was when Walton announced quite casually that he wanted a woman. He might have been talking about buying a tie or a pair of shoes. He even – " Spavin had now blushed bright crimson – "seemed surprised that I vehemently rejected his invitation to join him."

"Embarrassing," said Webber.

"Embarrassing and insulting. He laughed at me. I'd rather not repeat his exact words. He as good as implied that . . . well let us say that he obviously didn't know that I had been a very happily married man. He told me that it was his invariable practice whenever the opportunity presented itself. I assume he meant whenever he was away from his wife, poor woman."

"How very unpleasant for you. I suppose he didn't mention where he intended to – er – receive these favours?"

"As I drove away in a taxi-cab – " Spavin's face was now a picture of outraged shock – "I saw him approach and speak to a passing woman. She looked, I promise you, perfectly respectable, quite smartly dressed. I thought she would slap his face but she appeared to talk to him quite amiably, and then they walked off together, as though it was the most natural thing in the world!"

Which for some people in Bond Street, reflected Webber, it probably was. He smiled sympathetically. "Did you know, by the way, that he had written a book?"

Spavin appeared to force himself to concentrate: "A book?"

"About his experiences in the antique trade I believe."

Spavin's face lost its colour like a bottle drained of wine.

"No," he said. "No, I didn't know that."

That night Webber spoke to Mrs Thomas at Father Girard's house.

"I feel a bit awkward Lizzie, phoning the presbytery at ten o'clock at night, are you sure it's all right?"

"Quite all right, the phone is out in the hall, the boys are watching boxing on the telly. Listen, you needn't be afraid of phoning me at the hotel, they really don't speak English."

"You're sure?"

"Yes I've tried them with a few simple insults, no reaction, not a flicker. John, you might as well know. I've told them why I'm here. I'll never get anywhere if I don't come out."

She had expected displeasure, probably a rebuke, even a command to return. Instead he said: "I thought you would. You're right, I see that. I don't like it, but you're right. I'm not even going to say be careful."

"You've just said it."

"Any news?"

She told him about the hospital. "Make any sense?" she asked.

"No, looks like a dead end, never mind it was worth trying. These people who run the hotel – what's their name again?"

"Bouvier."

"These Bouviers, how did they react when you told them why you were there?"

"I think they're frightened. At first I thought they were hiding something but I don't think it's that. They're only worried about the hotel. They had a bellyful with the press at the time, bad for business. They don't seem to know any more than the Pichon woman did."

"You say woman, what was she like? To look at I mean."

"Forty-one, plain but not ugly, spinster, no family, at least none that she ever mentioned to Father Girard. She probably had a bit of a crush on him, it's common enough. She had no men in her life that he knows of."

"David Walton might have made a pass at her." He gave her Spavin's account of the Bond Street incident. "If Walton was as promiscuous as that – and it seems possible – he might have made a fool of himself, if the opportunity came up."

"Daft place to try it."

"Depends how randy he was, perhaps Mrs W caught him at it."

"And she just happened to have an incendiary bomb handy."

103

"She could have planned it. I don't imagine it would have been the only time. The Pichon woman is only a possibility anyway. The motive stays the same."

"It's a funny old way to kill someone John."

"Bad thing, jealousy."

"I don't question the motive, it's the method I keck at."

"Well if she didn't, someone did, unless you want to go along with the pipe ash."

"What did you have for dinner?"

"Tuna-fish pancakes – very nice."

"Good God."

"Yes lovely. I came out to Finchley to see Ted, Betty very kindly gave me supper. That's where I'm phoning from."

"Sorry, give them my love. Ted's trial just about over isn't it?"

"It should have been, they're back to square one, someone tried to nobble the jury so it's got to be a re-trial."

"Poor Ted."

"He's not very happy. Look this call is running up." He listened while she outlined her next moves. The newspaper office and Julie Pichon's neighbours. He advised her not to try the local police. "You won't get anywhere with them I promise you, they'll close up like a clam. We'll leave that to Ted – he's got some pull, the tame mole I told you about. I'd like to know if there were any other English visitors around that Easter, but I shouldn't think there's much chance of finding out, not after this long. I think hotels had to report all foreigners to the police at one time but Ted says they've stopped doing that. Are you still there?"

"I love the way you economize on a phone call."

She sensed the grin on his face far away in Finchley and missed him suddenly and protectively. Tuna-fish pancakes had been a shock for her. She would be glad when she had finished in Le Bosquet and could go home and be with him.

"Lizzie love, don't hang about over there longer than you have to. Contact Ted here when you get back, he'll know where I am. Give my best to old Bernard, how is he?"

"A touch of gout, nothing serious – yes I will. God bless."

"God bless."

For some time she stood by the phone in the gloomy hall, gradually aware that the television in the room had been silent for some time.

When the door of the room opened it was Father Girard who stood there.

"Madame Thomas, Father Bernard and I have something to say to you."

✣ SIXTEEN ✣

THE ATMOSPHERE IN the room was plainly that of embarrassment. Most of it came from the young priest who, having offered Mrs Thomas a rickety armchair near the smokey fire, had seated himself awkwardly at a table in the middle of the room, his face was strained and without its usual healthy glow. It was Father Bernard with his gouty foot raised on a small pile of books who broken the silence.

"Elizabeth, Father Girard has told me certain things in confidence and I have decided that I have no option but to break that confidence." He caught her look of quick concern directed at the younger man. "I need hardly tell you that it in no way concerns Father Girard's calling as a priest, not, that is, in an ecclesiastical manner. Indeed, it is something that he was expected to confide to you. He had made up his mind to say nothing, but I believe he now understands that his decision was one of misguided loyalty to me. I have told him also that I believe his action might have placed you in a position of some danger. He finds that difficult to believe. I hope I have convinced him otherwise."

Father Girard looked like a football player receiving a rebuke from his trainer, uncomfortable and hardly convinced.

"I was asked to suggest to you, Madame, that your presence in Le Bosquet was unwelcome, that your inquiries could only be a disruptive influence among us. It was done very politely, very subtly. I thought about it and decided to ignore it. It seemed to me that there was an element of blackmail involved and I could not countenance that."

He looked miserable and she felt sorry for him but waited for him to continue.

The word blackmail hung in the air.

"Tell her," Father Bernard said.

"My work here," said Girard, "like that of any priest in a small community, is by no means confined to purely pastoral duties. I spend more time sitting on committees than I want to, but it has to be done. Le Bosquet is a poor town. I don't complain, if money is needed I'm not ashamed to beg for it. It is not always easy and there are many demands, it is difficult to assess priorities but I try to do that too. People are more important than buildings and the fabric of my church has always had to give place to more pressing claims. There was some damage from the last war, patched up, but never properly tackled. Quite recently I received an offer, a very generous offer which would have gone a long way to restoring it properly, even handsomely."

"And now you have been told that the offer will be withdrawn unless you can persuade me to go?"

"It was not put so crudely but yes, that is what they meant."

In the pause that followed she sought to catch Father Bernard's eye but he continued to watch the boy at the table.

"Why danger?" she asked.

"That word is Father Bernard's, it was not used to me, and Madame, I still cannot bring myself to believe that. The offer was made by, or at least on behalf of, a most respectable group of individuals, businessmen of some standing in our community. I cannot believe that my rejection of their financial help could have in any way compromised your safety. It is unthinkable."

"And yet you yourself mentioned blackmail," she reminded him.

"I do not approve of conditional charity. There was no threat," he said stubbornly. "If such a threat had been hinted at can you suppose I would have refused the offer and said nothing to you?"

The old man eased his foot off the pile of books and winced as he lowered it on to the floor. Illogically the action annoyed her, as though he was responsible for placing her in a position which, far from frightening her, only made her feel angry.

She rose and gathered her handbag and the notebook she kept for her telephone conversations with Webber. It was a pity that she had not been told all this nonsense earlier, then she could have discussed and assessed it calmly and objectively with him. Now she did not feel in the slightest degree objective and certainly not calm, but she knew that it was a time to make a

107

conscious effort to be both. Her mother had deeply mistrusted the Church of Rome and consigned all its devious machinations to a fierce Protestant hellfire. It was a view she herself had abandoned in childhood and now virtuously refused to re-examine with sympathy.

"Businessmen of respectable standing? You must accept their money, Father. It will be all right I promise you, my work here is finished now. Just now on the telephone it was decided, I was about to tell you so. You can assure your benefactors, let them assume you have persuaded me, that could not be considered even a small sin I'm sure."

She hoped that the expression on Father Girard's face was purely one of relief. Greed she was sure would count as quite a big sin.

"Since I'm leaving, and purely as a matter of interest, will you perhaps tell me the name or names of your respectable businessmen? No? No of course, I quite understand, one should not boast of charitable deeds. One should do good with modesty, by stealth even."

That was reasonably calm and almost objective. Now she wanted to get away without losing control. Father Bernard insisted on coming into the hall.

"Elizabeth . . ."

"Not now lovey–save it. You won't be staying on? Good. Come and have lunch at the hotel–lateish, I've got a few chores in the morning–now don't quibble, I'm fighting for calm. Say about two o'clock."

"My bus . . ."

"Forget the damn bus, I can get back from Calais just as easily as from Boulogne, we'll take a taxi, I'm on an expense account remember. Oh do go back and sit! You look like a stork standing on one foot like that. Was I rude? To him I mean."

"Not really, not for you. I was quite proud of you."

"Smooth it over, you're right perhaps he should have gone in for football instead."

"You want me to find out about the bribe don't you?"

She paused in the adjustment of her hat in the hall mirror to thrust a frizzy curl beneath the orange felt. Her face when she turned to him was very serious.

"You must," she said. "You know you must."

In Berrywood Gardens, Webber accepted a nightcap of whisky before catching the last tube train.

"You should have pulled her out," Snow said.

"She doesn't pull easily, she digs her heels in. I gave her a nudge, it should be enough. It's a blank over there I'm afraid but at least it hasn't turned nasty thank God."

Later he was to remember saying it.

In the morning she had recovered her good humour and congratulated herself on her restraint of the previous evening. Far from having a sense of foreboding that someone was actively suggesting that her presence in Le Bosquet was resented, she felt only a mild excitement. She allowed herself not the slightest doubt that Father Bernard would find out who it was, his loyalty to her was unquestionable. The young priest would be no match for him in a contest of wills. She had more sense than to think she could pursue the matter on her own but it would be something to take back to Webber.

For the first time the morning promised a warm spring day. The sky was a clear blue with only the mildest breeze stirring the flags on the promenade, the sand of the beach washed smooth and clean by the retreating tide, frilling white in the distance. It was seven o'clock. The morning lay before her, ample time she hoped for the last few things she had to do. She was glad to be relieved of the local police. Somehow the ones she had seen about the town had not inspired her with confidence. Not like Webber. Part of the excitement was knowing that soon, perhaps even before the day was over, she would see him again.

So far she had treated the bathroom with respect. Now with her head full of other things it took its revenge. The bidet had received her cautious descent with deceptive humility but evilly repaid her consideration by slapping a near scalding jet of water up her bottom. Her anguished squawk was heard by Madame Bouvier passing outside in the corridor with an armful of linen. She arrived white-faced in the doorway to find her guest mopping up.

"Sorry, panic over, took me by surprise."

Madame Bouvier sank on to the bed her face the same colour as the clean sheets she still clutched. "Oh Madame! I thought . . ."

"It's nothing, my own fault, careless, stings a bit, nothing a dab of talc won't cure. Here, sniff this," she administered her smelling salts to the woman. Honestly! As though she hadn't enough to occupy her last day without coping with hysterical women.

"Such a loud cry Madame! Forgive me, it was a shock."

"You should have been sitting where I was."

Perhaps it wasn't hysteria, perhaps it was plain fear in the woman's white face. Now she was over reacting herself. That stupid little priest. No time to be fanciful: a time for businesslike normality, she would shake the silly creature with orders and sense. She was leaving, she told her. She would require breakfast and a late lunch for herself and Father Bernard. No, she would arrange her own taxi and would want an itemized bill which she would settle after lunch.

"Yes Madame."

First the beach. She could do it while they prepared her breakfast.

The seafront and the row of hotels looked smaller than she thought. The long line of her footprints in the sand marked her passage to where she guessed the Waltons had come themselves or at least as near as she could judge from her memory of the photograph in the newspaper. At one of those windows in the L'Aigle Royal Julie Pichon had stood looking out, a maid carrying a breakfast tray.

Mrs Thomas produced the small camera she had bought and duly entered in her expenses. It was a simple camera, but anything more complicated would have defeated her. She ran off the film methodically, all twenty exposures, in a sweeping arc along the front, round to the sand dunes, dipping down to the sun sparkling on the sea. In the tiny viewfinder her shadow stretched along the sand towards the hotel. If anyone was watching her from a window then they had taken care to conceal themselves. On the promenade an early-morning cyclist pedalled slowly on the front with long loaves of bread stuck in his jacket. Once, among the sand dunes in the distance, she thought she caught a movement but when she lowered the camera there was nothing. The cyclist turned and disappeared into the town and she was alone. She stood and glared about her with something of defiance at the empty morning. If she was inviting a bolt from the blue it didn't come.

110

In the hotel the atmosphere had returned to normal. Madame Bouvier seemed quite recovered with a jollity bordering upon open relief, she even invited Mrs Thomas into the kitchen to inspect and choose from a selection of fish laid out on an impressive marble slab.

"They are very good Madame Thomas."

She could see that, fresh and shining with the smell of the sea. She looked wistfully at the gleaming kitchen. It would have been wonderful to cook the lunch herself. Father Bernard was right, the woman was adequate, no more. If only she could persuade her to keep it simple. No, that would not be correct, you should never presume to offer advice in a kitchen, an unforgivable sin. She chose a plump sole and fell from grace.

"Filleted I think, in a little butter, and perhaps a suspicion of Calvados?"

A curious look, almost of pleading, came over Madame Bouvier's face and was gone almost at once. It was as though she was looking for some courage to talk. Mrs Thomas had seen the look before but the courage had never come. The Bouviers had answered all her questions politely and told her nothing. If they knew anything then the fear that held them back was very real. She would learn nothing from them. Just the same she waited quietly until the woman's silence lengthened into embarrassment.

"You were going to suggest a little cream perhaps?" she said brightly. "No thank you – no cream."

"Very good Madame."

For breakfast she settled for coffee and bread with oversweet orange jam unrecognizable as marmalade but she had a lot to do. Irritatingly there was no reply from the number Paul Colbert had given her and she found another taxi to drive her to the address where Julie Pichon had lived. Shack was an unkind description for the drab prefab bungalow built by the Commune as a temporary measure after the wartime bombing and lived in by the poor and underprivileged of the town ever since.

She had not expected to discover any great secret in Julie Pichon's life but she remembered Webber's working theory that you didn't skip a boring chore. She had not looked forward to it, picturing herself knocking on doors to a suspicious, even a hostile reception, and in that she was wrong. After the Bouviers and Father Girard she was treated with warmth and interested concern. She was mercifully spared the door-knocking. Most of the women of the bungalows had taken advantage of the bright sunny morning and the tiny patches of gardens were full of children playing noisily while their mothers loaded clothes lines with the family wash. Perhaps visitors were a novelty and strange foreigners with strange clothes something not to be missed. Mrs Thomas had not been born and brought up in a Welsh village for nothing. She blossomed.

"Ah! The poor Pichon? Madame has known her from the hotel? As a guest in the past? (It was only a white lie, you had to have reasons for questions.) Yes, yes sad indeed – Agathe! Don't pull the lady's skirt, not with those hands! She loves bright colours Madame. Go away all of you!"

The ragamuffins retreated to a nose-picking semi-circle while their friendly big-bosomed mothers gossiped in the sunshine.

"Yes, she was a good creature, Auntie Julie the kids called her. She was a kind neighbour too, a chatterbox but kind, and did her job well at the hotel did she? Yes, yes she would, she would, a hard worker, she would have made a good wife for some lazy layabout. Ah well! Perhaps she was lucky. Agathe! Must I tell you again? Any more and I'll make you wash poor Madame's skirt yourself. She hates clean hands," her mother confided.

"It doesn't matter, does it darling?" Mrs Thomas gathered the child up into her arms, a barefoot bundle of dark-eyed mischief, now suddenly quiet and solemn. "And was she nice, Auntie Julie then?" she asked the urchin face.

The strange woman's arms and the sea of faces now so unexpectedly on a level with her own disposed Agathe to shy secrets. She nodded and then cupping her hand close to Mrs Thomas's ear confided: "And she was very rich."

112

❦ SEVENTEEN ❧

THAT SAME MORNING Webber had a visitor at the Glockemara. She arrived without an appointment and he was grateful that most of the tourists had already been collected by their sightseeing coaches and that the residents' lounge was comparatively quiet. The room had never aspired to luxury and now with the sun on the tired carpet and the stained upholstery of the armchairs the quiet elegance of Jessica Elberg's clothes made it appear shabbier than ever. He offered her coffee and was glad when she didn't accept. Somehow she appeared to him more at ease than at their first meeting in her own home and her frank appraisal of the room amused him more than it embarrassed him.

"It's listed as tourist-class," he smiled at her, "but it serves pretty well. Have I destroyed my image?"

"No, on the contrary, I'm impressed. Hans would willingly have accepted something much grander I'm sure. I'm not disturbing you I hope?"

"You're my employer Mrs Elberg, if I say no, not at all, you might think I wasn't earning my fee." He was quite pleased with that. It acknowledged his duty to her, he thought, but with a gentle nod at a day's work ahead. "All the same," he added helpfully, "I hope I can tell you anything you want to know. After all you can hardly tell me that you were just passing. I'm sure Notting Hill Gate is a bit off your usual ground."

"Yes it is, you're right, I got your address from Miss Evans and came early. Obviously I'd like to know if you have any news."

"No I haven't, but I can say this, I don't believe that your original doubt about your parents' death was misguided."

"But you don't want to tell me why."

"Mrs Elberg, policemen are no different from anyone else. It's not that I won't, or even that I can't. I'm sure that something happened to your parents that ought to be investigated as fully as

113

possible. I told you when we first met that there was always the possibility that they met their death in the way that the French authorities said. Now I don't believe that, and if I can, I intend to prove it and to find out what did happen and if possible why and, God help me, how. If I fail, then I shall be very disappointed and you will have wasted your money."

Except, he thought, it wasn't strictly speaking her money but Elberg's, unless Snow was right and she was sitting on the lot. Either way there ought to be enough to cover the expenses, at least he hoped so. It wasn't something you could ask her about, a different scene, something for the fraud boys, and from what he had seen of Elberg he didn't envy them much.

"You mustn't be disappointed," he told her. "Mr Elberg mentioned that he'd like a weekly report, well you know it's not quite like his company reports, but you'll both know how things are going as soon as I can tell you something. Perhaps you might mention that to him? You told him you were seeing me?"

He hoped he didn't sound over-casual. It was the first time he had heard her laugh. Not with any hint of bitterness but with genuine amusement.

"Mr Webber, I don't see a great deal of him you know, not even at the best of times. When he's really busy I practically have to make an appointment. I suppose Miss Evans might mention it to him. She's my great link, I'd be lost without Miss Evans, luckily we get on very well together. She is a very bright intelligent woman but then she would have to be, Hans always employs the best. I mustn't keep you but there is something you might perhaps be able to tell me. Have you by any chance seen Donald yet?"

"I shall be, at least I hope so. I want to see Mr Swan, your father's partner, I'm going to see your brother when I'm up there."

"You've spoken to him then?"

"I telephoned him at your parents' house – his house – shortly after I met you, just to see if it would be convenient."

"Oh well that's all right then. I wasn't really worried, he's always been difficult to get hold of, he's a traveller for the firm you see."

"You've been trying to contact him?"

"Only for a day or so, it's nothing unusual for Donald he's usually on the road somewhere or other." She glanced at her

114

watch and rose to go. "You might remind him that he's got a sister when you see him."

He considered asking her if she knew about the book her father had written but decided to wait until he had talked to the brother. There wasn't much chance of getting anyone at the Glockemara to find a cab for her and he stood outside on the pavement with her to catch one passing. She shook his hand as one drew up in front of them.

"I'm glad I saw you. Sometimes it's good to talk to someone who knows. Donald would have been a help, you've had the brunt of me instead. Wasn't I lucky, you might have been in France or anywhere. Will you go to France?"

"I have an agent working over there now."

"You must be very busy. I'll try not to pester you, I promise." She caught his arm impulsively. "I trust you – don't give up."

She didn't wait for any reply he might have made and he watched the cab turn in the road and drive away. Perhaps 'agent' was rather overplaying it, he thought, a bit cloak and dagger, not Lizzie's style. He hadn't been able to think of any other word for her except 'operative', and that was even more melodramatic. Neither of them really suited her. He grinned suddenly. "My own personal nosey parker" would have done nicely.

Mrs Thomas's appointment with the editor of the local newspaper, churlishly granted on the telephone, was for half past ten. The offices were in the only square Le Bosquet possessed, on the commercial side of it, huddled between a shoe shop and the local cinema. The small window was filled with photographs of the life of the town, civic banquets, the local fête with children throwing paper streamers. On the grander side of the square stood the town hall. With no competition from the municipal buildings on either side of it, the flaking baroque stucco gave it an air of dignified authority over the market stalls ranged about the cobbles of the square itself.

She was early, the town-hall clock showed another seven minutes to the half-hour. She strolled among the stalls pausing to admire the vegetables and cheeses. Apples might be useful for the journey. She was selecting what she wanted with fierce concentration and not expecting to hear herself addressed softly in English and in a cockney accent.

115

"Good eaters those, you'll like 'em. No, you keep looking them over and just listen. It is Mrs Thomas? Thought so." He was half turned away from her, picking over a selection of early lettuce. "Let's see, your appointment is for 10.30. It won't keep you long, I'll tell you that for starters. There's a bar called the Festival in the rue Creton – down at the end of it. It's not far, I'll wait for you in there, OK?"

She watched him stroll away, a man of medium height in a belted raincoat with bulging pockets. Not a remarkable face, judging by the short time she saw it, brown hair, balding, a London rush-hour face. At her feet a wooden crate held a huddled bunch of live chickens, their feet trussed together with tight string.

The man in the raincoat was right. Her interview with the editor took less than ten minutes and was coldly polite, almost to the point of rudeness. He could tell her no more than he had told Father Girard. She watched the roll of his thick red neck swelling over his shirt collar, the tufts of grey hair in his nose and ears. It was an unpleasant accident, he said, enough to derange any unfortunate eye witness. The woman Pichon had given her evidence at the inquiry and it had been duly recorded and attested by the juge d'instruction, the examining magistrate. That was the report they had printed. And now if Madame Thomas would be good enough to excuse him, he had a busy morning ahead of him. He looked almost disappointed when she rose and thanked him without attempting to question him further, as though her reputation had preceded her and had been exaggerated. And in this he had underestimated her. She did not question him because she could see plainly in his face that he was telling her what he had already intended to tell her. She also thought he was lying.

The bar wasn't crowded. It was too far away from the square to catch the market people and workmen in overalls sat at the few tables that were occupied. In a corner two youths concentrated on an old-fashioned pin table with thumping lights. She saw him sitting alone in a corner and he stood politely as she joined him and sat and accepted a coffee. It was a kind face, quizzical but open and friendly. His eyes were toffee-colour with laugh lines at the side but the bags underneath were heavy and dark. She was surprised how relieved she felt to hear English spoken.

"You could be Press," he said, "but I doubt it. Police was possible but you're a bit old for the Old Bill. No offence."

116

"The Waltons' daughter didn't like the verdict, so she hired a private detective," she told him. "He sent me here because I speak French."

"Yes, that fits." He lit a cigarette and inhaled deeply. "Any luck?"

"I wouldn't be very bright if I didn't ask you who you are."

"That's right, you wouldn't be. Marks, Micky Marks. I used to be a freelance photographer. I married a girl I met in Phnom Penh, a nurse, she'd seen enough war, she wanted to come home and live here in Le Bosquet. It was a condition, know what I mean? I'd had enough too, Cyprus, Africa, Vietnam, the lot. So I said yes. Now I work for the local rag, accepted but not loved, they're a clannish lot up here. Trust me?"

"Yes."

"You can. So then, any luck?"

She told him as accurately as she could right up to her encounter with Julie Pichon's neighbours and he listened without comment, chainsmoking, with only the thump of the pin table in the background. Once he stopped her and asked if she wanted a drink. They didn't have Guinness so she settled for a glass of beer and he fetched it from the bar with cognac for himself.

"What will you do, catch the ferry from Calais?" he asked.

"Either that or the hovercraft, it's no problem without a car."

"Good, get the first one you can. Here stuff this lot in your handbag," he produced a fat brown envelope from his raincoat and slid it across the table towards her. "Don't look at it now, just get it in your bag." She did and he seemed relieved.

"I must have got there that morning just after the fire brigade," he said. "I tip the girl on the switchboard and she rings me if it's a decent fire. When I got there the fire-engine was bogged down to its axles in the sand. Some of the boys had run over to where they were with a couple of hand extinguishers. They hadn't used them, there wasn't much point. It looked better through the camera, it always does for me, then it's just a job, automatic. The same as any assignment, you wouldn't get me to watch some poor sod in front of a firing squad but I've photographed it. At least an execution doesn't smell, I had to stand upwind of them that morning."

"How much wind was there?"

"Not enough to kill her with tobacco sparks. I'd say a light breeze, no more. I shot off a roll of the Olympus and by the time the police arrived I'd shoved it back in my pocket and was using

117

the Nikon. I went on using it until the police cleared us away for their own tame photographer."

"If it wasn't an accident what do you think killed them?"

"I didn't say it wasn't an accident. I don't know do I? But the last time I saw a barbecue like that was in Vietnam and that was napalm. Not common in northern France."

"No."

"I'll tell you something else. Through the camera it didn't seem so obvious, but it did when you had to look at them and it does on the photographs too. I'm jumping a bit but you'll see it for yourself when you look at them. I'd save that until you get back if I were you, it might be a rough crossing. What's your boss like, your Mr Webber?"

She told him, without mentioning Snow.

"Good, not a bloody amateur, that's something. Tell him that's all the stuff from the Olympus, contact prints but the negs are in there too, not so bulky and he can blow up anything he wants, it's quality and needle-sharp. I've put a note in too, date, time, and signed to prove I took them."

"You haven't asked for money." She didn't make it sound suspicious because she wasn't, only curious, which she was.

Marks glanced at his watch and then round the bar. "Time's a problem, I'm supposed to be covering a wedding soon, no it's all right, I can make it. First, there's no catch. I'm a realist but not a philanthropist. Wars? I wouldn't have gone through that lot out there without knowing a good story when I see it. I thought the old man, that mean old bastard we call the editor, would see it too. OK, too gruesome for local family paper but he could have flogged some of that stuff world-wide, and for real money, but he never did."

"Why didn't you sell them yourself?"

"Don't think I wouldn't have, technically they're not my copyright for one thing, that belongs to the paper, but that's not the real reason, and remember I kept all my Olympus stuff, nobody knew about that – they still don't. I could have quit the rag and gone freelance again and flogged them all over, foreign Press, TV companies, America, Germany, the krauts pay top, always have, the messier the better."

"So what stopped you?"

Marks smiled. "Would you believe mother-in-law problems? French families are very close love, you wouldn't credit. There's not enough work for me in Le Bosquet without the rag and Mama wants her little girl near her, know what I mean? So when the money's gone – what then? That would have been my lot. Put it another way. You think I could have kept my mouth shut, sold my stuff on the side and kept my job on the rag? No way darling, there was too much interest in the case. In my book I reckoned it for two things and I didn't like either of them. One it could have been dangerous and I'd had enough of that, and two, when they traced the snaps back to me that would have spelt local scandal for sure. My wife's old Ma wouldn't like that, know what I mean? She'd never let Jeannette forget it, 'That's what comes of marrying a foreigner.' All that jazz, wind her up and you can't stop her. Also I love Jeannette – so forget it. Forget the lot, forget the cover-up and all. I'm a photographer not a bloody detective."

"You think there was a cover-up?"

"I'm damn sure there was. Oh Christ, it's getting late. Listen. Item, Brieux, the editor, never sold a single snap and he could have, and legally. Something stopped him. He says the police confiscated the lot. OK, maybe, either that or someone paid him. Item, the juge d'instruction, that's the one in charge of the inquiry, got promoted. They're always vulnerable over here poor sods, they've got influence but a silly salary, promotion is very tempting for them, know what I mean? Item, the police doctor is difficult to question because he's on an errand of medical mercy in Afghanistan – fancy a trip out there? What about the new kitchen at the L'Aigle Royal? Perhaps that's why they didn't chat a lot?"

"And Julie Pichon, you think they bribed her too?"

"Yes, but I think they were clever, give her too much and she couldn't have coped, people would have noticed. Remember what a child thinks is rich is peanuts. The bicycle was new, did you know that? Poor little cow, a new bike and enough to treat the neighbours' kids to sweets! They still got it wrong with her anyway, she still talked too much and, if I'm right, they killed her – well they'd have to, wouldn't they?"

"The Foreign Office in London have some photographs."

"Might be some of my Nikon stuff but I doubt it, more likely the stuff the police boy shot. Might have been tidied up, I don't know, I never saw them. All I know is that my photographs are clean, if you can call a mess like that clean. They ought to be

119

looked at and looked at professionally, studied, know what I mean?"

"Mr Marks – Micky, I'm puzzled. If we use these photographs and it comes out, you'd still be in trouble wouldn't you?"

"No darling, I won't because I'll be dead. Two months, perhaps three. I've got cancer, love. Sorry, how else do you tell it? Jeannette doesn't know. I've put my address in with the snaps. An inquiry like yours, it's not like you was going to flog them to the Press but perhaps if anyone's dropping a bit of cash around you might see if you can slip her some of it, quietly, without her mother knowing. When it's all over eh?"

Mrs Thomas tried but no words came that she could use. Marks pushed the remainder of his cognac across to her and she drained it.

"What was it you thought you saw," she said at last, "on the photographs?"

"It was the way they looked," he said. "Not the faces, you couldn't tell from those. No, it was the arms, like two boxers in the ring. Like they was fighting each other."

✍EIGHTEEN ❧

Snow phoned Webber early the next morning.

"John I'm at the Yard, how soon can you meet me at the pub in Strutton Ground?"

"Half an hour? Hang on, no, an hour to be safe, it takes me longer to dress than it used to, anyway what time do they open?"

"Any time for me, ring the bell, the governor will let you in. Don't wait for breakfast, he'll do us some sandwiches."

Snow was waiting for him in the back room with the fire lit. The ginger cat had already claimed its position in front of it, singing quietly to itself in the bonus of unexpected warmth. It was a typical spring morning and the weather had turned wintry; cold with hail showers and a distant grumble of thunder.

Snow looked tired, more than tired Webber thought, anxious and drawn. He was looking through some notes he had collected from his office.

"Not much I'm afraid John, but I'm going to be busy for a while." He pushed them across the table to Webber. "Routine, but it's some of the stuff you asked for, Trina Murphy the chauffeur's first girlfriend; she shares a flat in Putney with four other girls, works in a supermarket, it's all there. She's clean by the way, nothing in CRO's and no known connection with any of the Irish naughty boys, unless of course she's a sleeper, and you can never rule that out these days. Any particular reason why you wanted to know about her?" He looked sheepish. "Perhaps you told me, I've forgotten I'm afraid."

"No, just background, the old story, anything might be useful. Something wrong Ted?"

"Yes, I've had a letter threatening the kids unless I ease up on my evidence at the re-trial."

"A bluff?"

"I can't risk it John. They sent it to Finchley not to the Yard."

121

"They play really dirty don't they? Don't rely on protection, get Betty and the kids out of it—sharpish."

Snow nodded glumly. "There's a list of safe houses, not many, most of them are full of Irish informers. I'll have to take what I can get and do a bit of praying. How safe is a safe house John?"

The landlord came in with a plate of sandwiches and two mugs of strong tea.

"Only corned beef I'm afraid Mr Snow—do for you?"

Webber paid him and waited until the door to the private room had closed behind him. They ate in silence and Webber was ashamed to find his thoughts wandering away from Snow's problem and on to his own. It was the cat which channelled them back to Snow and a bright idea. Like all good ideas it was simple. The cat had politely but not enthusiastically accepted his offer of a piece of corned beef and was washing its face. It had turned one of its ears inside out and for a few moments it remained like that, puffed out like a dandelion clock. He had seen Lizzie Thomas's cat do the same thing many times. It reminded him of Flaxfield and their homes they had left empty behind them. From that it was an easy step to a simple solution.

"Are you sure John?"

"Of course, no problem, my place could do with an airing, plenty of room for Betty and the kids until the trial's over. Aggravation Ted; it'll pass, unless the case is a blow-out."

"It won't be, not with the evidence. He'll get his porridge thank God, ten, fifteen years with any luck and with his form."

"Well this is it then, you're laughing, smiling anyway. I'll phone Lizzie's daughter, Doreen Trottwood and her husband, they run the local antique shop." He fished into his briefcase for his keys. "Front door, back door, but tell them to check in with the Trottwoods first. Where are they now, not Finchley?"

"No I've closed it up, the local coppers are keeping an eye. Betty and the kids are waiting at the Yard. I'll get a driver to take them down in a nondescript." For the first time he appeared to enjoy the sandwiches. "Thanks John, better now."

"I can imagine."

"How is Lizzie, heard from her again?"

"She ought to be back soon, a couple more calls, the newspaper and a few neighbours and that should do it. What's happening to your telephone calls by the way? She might try to contact me through you."

"They'll come to me through my office – re-routed. Don't worry I'll get them, I'll get a pad in a Section House for sleeping during the trial. Be like old times."

"Lizzie's not touching our French police comrades. A waste of time."

"And very wise too, they can be very stubborn. Lower ranks especially, they tend to set solid once they've made their mind up."

"Or had it made up for them. Any news from your lad in the Foreign Office?"

"I've asked him to stand by for a meet. I'll fix it once the trial gets going, I'll know how to plan things a bit better then. And you?"

"I'm off to see Swan, Walton's partner." He tidied Snow's notes and put them in his briefcase. "Anything else here?"

"No, mostly Elberg stuff from the fraud boys. I did ask them for everything they came up with so I could hardly refuse it." He grinned at Webber over his mug of tea. "Make a nice book at bedtime for you. Sorry, don't ask me what's in it, I've had things on my mind."

After Mrs Thomas had left Micky Marks, or more accurately obeyed his instructions and waited a few minutes before following him from the Festival Bar, she stood in the narrow rue Creton undecided as to what to do. The cheap cognac had left a bitter taste in her mouth and done nothing to cheer her. She thought of the photographer, his raincoat pockets bulging with his cameras on his way to the wedding, and then arranging the happy group on the steps of the church.

It wasn't yet twelve o'clock. She could go back to the hotel but she had already packed and it was too soon to settle her bill. Besides she knew that she would be tempted to look at and examine the photographs and she didn't want to do that. A quick glance at the contents of the envelope after he had left the bar had been enough to show her that it did indeed contain what he had said strips of negatives and contact prints, mercifully too small to reveal themselves clearly at a cursory glance. In spite of her shock of sadness that he was so ill she felt a sense of elation and excitement. Even if they turned out to be of no practical use, she would go back to Webber with something concrete,

123

something to show him that his faith in her hadn't been misplaced. The elation was tempered by the unpleasant sensation of tingling and burning on the inside of her legs and on her bottom where the plumbing of the hotel had attacked her. Talcum powder was the answer she decided, and she looked around for a pharmacie. The rue Creton looked unlikely, small and almost deserted, it appeared to be mainly residential apart from a baker's shop and another bar and tabac opposite the Festival. It was from this bar that she now saw Paul Colbert emerging, clutching a newspaper and packets of cigarettes, as pleased and surprised as she was herself.

He was the antidote she needed, cheerful and chatting about the good weather and the price of his cigarettes, but business was improving he said, it was the good sunshine, already he had had one customer today, not much of a tip, but then not everyone was as generous as she had been. And then (mock disappointment) but she had promised to use him for her work in Le Bosquet, a special rate! She had not forgotten her promise? He looked about him with the sudden conspiratorial interest like the boy-hero detective in a film made for children.

"The inquiry Madame, you have discovered something?"

He looked so earnest and serious that his face was comical. She resisted the temptation to laugh, she liked the boy and had no intention of making him feel ridiculous. He was disappointed enough when she told him that she had indeed tried to telephone him that very morning.

"A pharmacie? Yes, come," he would show her, it was not far, a short walk only, near where he had parked his taxi. Le Bosquet was a mess since they had ruined the traffic flow with their stupid one-way streets.

On the way to the taxi she fended off his questions with non-committal replies, not wanting to discuss it with him. It was her own fault and she regretted her earlier indiscretion when she had first talked to him about Julie Pichon. You couldn't blame the boy, but Father Bernard had been right, and Webber, she knew, would have been appalled. She did her best to make amends by asking him to drive her to Calais in the afternoon and could not bring herself to refuse when he pleaded to be allowed to take her for a farewell drive in the sunshine. The boy had taken a fancy to her and she hadn't the heart to disappoint him again. Then he could take her back to the hotel and her lunch with Father

Bernard. Mollified, he pointed to where the taxi was parked and said he would be waiting for her.

The pharmacie took longer and was a more complicated exercise than she had expected. The woman ahead of her delayed her with endless questions about the correct dosage of the prescription she was collecting. When finally it was her turn, it took some time before she could explain to the white-coated man in charge that she would be grateful if she could retire with the tin of talcum powder and avail herself of the privacy of his ladies' lavatory. There was no public facility he told her, but under pressure and recognizing a superior will to his own he reluctantly conducted her to the staff lavatory in the rear of the shop from which some ten minutes later she emerged dusty, triumphant, and soothed.

Seated in the front of the taxi with Paul she allowed herself a sigh of satisfied content. It was nearly over, the French connection, and there was no more that she could do. After a pleasant drive she could relax over lunch with Father Bernard and Paul would take them to Calais where she could see the old man safely back into the Hospice Ecclésiastique. Then the boat, and then home and Webber. At least she hadn't disgraced herself. Perhaps it wasn't Webber's way or Snow's, but if she hadn't announced the object of her visit she would have discovered very little, certainly she would never have been contacted by the photographer. Perhaps what she had discovered wouldn't be of any practical use at all, but it was something, she wasn't going back empty-handed. She sat upright, clutching her handbag with both hands, quietly elated. They were out of the town on a side road with flat ploughed fields stretching around them to where in the distance she could see the sun streaked in silver on the sea. Busy and pleased with her own thoughts, it took her some time to realize that her companion was unnaturally silent. Children, all of them, whatever their age, men sulked when they felt slighted or ignored.

She could afford to be generous and she set out to be kind to him. People forgot how easily kids could be hurt and how seriously they took things. She remembered the few things he had told her about himself and asked him about his mother and their partnership in the taxi business. He had never talked about his father and she avoided any mention of him herself, instinct warning her that it might be a sensitive subject. He might be respectably dead but he could equally have abandoned the marriage or indeed never have existed except as a casual lover.

By the time they had reached the cliffs she had almost succeeded in restoring him to something like his more normal good humour. Kindness and understanding, she told herself, seldom failed to break down barriers of hurt pride. She even ventured to tease him about joyriding when he might have been more gainfully employed until the time when he was to drive them to Calais after lunch. Almost at once she wondered if that was embarrassing for him. Perhaps she had assumed too much and he had intended her to pay for her farewell drive in the sunshine? She was relieved when he did not react. Instead it seemed to please him. He had pulled off the road into the same place that he had stopped before. Jumping out he came round and opened the door for her. He was smiling now, his childish sulks forgotten.

"Come and look. Shield your eyes from the sun on the water. See there – on the horizon?"

She did as he told her, concentrating, and when she had adjusted to the glare, she could see the faint line of the English coast.

"England," he said. "Soon you will be home again."

"Yes soon."

He held out his hand and they walked in the warm sunshine. The air was clean and the grass bright green.

"You see," he said, as though in answer to a question, "it is I, Paul, who is the patron. A business needs a man. I do not need to ask permission when and where I can drive."

It wasn't said with any emotion, she noticed, but only as an explanation of his status, and she saw too that he wanted to talk. An only child, his father had deserted them for another woman when he was eight. As soon as the law allowed he had left school to take the place of his father and when his mother had saved enough for a deposit they had bought the first taxi to drive the tourists in the season. A second-hand taxi, old and unreliable, a bit of a joke with the other drivers in the town. When it went wrong he had worked in a garage in the daytime until he had learned enough to put it right in the evenings when he had finished work.

"And now you have another." They paused and looked back at the taxi shining in the sunlight on the grass. His pride was unmistakable.

"Yes, a new one. Beautiful yes?"

126

One day, she thought, he would talk like that about a girl and not a new car. His youth and enthusiasm touched her, reminding her of the time when she had been young herself and listened to the French boys laughing and shouting in her mother's house.

She was glad to let him talk, relieved that his mood had passed.

"You must be very fond of your mother."

"Oh yes, always. But now that I am a man it is easier."

Far out in the Channel a sea mist had rolled up under the sunshine and they could no longer see the line of the English coast. When the grass gave way to a gravel path it led them round to where the grey German blockhaus squatted on the cliff-top. Even in the bright sunlight she hated it and was relieved to see a notice at the entrance saying that by order of the Mayor and Commune it was closed until further notice. They stood and stared at the barred steel rods with the empty pay-box beyond.

"Idiots," the boy said cheerfully. "There is another way. Come, I'll show you, you will find it interesting I know."

❧ NINETEEN ❧

WEBBER DISLIKED DRIVING. He missed the official car with the police driver which in the old days would have taken him wherever he travelled in comfort. He disliked motorways too. At midday he left the M6 for the M42 and turned off it with relief where the sign pointed to Solihull and the house where David Walton had lived with his wife, and where he now hoped to talk to their son Donald.

It was a part of the country he had not seen before and he was impressed. Rich rolling meadows and woodlands, Shakespeare country, the centre of England. He had expected industrial gloom and mean suburbs and the obvious prosperity of the houses set in their large gardens surprised him. There was no gateway leading to the Walton house and a short drive up a curving private road thick with shrubs and conifers on either side brought him to the front entrance. The house had once been a Victorian vicarage and looked it; red brick, solid and uncompromising, it would have been gaunt and ugly without the softening cover of the Virginia creeper.

It took him some time to ease the cramp in his legs after the long drive and he walked a few paces, staring at the house and coaxing his stiff joints to move more smoothly. What was it, he wondered, that told you a house was empty and that no one would answer a ring at the door? It didn't surprise him.

After Jessica Elberg's visit he had tried several times to telephone her brother again. The phone had rung and echoed round the house and no one had answered. Sometimes people chose not to answer a telephone, standing and watching the instrument until the caller got bored and hung up and eventually stopped trying. That was why he had come to see for himself.

The front door was sheltered by a porch jutting out into the gravel path like a Swiss chalet in miniature, the side windows private and impenetrable with designs of coloured glass. Through the pale yellow wing of a swooping bird he could just make out a limited area of the inside of the porch. On the tiled floor a few letters, mostly bills he thought, judging by the look of the envelopes. Difficult to tell how long an absence they represented.

On his way round to the back of the house he looked in at the windows. Lace net curtains made it difficult to get a clear view. Where there were gaps he saw no sign of disorder. Comfortable, unremarkable modern furniture with a few older pieces. One room, possibly a dining-room, had a mahogany table with a potted fern near the window-pane. The fern was unwatered and nearly dead. The surface of the table was covered with dust. How long would a fern last without water? A week? A fortnight? He had spoken to Donald Walton about ten days ago. That would fit.

He could see no sign of any other houses nearby, the trees and the shrubs dripping with the overnight rain hid them from him. He completed the circuit of the house. There was no sign of any forced entry. There was a burglar alarm but it was old, anyone with even an elementary knowledge could have silenced it. A professional could have rendered it useless even before it went off. There were clean empty milk bottles at the trades-man's entrance by the kitchen but no accumulation of fresh milk. At the back of the house a large lawn with an old cypress tree sloped down to a meadow. Surprisingly the grass of the lawn seemed to have been cut quite recently. He guessed it was the work of a jobbing gardener, incurious perhaps, and paid for a weekly visit. The kitchen garden extended into the meadow so presumably that land had belonged to the Waltons too, bought perhaps to prevent the encroachment of the housing estate he could see in the distance.

In a far corner of the meadow stood a curious barn-like building with twin towers like bottles jutting from the roof. It reminded him of the oast houses of Kent. Perhaps they grew hops in Warwickshire too. It looked derelict. The windows, he noted, were built high up into the wall so it was unlikely that a closer inspection would have made him much wiser. Besides the path across the meadow was overgrown with long wet grass and he didn't fancy driving on to Hanley to see Swan in wet trousers.

The garage at the side of the house was locked. It might or might not have contained a car. From the glove compartment of his own car he took a reel of black cotton and some black-headed drawing pins. More from habit than anything else he marked the garage doors stretching the cotton taut and low across them. He did the same to the doors of the house. If he had to come back he would know if someone had been there before him. He grunted himself into the car, consulted his map and retraced his morning journey to the road junction which would take him on to Swan.

By one o'clock the M6 had steered him around the maze of Birmingham and set him off northwards in the direction of Stoke-on-Trent and Hanley. The filling-station where he stopped for petrol warned him of the type of food he might expect on the motorway and he took their advice. He found a pub on a minor road and from there phoned Swan to confirm his appointment.

He was waiting for Webber in his dark untidy office in the factory building of Walton and Swan when Webber eventually found it in a bleak back street of Hanley shortly after two o'clock.

He liked Swan at once, the eyes were honest he thought, unless he was a good actor and had something to hide, but the first impression was encouraging. Wary though; he might have to lean on him a bit. He looked about seventy but was probably a bit younger. A mane of white hair tumbling on to his suit collar from a high forehead and the jutting aquiline nose gave him the air of a musician more than a working potter. When he spoke, which wasn't a great deal at first, his voice was quiet, with the flat tone of the West Midlands.

Webber made his exposition brief but clear, he avoided any area of speculation or of sensationalism. Jessica Elberg had been distressed and shocked by her mother's and father's deaths. Coming home from abroad she had found it increasingly difficult to accept. That was why she had employed him to make inquiries. He showed Swan the paper she had written for him to establish his right to inquire on her behalf. Swan folded it back into its original creases and returned it to him.

"It must seem strange," he said, "making inquiries about people you never met. People you never knew."

"No, not really, not for me. It's been my job for a long time. You ask questions and listen. If you're lucky people help you. That's why I'm here, you knew them both as well as anyone did."

130

When Swan stood he was taller than he had seemed sitting at his desk. "Come and have a look round," he said. "It's nothing much but there aren't many of us left now, not factories of this size. Most of them got caught up in mergers of one sort or another. We didn't have to, and that suits me. It suited David too."

There wasn't much to see. Workshops and equipment that with only a few exceptions looked as though it had been in use for many years before the age of automation. A back yard was stacked high with the raw materials of the pottery. Clay in plastic containers from Devon and Cornwall and drums of metallic oxides for colouring. It didn't take Swan long to walk him through the various processes until the efforts of the modest workforce were stacked in the warehouse racks where the raw clay had been transformed into stacks of household and kitchen pottery.

Back in the office a girl brought them tea and biscuits, her hands and arms ghosted white with dried clay powder. Swan blew some of the dust off the biscuit plate.

"It won't poison you; it would have done way back. We don't use lead in the glaze any more. Too many rules and safeguards, damn great extractor fans and face-masks. When this place started in 1850 it was all lead. Not many of the workers lived into middle age, a lot of them were dead at thirty. That's one change, that and the ovens, we use electric now, no more coal-firing. Mind you in 1850 they were artists. Like David, he was an artist. Do you think they were murdered?"

Webber gave no indication that the quesion had surprised him and he answered without hesitation: "Yes, I may never prove it, but yes I do. You were right, I find it difficult to see him as a man. I can't see either of them yet, even the daughter couldn't do that for me."

"What about young Donald?"

Webber told him about his visit to Solihull.

"Gone to ground. I'm not surprised."

Webber left it, with an opening like that Swan would be better on his own, taking his time.

A workman came in and asked a question about the delivery date for an order. Swan sorted it out for him, finding the customer's letter without difficulty among the scattered mess of papers on his desk.

"Not easy to talk here. My house isn't far, we'll be more private there."

They went in Webber's car, Swan directing him on the short journey to the pleasant tree-lined avenue. Detached, with a small well-tended garden, it wasn't as grand as his partner's vicarage, suggesting modest comfort rather than affluence.

The room where they sat was large and surprisingly neat and tidy, the covers on the chairs and sofa clean and fresh.

"I have a woman who comes in," Swan said seeing Webber's look. "It suits me, wives expect to live in I'm told."

"You must have had some doubts about their death," Webber said, "or you wouldn't have asked me."

"If they were murdered? Yes, I had doubts. Frankly I'm surprised that your inquiry is private."

"The French verdict was accidental death, the case was closed."

"So I read."

"But you still have doubts."

"It was a shock. Jessica wasn't alone in that. In time I suppose I would have accepted it."

Once more Webber left him without prompting. Swan, if he had anything to reveal, would do it in his own way and Webber knew that he wanted to talk. That was why they were sitting together in the man's house. That had been his choice not Webber's.

"Or in other words," Swan continued, "I hoped that whatever had happened wouldn't affect me. Like most people I'm selfish, perhaps more than most if you like. I'm well settled in my life and I wanted to keep it that way. Now I don't think I can, not since you told me you wanted to talk to me. At one point I decided to tell you nothing, but I got frightened. I didn't know how much you knew and if I held things back I thought it might all blow up in my face. I didn't want that."

"It does happen," Webber said, "not always but more often than not."

From then on as he listened to Swan he blessed Ted Snow and the thorough way he had prepared his original notes. He knew then for sure that what Arnold Swan was telling him was true, because at any point where his story coincided with Snow's notes they fitted like pieces of a jigsaw. What Webber was grateful for was the larger portraits of David and Jane Walton. It meant

132

sitting through some things that he already knew but he wasn't complaining. Sometimes he asked a question but mostly it wasn't necessary. Swan wanted to talk and he left him.

"How soon was it," Webber said, "before she knew that the business wasn't going the way she wanted it to? For David I mean."

"Quite soon I should think. Oh it wasn't a financial failure she saw to that. She was a worker, she got the orders and saw that they were carried out. We've never made a fortune but we never made a loss either. She was good with the books too. What she found was that it wasn't right for David. She thought she'd married a good solid working potter but she'd got a dragon by the tail had Jane. That's why she brought me in from Smith and Lakin."

"What kind of a dragon?"

"He was a kid when I first knew him at Smith and Lakin, an apprentice, about fifteen I think. Apprentice was the wrong word for David, he didn't have to learn, show him something once and he'd do it himself straight away – only better. He wasn't conceited, he just knew, a natural. I think some of the lads disliked him for it but he never seemed to care or notice. He was good-looking and a spunky little bugger. The girls were mad about him and I think he just took his pick. That caused trouble too but he didn't care about that either. Old man Lakin knew talent when he saw it, that's why he sent him to art classes."

"And he met Jane Bennett there."

"Yes, he met Jane there. She was in charge of the senior class and about eight years older than he was, but like Lakin she saw that he was something special. She took him under her wing and encouraged him. When he was twenty she married him."

"A happy marriage?"

"Oh yes, I think so. People said it was her money but it was more than that. She had faith in him, she opened doors. If she knew about the other women she chose to ignore them. She told me once that he was a genius and that they had different rules. That was the nearest she ever got to criticizing him. I don't think it was a criticism really. It was only a comment. Later on she lost control of him. But that was much later."

The sun was shining outside the windows but Webber didn't find the room uncomfortably warm. He watched Swan rise and

133

open the French windows and stand for a moment in the fresh air. Sitting down again he said:

"Someone's been investigating the business – tax returns, VAT. Was it you?"

"No," Webber said. "No, it wasn't me."

Technically it was true and if Snow's inquiries worried Swan it was best to distance himself from them. He wondered how he had found out although he wasn't surprised. In small communities gossip was quick to filter through.

"You knew that David left most of the business to me?"

"Yes, I knew that."

"It was quite straightforward. We all did it together, part of our original agreement. If I died first my share would have gone to him. His went to Jane and she made a will in my favour. It was what we all thought was fair. After all I left a good job with Lakin to come in with them."

"Did the children know about that arrangement?"

"Yes, it was no secret. Jessica didn't need it of course. Donald got everything else from the estate and the house in Solihull. He got a small share of the business and a guaranteed job for life if he wanted it. I've got no family, when I die my share of Walton and Swan reverts to him."

Webber saw something like relief in his face and felt sorry for him. He was a beneficiary in his partner's will. A will made long ago as part of a perfectly sensible business deal, but he had it on his mind and it worried him. He could have reassured him there and then but he preferred to leave it. It was a bit callous but fear could prompt confidences and Swan hadn't told everything yet.

"You said she lost control," he said, "that she was frightened for him."

"She thought I was to blame because I wouldn't help her. It wouldn't have done any good. I couldn't have stopped him any more than she could, but I washed my hands of it and she blamed me for that. Once she said, 'One day he'll go to prison or get himself murdered'."

❧ TWENTY ☙

INSIDE THE GERMAN blockhaus she was fascinated in spite of herself. There was no problem about getting in, the boy led her round to a wooden door half-obscured by ivy and nettles. It wasn't even locked, the hinges had rusted and fallen but it opened easily when he lifted it bodily and pushed it over the ridge of grass and moss. It was the way they had sneaked in when they were kids, he said. He knew where the light-switches were too.

No wonder they'd closed it. It smelled of decay and the neglect of unprofitable years. Only the bare concrete shell with the cramped living-quarters remained. The massive gun which had lifted ton-weight shells across the Channel to England had long since been torn out for scrap, leaving the scar open to the sky. The room where they stood had tiers of wooden bunks climbing the wall. In the remaining space was a jumble of rusting iron and steel objects. Only the occasional faded card identified and separated them from a scrap-heap. A British parachutist's folding bicycle, signal rockets and field radios in rotting webbing, the battle-twisted guns and mortars of allies and enemies, and on the wall behind them the posters and decrees of the occupying German liberators:

'Frenchmen, we come in friendship for the glory of a greater Europe. We are your friends. Know your enemies, any civilian aiding them will be shot.'

"Madame, Madame!" The boy's voice called from a distance, echoing from another room. "Come and see the uniforms and the guns."

They shouldn't be there, she should have stopped him. She ought to have known better. If they were discovered the boy would get into serious trouble and it would have been her fault.

"No Paul, we must go or I shall be late. Paul? Paul, where are you?"

135

Water had run down the concrete walls of the corridor, the feeble electric bulbs caught the green slime where it streaked the rough grey concrete and spread out over the crumbling slabs of the floor.

"Paul?"

When she turned a corner she faced a German soldier. Only for a second did her heart leap. The figure was a wax model. It would have looked better elegantly clothed in the window of a shop in the town which was indeed where it had first come from. The sad androgynous face and the angled wrists above the delicate hands looked ludicrously out of place in the field-grey greatcoat and under the steel helmet. One hand supported a rusted rifle, the little finger cocked genteelly, more at home with a teacup or a tennis racket. Someone had stuck a flower in the barrel, long dead, the petals dry and brown.

"Paul?"

The wax soldier was guarding the half-open door of the room, the light in there was dim but brighter than in the corridor. Not really guarding it, only pretend, like a silly game, amateur theatricals with hired costumes; if she wanted to join in, she could pretend to be frightened. If she walked in the room and he jumped out at her from behind the door she wouldn't have to pretend.

"Paul?"

He didn't jump. It looked like an officer's room, with a desk and maps on the walls and racks for files. Or a guardroom perhaps, more museum now, wax models again, Canadian and French soldiers and an RAF pilot, fixed sightless smiles, staring at nothing, like polite guests embarrassed at a joke in bad taste.

The boy was sitting at the desk, his head bent over a metal case and its dials; a jumble of wires and plugs snaked out over the dusty surface of the desk.

"Paul we must go."

She made it sound easy and casual, angry with herself for allowing herself to be party to a ridiculous escapade. When he looked up his face in the dim light was as pale as the wax figures. It was a relief to see the life in his eyes; not sightless like theirs. He looked at his watch.

"Yes we must go. You will not be late even so; but we must go." He held up a loose wire from the apparatus in front of him. "This was their command radio. A receiver and a transmitter.

How crude they were, so many wires and all valves, they had no transistors then. Imagine."

Like a boy with a toy, she thought.

"Does it still work?"

He looked at her with something near contempt, shaking his head. "No of course not, no batteries, and some of the valves have been stolen. I could repair it," he said it without boasting, only stating a fact, "but these parts are not to be found now, otherwise . . ."

That was when she saw the gun. A pistol on the desk in front of him, half hidden by the radio. She didn't know anything about guns, only that it was big and real and gleaming with oil. Not rusty. Not a toy. But he was talking about repairing a radio, nothing about guns. Perhaps the gun was always there, part of the museum and nothing to do with Paul and nothing to do with her. In seconds he would stand up and they would walk out together and she would be ashamed in the sunlight and the open fresh air from the sea.

"And your English photographer. He is a policeman too?"

"My English photographer?" She was repeating it stupidly, not to gain time or to evade it, but because sudden fear robbed her of any coherent thought. She could hear him talking and she watched his face, she watched it as though she was listening and understanding. She didn't look at the gun, she knew that it was within inches of his hand and that it was already pointed towards her. However quickly she moved she could never reach it before he did.

"The man with you in the Festival Bar, the Englishman."

"A policeman? How could you think anything so foolish. Mr Marks is an old friend, Michael, we call him Micky, I've known him for years."

She wondered at the quiet conversational tone of her voice. "You've been watching too much television my boy. A policeman indeed! He's been a photographer all his life, I know his wife too, Jeannette, I am godmother to their children for heaven's sake, because I speak French. He's an old friend, Paul!" She wanted to turn her back on him then and walk away but her legs wouldn't obey her. They held her up but they wouldn't move.

He was standing now and shouting at her: "They are Jews, they go to the synagogue. Jews don't have godparents!"

"Paul listen . . ."

137

"And they have no children."

He hadn't touched the gun, he wouldn't touch it, a stupid hysterical boy playing fascist games.

"He told you. I got a prize, first prize, a silver cup, it was in the paper – a photograph, my photograph! He took it. AND HE TOLD YOU!"

None of it made sense to her. She said nothing, not moving because she was afraid to provoke him to violence. For seconds they were as still as the wax figures around them. Then he sat again, but his eyes never left hers. Without the desk between them she might have gone to him, put her arm round his shoulders to break the hate and terror in his face. To comfort him, to stop him trembling. To stop him picking up the gun.

When he spoke he was quiet, not shouting. "In the pharmacie, you phoned the police, you told them – that's why you were so long."

He was talking, that was something. Told them what? It didn't make sense but it was something. She'd lied to him once and been found out, but if he was afraid of the police then it was a straw in a nightmare and she clutched at it praying that she would make sense. Pick a card. Any card.

"They won't hurt you, I won't let them, we can go to your mother first. We'll go to her together."

The vomit, when it left him, did so without any heaving or contortion. Only his head lowered slightly so that it spilled out onto the dust and the wires on the desk. Some of it went onto the gun. Before she could reach him it was in his hand and pointing at her.

She saw misery and shame in his face now but not hatred. When he fired the gun the noise was so great, trapped within the concrete walls, that it deafened her and what she saw was like a silent film. The great mess of blood on the tunic of the RAF pilot covered the top of his chest with such force that the figure rocked back on its heels and crashed stiffly and silently against the wall of bunks before slipping slowing sideways in an awkward parody of sudden death, the smile of polite amusement still on its face. She couldn't see Paul's face, only what was left of the back of his head where it had fallen forward on to the desk. The gun was still in his hand where the recoil had knocked it back out of his mouth. The sharp firework smell covered the heavy sweetness of the blood, but the vomit, stronger than ever, filled the room with

138

the reek of beer he had drunk in the bar and the scent of mint humbugs.

Outside she remembered to lift the door back over the grass and the moss. She took great gulps of air and knew that she must not give way. Hysterics and panic were luxuries she couldn't afford. The one overriding thought in her head was that she must get out of France and back to England. Once she allowed herself to get caught up in a police inquiry she could be trapped for weeks – perhaps months. And the first thing was to get away from the blockhaus. She was relieved to find that her legs had regained their strength and carried her firmly along the sunken gravel path and up on to the grass mound of the old earthworks. The cliff was deserted, only the taxi still stood parked on the layby. It was some way from the main coast road and she hoped it might not attract notice before she was out of it all and away. For a moment she considered moving it, driving it over the grass to the edge of the cliff and then letting it run over the brink onto the rocks below. Someone might see her; it was too much of a risk and she abandoned the idea.

On the coast road it seemed unlikely that she would find a bus service and she walked back in the direction of Le Bosquet for some distance before she felt it safe enough to thumb a lift from a woman driving a pick-up truck filled with boxes of cut tulips. She was grateful that the woman seemed incurious and accepted without question her explanation that she had walked farther than she had intended.

Father Bernard was waiting for her at the hotel. Incredibly she was only a few minutes late. She now faced the most difficult test of all. She had already decided in the pick-up truck that she would say nothing to him until such time as she could leave the hotel without seeming in any way rushed or distressed. It would not be easy but it had to be done. She could rely on herself but it was too much to ask of the old man. There were things to do and she must do them as she would have done after a pleasant morning in the sunshine. She still didn't know to what extent the Bouviers were involved. She did know that to them her behaviour must seem normal and unexceptional. It was a calculated risk and it must be taken. It seemed unlikely that anyone would investigate the blockhaus until Paul Colbert was reported missing and his taxi discovered, even then it was possible that they wouldn't immediately think of searching the locked and barred blockhaus. If they suspected foul play they were more likely to search the shoreline beneath the cliff. Later on, when the police started their investigation, it was possible that someone would remember seeing her with Paul Colbert, either talking to him in the rue Creton or later getting into his taxi. By then, with luck, she would be back in England, and even if faced with such evidence she was prepared to deny all knowledge of his death. She was already rehearsing her story as she advanced on Father Bernard. She had used the Colbert taxi for some shopping in the town and then had dismissed him.

She greeted the old priest as calmly as she could and was pleased with her control in front of Bouvier at the reception desk, where he had taken charge of Father Bernard's suitcase. She asked for her own luggage to be brought down from her room and for her bill to be presented to her after lunch. The dining room was busier than usual, filled with market people and their wives, spending some of their morning's profits. It made it that much easier for her. He ordered wine and she was grateful for it. She even forced herself to eat some of the fish.

"Calvados," murmured Father Bernard appreciatively. "Interesting, she is improving."

"Could you manage a little more? I'm not very hungry I'm afraid. She has taken trouble and I wouldn't like to offend her."

He accepted it smiling. "Excitement? Ah, how fickle you are Elizabeth! You will return to dear John and forget all about me."

She let him chat, grateful that he was in an expansive mood and enjoying his food and wine. With luck it would take her safely through the meal until they could leave without any appearance of rush or undue panic.

"You approve of the Sancerre, Elizabeth?"

The wine had been his choice and she hadn't mentioned it.

"Oh dear, I'm sorry. Yes I do, you know I rely on you for wine."

"The Loire is much underestimated I think. A Muscadet would have been delightful but perhaps just lacking that slight shock to the palate which makes for adventure."

He looked at her through his ancient steel spectacles with sympathy and love, covering her hand on the table with his own. "But then I think perhaps you have had enough shock and adventure for one day?"

140

"I don't want to talk here," she said. "Will it look odd if we don't take coffee?"

"We can say you have a sailing to catch."

The Bouviers wished her a safe journey and watched her leave with undisguised relief as Father Bernard hovered solicitously behind her and they got into the taxi.

The journey to Calais seemed endless, and because of the driver it passed in silence. She was thankful that Father Bernard didn't remark on the absence of Paul Colbert. Not until she had brought her ticket for the hovercraft, the next one due to leave, could she talk. They sat outside the waiting-room on a wooden bench surrounded by screaming seagulls and children.

"How did you know?" she asked.

❧ TWENTY-ONE ❧

"It wasn't very difficult," he said. "No appetite and you drank your good wine like water. It wasn't like you. I haven't, my dear, spent a lifetime hearing confessions for nothing. I didn't know what it was but I suspected it was something serious."

She sat on the bench in the unsuitable clothes which she had been wearing since she got up. That seemed a lifetime away. Her shoulders drooped over the handbag clutched with both hands on her lap. She felt crushed and exhausted. It was reaction, she knew that. As a small child, scarcely more than a toddler, she had wandered to the bottom of a neighbour's garden and watched unnoticed as they cut the throat of a pig she had counted as a special friend. She remembered the screaming again now, the eyes rolling in terror and the bright blood. Someone had carried her back to her mother who told her not to be such a cry-baby and given her a cotton reel to play with.

"Yes it was serious," she said, and then told him about Paul Colbert in the blockhaus.

Far out on the sea the hovercraft was a distant speck, the roar of its engines barely audible. They watched it grow slowly nearer and louder as he listened to her without interrupting. When she had finished it never occurred to either of them that her flight across the Channel was anything but expedient and sensible. Pragmatists, both of them, they had more faith in their own judgement than that of others.

"Poor young man, he must have been very much afraid of something to do such a terrible thing. I wonder what he thought you had told the police."

"Or what the photographer had told me."

He nodded, his eyes alert in the sunlight from the sea.

"You are right to go. It is no longer safe for you here in France. Now it's my job to do what I can for you and John. I'll see the mother of course, and your Mr Marks as soon as the body is discovered."

"That might take days, weeks even."

"No no, the police are slow but not that slow. If necessary I shall phone them anonymously, I see nothing wrong in that."

"It could be dangerous for you too, people have seen us together remember."

"A priest is allowed to ask questions Elizabeth, it is part of our trade. Even if they have seen us together, what of it, eh?" His elbow prodded her gently in slow motion. "I shall let it be known that we are the sad fire of an old affaire! It is not unknown. Our old love was quite respectable, possibly even unconsummated, although perhaps I shall not say so. Let them think what they like. People long to believe the worst, and if I am thought to be a lecher they will be too busy gloating to think me a detective. I shall be quite safe I promise you."

He had always been able to distract her with nonsense. It was one of the reasons she was so fond of him. That and his passion for truth. Perhaps above all for his plain common sense.

"I don't think you should go back to Le Bosquet all the same," she said. "I shall feel happier if I know you are here at the Hospice. Here's some money for taxis and expenses." She fished in the handbag for it. "I don't want you hanging about for buses or skimping on meals."

He took it without embarrassment, pointing out that if anyone was watching them it would add strength to his story. "Not only a lover," he said with satisfaction, "but a lover who gets paid! Thank you, yes I confess I would prefer not to impose on Father Girard so soon. A good man, not a great thinker but kind enough in his way, however a man gets used to his own bathroom and lavatory at my age."

The hovercraft was still some miles from the shore but now clearly visible, the four great propellers blowing a plume of white spray behind the bright red of the cabin deck. Soon she would have to leave him to clear customs.

"Yes, you'll have to see Girard of course. Do you think he will tell you about the businessmen who tried to bribe him?"

All through lunch he had waited for her to remember that. More than anything it had signalled to him the measure of her distress.

"He has a working knowledge of God," said Father Bernard, "but his knowledge of his fellow men is as yet elementary. I had to explain the principles of duty to him. Not an easy task with one so young and inexperienced. Luckily I was able to use football as an analogy. No player of merit, I believe, hangs on to the ball selfishly when he might usefully pass it on to a colleague."

It would be a pity to scream with impatience at him when with only a little more control she could part from him amicably.

"He told you?"

'Businessmen of respectable standing you remember? In fact Father Girard was approached by only one man, a man who was most certainly of some standing in the district. Le Bosquet has always been a poor community. They have only the summer tourist trade and then for the rest of the year nothing. Oh, some agriculture in the surrounding countryside, but peasant farmers tend to employ only their own families. In the cold months there were many people without jobs and no industry to supply them. Then about three years ago their luck changed, something to do with Common Market policy and the distressed areas of Europe. They built a factory about five miles away and the unemployment in Le Bosquet has fallen dramatically. It was the managing director himself, a man called Koenig, who approached young Girard – at a Rotarian lunch, he told me. They are, I believe, a most highly regarded charitable foundation. Of course there are bad men in all walks of life but frankly I'm surprised that a man in his position would have made such an approach himself."

"Cocky," she said, "he never thought Girard would talk, and you heard what he said, 'It was all done very politely – very subtly'. Big boys like that are very sure of themselves. He'd deny ever mentioning my name if he was ever faced with it directly. Cocky." She shot him a quick look of apprehension. "You wouldn't be so daft as to try anything silly I hope?"

"I am one of God's natural cowards. It is His gift, I would not presume to abuse it."

"A few discreet inquiries perhaps?"

"That is what I intend."

They watched in silence amid the roar of the engines as the hovercraft defied the laws of nature and glided out of the sea, on to the beach and up on to the solid concrete behind the barrier. The improbable machine, he reflected, was not unlike Elizabeth herself, charging ahead with formidable power over anything that lay in her path. For a woman who had faced death only a few hours earlier she was remarkable.

She gathered her possessions and gave him clear, concise instructions as to where and how he might best contact her. On the whole she thought it would be best to telephone her daughter in Flaxfield.

"I don't confide in her you know – too much of a gossip, but she'll know where I am. I keep in touch because of Bunter."

After John Webber he knew that Bunter the cat held the highest place in her affections. Father Bernard was content, even proud, to accept any place in her personal hagiarchy. He embraced her warmly and watched her advance upon the customs barrier. At the back of her mustard-coloured skirt the small damp patch he had noticed earlier in the hotel had now dried and was less obvious. It happened he knew with both fear and laughter, but that morning he did not think she had been laughing.

He stood patiently all through the long unloading and loading of the cars but not until he had watched her safely aboard and the craft was a silent spur of foam on the horizon did he turn and leave. He was not jealous of Webber but he envied him.

In almost every successful case Webber could remember there came a moment he could look back on when he knew he stood a chance. When Swan told him that Jane Walton had a lived in fear of prison or death for her husband, that was such a moment.

"It started with David's exhibition," Swan said. "That was soon after she set him up in business. Remember she had been his art teacher and she had tremendous faith in him."

"What sort of exhibition?" Webber asked.

"It's a good question. Pottery of course, but not easy to describe. Not the usual run of stuff that you get with studio potters. They usually go in for jars and vases, Japanese-influenced, a bit wishy-washy I've always thought. David's stuff wasn't like that, he liked figures – groups I remember – and some that were more like portrait sculptures than anything else, then just when you felt you were getting the hang of his style there was a whole string of abstracts, a bit like Henry Moore. It was a quite astonishing display of versatility. Like a precocious child showing off."

"Did you think it good?"

145

"Yes I did. To be honest a lot of it was rather above my head, but I'm not a judge, I'm a working potter not an artist. I'll tell you this, I could appreciate the sheer technical skill, that's something I do know about, and that was bloody marvellous. This was pottery, remember, not sculpture, everything had to be fired in a kiln and with some of the really complicated pieces that took some doing I can tell you. Jane did him proud, hired a whole art gallery in Birmingham and invited anyone she thought would come, local bigwigs, the Press, the lot."

"And did they come?"

"Yes they did, the regional press were polite enough. Local boy, that sort of angle. I don't think they understood it much either. The London papers didn't cover it at all, not interesting enough for them I suppose. However there was one very important review. You've heard of an art magazine called *Dilettante*?"

Webber nodded.

"Glossy and expensive but it carries a lot of clout in the art world." Swan went over to a bookcase and brought an ancient copy of *Dilettante* over for Webber to see. "Nobody realized their critic was there and you'll see that the article is anonymous, that was their policy in those days."

The magazine had been quite generous – in terms of column inches that is. The article covered almost half a page. It was headlined 'Pretentious Rubbish', and was vitriolic in its abuse of David Walton's exhibition. It was a hatchet job and the critic had spared him nothing, ending with a contemptuously dismissive, 'too clever by a quarter'. The magazine was dated November 1952. David Walton would have been twenty-two. Webber tried to imagine the young potter's feelings the first time he read it.

"Unkind," he said, aware that it was an understatement.

"It was vicious, David pretended to laugh at it but he was hurt – stung. I knew him well enough to see that. He never tried anything like it again. It was bad for Jane too – worse for her in a way. She had some grand ideas about suing the magazine for damages but of course that was daft. It was one man's opinion and in law there wasn't a case."

"Did they ever find out who wrote it?" Webber asked.

He wasn't surprised at the answer. The old-womanish pedantry of the author hadn't altered much in thirty-odd years.

146

"Jane made it her business to find out. It was a man called Spavin. James Spavin."

Thirty years ago . . . Webber pictured Spavin and David Walton meeting for the first time all those years later. Would the article have been mentioned? He was beginning to see Walton clearer now and he guessed not. He would have said nothing, his pride wouldn't have allowed it. So Spavin had been left to wonder. Webber remembered his face when he'd told him David Walton had written a book.

The afternoon sun had thrown a pattern of leaves on to the carpet near the open window. A faint breeze in the garden trees moved the shadows like fish nudging each other in a stream. It was pleasant and relaxing and he looked at Swan with feelings close to affection which he had no intention of showing. Some people, he knew, were more revealing in a state of anxiety.

"Those wills," he said amiably. "The Waltons' wills – they were both legally drawn up I imagine? Properly attested and so on?"

Swan spent the next five minutes giving chapter and verse down to the names of the witnesses and the address of the firm of solicitors.

Webber let him see that he was listening with full attention and then asked quietly:

"When did David Walton start making fakes?"

৶ TWENTY-TWO ৻

IT WAS A guess. He could have been wrong and Swan would have denied it. He wasn't wrong, one look at the man in his armchair told him so. Very pleasant – lucky too. It would save time and with his man already worried he might do nicely. It was always a question of balance. Push him too far and he might panic and start thinking of that firm of solicitors.

"I wonder," Webber said, "if I might scrounge a tot of whisky? It's been a long day and I tire more easily than I used to. Why not join me?"

Swan didn't speak until he'd poured the drinks and he was back in his chair and then only after Webber's "Cheers" had prompted him to swallow some of his own whisky.

"They weren't fakes," he said, "well, not at first they weren't. Reproductions, that's what we made. Once the boom came in Staffordshire pottery it was a good market. People wrote books and articles about it and soon the demand began to outstrip the supply, especially for the Victorian figures. People liked them, they were bright and cheerful but when the prices for the original pieces went up they couldn't afford them. So we reproduced them at prices they could afford. Simple as that, and of course we weren't the only ones, lots of small firms were making them. Most of them never marked what they made – that's not illegal by the way – the trouble came when they turned up in antique shops and auction rooms all over the country."

"But that was illegal surely?"

"Oh yes, if they were sold as genuine, and of course they were, sometimes the dealers were just ignorant, but a good many of them must have known they were selling fakes."

"Or reproductions?"

"No, once they were sold as genuine they lost that respectability, especially if a dealer decided to help things along by giving

148

them a bit of false age. It's not a new idea you know. They were busy making Greek statues in ancient Rome."

"How was it done – with Staffordshire I mean?"

"It's not difficult: crackle the surface of the glaze with a quick change of temperature, a kitchen oven and a fridge is good enough with a bit of practice. Then you can rub them over with a stain of some sort, strong coffee or shoe polish. I'm told one dealer buries them in fresh cow-dung. A few artistic chips where they don't show too much and you've got a profit margin of about 1000 per cent. I've seen some of the stuff I've made myself in country antique shops tarted up like that and guaranteed over a hundred years old."

The whisky had induced a more relaxed atmosphere, some of the tension had gone from Swan's face. If that inclined him to full confidences it was good. Webber could easily recall him to a sense of insecurity and apprehension if he felt Swan was holding something back.

"What decided you to stop making reproductions? Were you frightened of becoming too involved?"

Swan considered. "Yes in a way, not so much because of what we were making but because of David and what he was making, and that was quite different. I was afraid that sooner or later someone would find out. If someone had traced his stuff back to the factory and there was I turning out reproductions . . . well it wouldn't have been easy for me to plead innocence would it?"

It depends how you define innocence, Webber thought. If innocence implied lack of knowledge then Swan was guilty by default even if he had taken no active part in David Walton's fakes.

"How were they different from your reproductions?" he asked.

Swan finished his whisky and replenished both their glasses.

"There was no comparison, chalk and cheese. When the saleroom prices for English pottery started to hit the headlines in the newspapers – that was the beginning. David was fascinated. He used to go down to London to view the stuff before the sales. He followed the prices like some men study form before a race. Not just the Victorian stuff either, he was just as interested in the early pieces, Sherratt, Whieldon, Wood, Walton, right back to the 1740s and salt glaze." He looked at Webber, wondering if he had made a mistake in confiding in him. It was too late now and the relief was a luxury.

"And he started to copy them?" Webber prompted.

"At first he passed it off as a hobby. He used the factory in the evening and at night. Jane thought it was his way of proving that he was a good potter; as good as anyone ever had been in Staffordshire."

"To prove something you need confirmation of course," Webber said. "In fact you'd need someone to tell you it was as good as the real thing, and the simplest way to confirm that beyond any doubt, I suppose, would be to sell what he'd made?"

"It started as a joke. He put a few of his pieces in a local auction, for the fun of it, he said."

"And?"

"The saleroom accepted them without question and catalogued them as genuine. That's when he should have withdrawn them, but he didn't. He wanted to see if they would fool the dealers and the collectors too. I'm sure that was true, I honestly don't think that money came into it. Not then anyway, later yes."

"And they sold?"

"Yes they sold, all of them."

"He'd made his point. I can understand that. So did he own up and return the money?" Webber already knew the answer, he was interested to see how Swan would justify what had happened.

"No–no he didn't."

"You could have though, couldn't you." It wasn't a question but a direct accusation and Webber's voice was deliberately sharp. It took Swan by surprise, forcing him to explain without pausing to consider.

"He said he was going to tell them, but not then, later. He said a provincial saleroom wasn't a true test. He wouldn't be satisfied until he'd gone right to the top and done the same thing in London. If he owned up too soon, he said, he would never know for certain." Swan was flustered and frightened, spilling some of the drink from his glass on his trouser-leg and rubbing at it with a handkerchief. When he'd finished he looked up at Webber but he found no comfort in his eyes.

"He was my partner for God's sake! My friend too. It was fraud man! What do you think that would have done to the business? It could have finished us!"

Webber let the pause last a full fifteen seconds before replying. When he did his voice was no longer sharp but conversational again, as though Swan's explanation made sense and he was satisfied. The man was doing nicely but he needed a nudge.

"I'm afraid," he said regretfully, "that the Fraud Squad are already involved." He watched Swan go pale. Well, it was true – in a way. Might perk things up a bit more.

Swan said fiercely: "I wouldn't have anything to do with it. I told him that. And Jane – she knew I wanted no part in it. I told him I was cutting out the repro trade and if he wanted to go on playing a damn silly game like that he could, but not in the factory and it was his affair but not mine."

Perhaps that was why Swan had shown him round the factory; no fakes, just honest pots and pans. Clean hands. Only it wouldn't be quite as simple as that.

"You must remember," Webber said, "that I'm no longer a serving policeman. I'm working for David Walton's daughter and I'm inquiring into his death. In so far as the faked pottery had any bearing on that, then it concerns me too. I have no connection with the Fraud Squad, not directly anyway. I won't pretend that I don't have close contacts in the force, it's only natural after the years I was with them. Sooner or later you'll have to tell someone the lot, and it might," he said cheerfully, "it might as well be me. Not a bad idea to have a friend at court."

Swan ran his finger round his collar and Webber saw that his face was damp with sweat.

"There might be a breeze in the garden," Webber said, "I'm a bit of a gardener myself, let's get some air."

The garden at the back was larger than the patch at the front had suggested. It was mostly lawn, but fussily broken up with flower beds. It was well tended, lawn edges trimmed sharp, the roses pruned and no sign of blackspot or mould, the beds bare of weeds. It made Webber's heart ache to look at it.

He let his eye wander over the rest of the garden. He was pretty well informed about the costs involved in gardening. Since his retirement it had become a heavy burden on his pension. Silver birches, well established, five of them, not cheap, nor were the exotic shrubs and rose bushes. Unless Swan spent every free hour of his day there he must employ a gardener, a good one too. Swan's hands had never kept this garden going; they were soft and manicured. So then, a woman for the house, a gardener, and under the open carport at the side of the house a gleaming Jaguar XJ-S.

"Your Icebergs are better than mine," Webber said generously, "nice roses, stronger altogether, it's not a good doer in

151

Suffolk. So where did Walton turn his stuff out after you stopped him using the factory? That barn place near the house in Solihull I imagine."

Swan had not made the mistake of underestimating Webber. "A friend at court" had had an ominous ring and if Webber was going to be on anyone's side Swan very much wanted it to be his.

"Do you know anything about potting?" he asked.

"Not a thing," Webber admitted cheerfully, "but I'm willing to learn, shall we try those chairs in the shade over there? I'm not very bright," he smiled beguilingly at Swan when they were sitting, "about technicalities I mean. You will be merciful I know."

"There's no great mystery about pots," Swan said. "People think there is, but it's pretty basic really. It comes down to clay and the potter in the end. In Staffordshire the actual method hasn't changed since they first started. Refinements that's all, purer clay and all the stuff we use for colouring is cleaner too. We don't use the old dangerous way of glazing with lead anymore and the ovens are electric not coal-fired like the old ones. That's really all you have to know. Lots of people have had a go at faking the early stuff. Some of them were very good too but they never stood a chance with the experts."

"Why was that?"

"They got the modelling right, more or less anyway, sometimes they took a mould from the original, it comes out a bit smaller but unless you put the two together and compare them it's very effective. Their big mistake was using all the modern stuff I've just told you about. Too clean, too good if you like, no impurities. David knew that, it sounds almost too simple, but he saw that to fool the experts he'd have to go back to basics. That pot bank he built in his barn is an exact working replica of an early one, right down to the coal-fired kilns."

"Why was that so important?"

"With a coal oven you get impurities in the glaze. In some of the early pieces you can even see bits of coal dust, wood ash too. They always used wood or charcoal to get the coal going. Not many people know that, but David did and that's the way he did it too. You can't rush it, not like pressing a switch. Five days up and five days to cool down, he followed that exactly."

There was no mistaking the pride in Swan's voice.

152

"What about all the stuff he used, the clay and the colours for decorating?" Webber was beginning to respect David Walton.

"He got the raw stuff from the factories, crude oxides before they refined the guts out of it. He dug his own clay from the old marl pits and mixed it with the white clay from Cornwall just like the early potters did. If they used moulds then he did too, but he made his own just like they did, and if the original had been modelled by hand then David modelled by hand."

"I don't wonder he fooled them."

"He didn't, not at first. There was something he'd forgotten."

"And that was?"

"Age, patina if you like, and that's the most difficult thing of all to fake, and I'm not talking about crude methods like coffee or shoe polish. Handle a piece for two hundred years and it shows. It's very subtle but it's there. David's early work was perfect – too perfect – it looked exactly like the originals, but the originals as they had looked when they first came out of the kiln. You could say there was nothing wrong with them except there was nothing wrong with them."

"And the experts spotted them."

"Some did, some of the big London salerooms, yes they were suspicious and wouldn't accept them. It was a big setback for him. But he got over that. It was nearly four years before he tried them again but by then he'd solved it. I never discovered how he did it but he did. There was no trouble with the experts."

"Just a minute. Wouldn't the people in the salerooms have remembered him?"

"He never took them himself, he was too clever for that. He used dealers to put them in for him with their own stuff, they were happy enough to get a commission and as far as they knew the pieces were quite genuine."

Webber thought of Molly Motherwell.

A blackbird in one of the silver birch trees staked out its territory with sweet defiance across the long shadows on the lawn. The whisky and the warm evening were a dangerous combination in the comfort of the well-padded chair but he forced himself to concentrate. David Walton must have made a great deal of dishonest money. He probably got most of it in cash from the dealers too. It explained a lot. The world cruise and the easy lifestyle.

"Why should Donald Walton go to ground do you think? You said it didn't surprise you."

"I think he's frightened."

"Did you know about the Elberg collection?"

"Yes, I knew David was helping him."

"How much of it is fake, do you suppose?"

"Your guess is as good as mine. It's been a long time since David confided in me."

Was he telling the truth? Webber looked at Swan in the other chair and decided that he was. He was too scared to lie now. He pressed on.

"Did he tell you that Elberg employed Spavin as an expert too?"

Swan's surprise had to be genuine. "No! No he didn't."

In the pause which followed the blackbird fell silent.

"But you did know that David had written a book and that someone has stolen it."

"Donald told me. He told me after his father was killed. That's how I knew he was frightened."

"The book I imagine would have exposed the whole affair. A sort of revenge would you think? And perhaps the ultimate recognition for his own talents?"

"It was something he wanted, yes. It would have made sense to him. He was like that."

Webber grunted, tugging at the thoughts in his head.

"Those early pieces, the original antiques, how many of them did the potters sign or mark?"

"Very few, the Wood family of Burslem in the late eighteenth century they marked some, not all but some. The Victorians even less. That wouldn't have been a problem for David though, simple lettering or a rebus mark impressed into the soft clay before firing, easy for him."

"I warned you I wasn't very bright about technicalities," Webber said. "You see what puzzles me is this. If Walton intended to take the credit for his work and if the experts couldn't tell it from the originals – how was he going to prove it?"

In spite of Webber's disclaimer it was a bright question. More than ever Swan wanted him on his side.

"I told you that most of the originals carried no mark," he said. "But David's did. David marked everything."

154

❦ TWENTY-THREE ❧

WEBBER HUMPED HIS chair round to face Swan more directly.

"A secret mark," he said, "had to be didn't it? Nothing obvious, but something he could point to with no room for argument when he published the book."

"Yes, all that," Swan said with no attempt to disguise his admiration for his partner's ingenuity. "Secret, yes, and certainly no one could question it, no possible room for argument. You were wrong about one thing though. It couldn't have been more obvious."

Webber waited, no longer drowsy.

"In one way," Swan said, "I misled you when I said that almost none of the originals carried a mark. In practice they nearly all did. It wasn't intended and not much good to us today but David saw it and used it. You see you can't press soft clay into a mould without leaving fingerprints – it's as simple as that! Every single piece that David made carries at least one of his prints somewhere. The style and the period didn't matter either, you can find prints on Staffordshire figures whether they were made in 1740 or 1840 – only they wouldn't be David Walton's. Only the fake figures he made himself could have those."

For someone in whom Walton hadn't confided for a long time Swan seemed remarkably well informed. He was beginning to relax too. Webber sensed it was time to push a bit. Apart from Walton's wife and his son, Swan was the only one who had known about the fakes right from the beginning. Webber wondered how much Walton had regretted that, and how much he had paid for Swan's silence through the years.

"I suppose," he said mildly, "I suppose you must have been mentioned in the book quite a bit?"

"I didn't kill him," Swan said.

155

Webber believed him. Why kill the source of a steady tax-free income.

"How long since you last saw young Donald?"

"Ages, it must be about three months since he came to the factory. He goes his own way."

"A nice easy job," Webber said wryly.

"A sinecure, I told you, it was part of the agreement, a job for life, but the firm never really needed him. We've never been short of orders, thank God."

"You never saw a copy of the book before it was stolen I suppose?"

"It's not very likely is it?"

"No, no it isn't." Webber rose with difficulty and wandered across the lawn leaving Swan to follow. He paused at the sleek car and regarded it with genuine admiration, his hands judicially clasped behind his back, like a potential customer in a showroom. "Very nice, they were always good but I think this is the best they've ever made. So tell me, did David still carry on with his lady-friends, so far as you know I mean?"

"I don't know that Mr Webber, I truly don't. I imagine so, a man doesn't change his character overnight does he?"

Webber let his hand stray over the black sheen of the coachwork. "But a happy marriage, would you say, for all that?"

"She was a remarkable woman, as remarkable as he was in her way."

"You probably knew him as well as anyone. Would he have published do you think? Blown the whole thing sky high and to hell with the consequences? He had a lot to lose didn't he?"

"And a lot to gain. David wanted recognition – fame if you like. There's not much point in doing something better than anyone else in the world if no one knows about you."

"A good old read," Webber said, "cause a bit of a stir eh? Salerooms with all their nice glossy catalogues going back for years, not to mention all the punters who bid up for the stuff, a few red faces among the experts too I dare say. I expect quite a lot of it finished up in museums too. Dear me, no wonder someone pinched it." He leaned forward peering into the car to admire the elegant layout of the controls. "Yes, very nice, a gentleman's car. Check it for bombs in the morning do you?"

"Are you serious?"

Webber straightened up and looked at Swan across the top of the car, his arms resting on the low roof.

"Yes, I am quite serious. In my book, for what it's worth, I reckon you could be a target. If you take my advice you'll clear out for a bit." He gave Swan, now ashen-faced, a card from his wallet with the Flaxfield address. "You can tell me where you are if you like, but I wouldn't spread it around."

The bus from the London terminus was due at Flaxfield at 21.15, and it was on time. By 21.20 Mrs Thomas had carried her suitcase down the familiar street and was gratefully drinking her first bottle of Guinness in The Bull. She had started to try and contact Webber by phone when she reached Dover. He wasn't at the Glockemara and he had left no message. She tried again when she got to the Victoria coach station in London with the same result, and so she had taken the bus to the village. If Webber was not readily available then she would settle for Flaxfield and Bunter. True, it would also entail seeing her daughter Doreen again, but that was unavoidable since Doreen and her husband Jimmy were looking after Bunter.

She sat in her own special corner under the ancient water-colour painting of the racing pigeon. In her green crêpe-de-Chine blouse, the mustard-yellow skirt and her Celia Johnson hat, she took time to unwind and marshal her thoughts. She was home. She graciously acknowledged greetings from some of the regulars but none of them had the temerity to join her and take the chair which by long accepted custom was reserved for John Webber.

The pub and the people surrounding her were more real than anything she had left behind in France. That same morning she had been close to death and now she was sitting listening to English voices talking about football and fertilizers. She wondered at her capacity to absorb and control her thoughts and emotions. Under the hat and the dark hair her face was white and drawn and the hand that lowered the glass on to the familiar table trembled. She knew it was delayed shock and was determined not to let it beat her. It was real, it had happened and she was home. It was enough for one day. The subdued sting of her flesh where the hot water had assaulted her was almost a comfort, a proof that she hadn't been dreaming. Webber would come and it would be all right. For a few days she would relax

157

and recover. A few days would be enough, she wouldn't push. It could, she thought sipping reflectively, be a good opportunity to show him that she was content for him to take command. A display of natural modesty and reticence. He would like that.

At ten o'clock she used the telephone outside the ladies' lavatory to phone the Glockemara again. He had not returned. The Bull closed at 10.30. It was just possible that he had driven down to Flaxfield himself. She tried his home and spoke to Betty Snow.

"No he's not Lizzie, oh help! Are you expecting him? Ted's here for the weekend but he's already in bed poor darling, he's exhausted after the Old Bailey. He said he'd spoken to you but nothing about John. The kids are in bed too."

She reassured her, it had been a remote chance that's all, no she hadn't spoken to him, she had no idea where he was.

"Poor Lizzie! Don't worry love, it's no fun being a copper's wife."

Chance, she thought, as she settled herself again with another Guinness. Chance would be a fine thing.

At 10.25 the landlord started to call 'Time'. She had a choice. She could go home and face Doreen in the morning, but that would mean a night without Bunter, or she could phone her now. She phoned her. Perhaps Webber would have received one of her many messages and contacted her. He didn't like late nights, he was bound to be back soon.

After he left Swan, Webber would like to have driven back to London where he could still have arrived at the Glockemara in time for a reasonably early night. Instead he turned the car off the M6 and made his way back to the house in Solihull. He stopped at the same pub where he had eaten earlier in the day. He ate bread and cheese and sausages, contenting himself with only half a pint of beer; the thought of being breathalysed by some eager young copper on the motorway didn't appeal to him. He'd been eager and young once himself. How long ago was that?

The pub was a survival from those same days when as a bright young man his superiors had sorted him out as a likely choice for plain-clothes work. Sometimes now, when he stepped out of his bath feeling young and refreshed, it was like seeing a stranger in the mirror. A body that had nothing to do with him.

The woman who came and sat at his table could have been 35 or 40, it wasn't easy to tell. Respectably dressed with discreet make-up, a neat unobtrusive handbag, a small suitcase at her feet. When she asked him the time to check her wristwatch her voice was educated. It seemed a genuine inquiry, not the traditional opening of a prostitute. He still thought so when he found himself listening to the tumbling story of how she had finally broken under the verbal cruelties and taunts of a husband who had found a younger woman and wanted to live with her. She wasn't sorry, only elated, at least that's how she felt now, tomorrow could take care of itself. The elation was a shout of freedom and she wanted to share it. No, she didn't want any money, she had money, enough anyway for a few days in a cheap hotel until she knew which of her sisters in London would have her. She would save her money for that, but if he was driving south perhaps?

She was a decent, vulnerable woman and too attractive, he knew, to be hitchhiking at night. The husband must be a wasteful idiot.

"Phone him," he said, "tell him to come and collect you."

It was a nice smile, shy but excited as though she only half-heard what he said. "I'll think about it. I promise. You've been very kind."

He had a wild image of her lying naked and comforted in his arms at the Glockemara and blushed.

It confirmed her opinion that he was a gentleman, sensitive to unaccustomed compliments. As a young man, she thought, he must have been very handsome.

Driving alone in the car towards the Walton house and warmed by the whiskies he had bought and shared with her he decided that he was a fool and that gallantry was a poor exchange for living. A police car cruising silently past him made him forget it and he was relieved to see it disappear round the bend of the road ahead.

In the gathering dusk the house looked more deserted than it had even in daylight. He pulled the car up under the trees of the drive without getting too close. The light in the sky behind the chimneys and gabled roof was pale green, fading into orange and then cheap blazing red like a holiday postcard. He took a torch

159

with him and walked towards the front door, his feet crunching on the gravel. The tracks of his own car showed clearly where he had parked and turned it that morning. There were no other tracks that he could see and a quick check with the torch told him that the mark he had stretched across the door was still in place and not broken. It was the same with the garage and the entrance to the house at the back. On the lawn the cypress tree was a black silhouette against the red sky and beyond it, in the deeper dark of the meadow, only the tops of Walton's brick kilns thrusting up out of the barn glowed like lighted cigars in the last rays of the sun.

He cursed his laziness of the morning and knew that he should have braved the long wet grass to look at it more closely. He did so now, soaking the bottoms of his trousers and freezing with fear when he disturbed a fox almost at his feet, a fox revealed only when he caught it in the light of the torch.

A wasted effort. Compared with the flimsy security of the house the barn was a fortress. Behind the gaps of the old wooden walls was a casing of solid steel. The place was reinforced like a safe. The windows high up on the north-facing wall were heavily barred and the only other breaks in the walls were the four large extractor fans; even those, he noted, were safeguarded behind welded grids. Behind the wooden barn door was another door of steel. No alarm system, you wouldn't need one. Without a key the place was like the Bank of England.

A north light for an artist; the extractor fans for a practical man to get rid of the poisonous lead dust. David Walton had guarded his secret factory well. There was no glimmer of light. Like the house the barn was deserted and, it would seem, had been for some time. The only tracks through the long grass of the meadow were his own and after satisfying himself that the barn was impregnable he retraced them back to the house. Somehow he was going to get inside.

The days when he could have done it legally were over. He checked to make sure that the car was out of sight from the main road and collected the things he needed from the boot. He removed the cotton marks he'd left, filling the holes left by the drawing pins with soil and wiping the smears clean with his handkerchief.

After thirty years he knew as much about breaking and entering as he did about his own job. He rang the front door bell not because he expected any answer but because it was classic routine, then he knocked politely on the door at the back for the same reason. It was on this side of the house, out of sight of the drive, that he would break in and hope to silence the alarm. He knew it was not a type that would alert the nearest police station but the bell would make a bloody awful noise, loud enough to reach the road and certainly the neighbours beyond the trees on either side. He remembered the voice of an old burglar.

"Then you try the door Mr Webber, always try the door, you'd be surprised Mr Webber how many people forget to lock a door. Always worth a try. I've known many a raw young man sweat his guts out with a jemmy when all he had to do was open the door."

Webber tried it. It opened.

❧ TWENTY-FOUR ❧

HE DIDN'T PUSH it wide open, only an inch, sometimes on old alarms you didn't break the contact and trigger off the bell for the first two or three inches. He closed it again carefully and selected a pair of wire-cutters and thin cotton gloves. He wiped the door handle clean with his handkerchief and considered. An open door could indeed mean, as his old burglar friend had told him, that someone had forgotten to lock up. It could equally be that someone had broken in before him. The frame of the door was clean, no sign of a forced entry.

Webber stood some five or six yards off and surveyed the back of the house closely, running the narrow beam of the torch around the window frames, concentrating on the ones nearest the drainpipes. The riot of Virginia creeper made it difficult to see clearly. A central window out of line with the others caught his attention. Between two floor levels: he guessed it was the window giving light to the half-landing of the staircase. He had no intention of trusting his weight to drainpipes or Virginia creeper.

From the ground the window looked innocently undisturbed. In the bag he had brought from the car he found his small Zeiss Dialyte binoculars and looked again. Now he could clearly see the thin black line where the frame and the window no longer fitted flush. Under the leaves he saw the jemmy marks where it had been forced. He wouldn't have to bother with the wire-cutters. Someone had already silenced the alarm.

Even so he pushed the back door open with his foot, keeping his hands free for the torch and the wire-cutters. The alarm was dead and the house stayed silent. He was free to examine it without raising his blood pressure. He resisted the temptation to switch on any lights, the less attention he drew to the house the better.

162

He stood in a small stone-flagged room, the old Victorian scullery used for boiling the household linen, an annexe to the kitchen proper. Now it was a store-room for logs, old tins of paint, stacks of newspapers. Whoever had done the search had made an effort to conceal it but the rings of dust on the shelves told Webber the story as clearly as if he had watched the intruder at work. Only the larger containers like tins of distemper had had their lids prised open and replaced hurriedly, such as no householder would leave them. A professional job too; a casual glance through the uncurtained window would not have aroused any immediate suspicion.

The kitchen, beyond the scullery, was protected by net curtains and only the area nearest the window had been restored to enough order to pass a casual scrutiny from outside. The rest had been turned over thoroughly. Remembering the advice of his friend in the trade he examined the rooms at the top of the house first. "I always check the bedrooms first Mr Webber. Someone might be a heavy sleeper, it's always a comfort to know you've got the place to yourself. Peace of mind Mr Webber, sir!"

The alarm wire had been cut on the landing window. Webber pictured him standing there after that short blast from the bell, ready for flight if the neighbours or someone from the road chose to investigate. Like Webber he would have known it wasn't very likely.

Every room at the top of the house had been ransacked. It wasn't vandalism, he'd seen that too. This was a search-and-find job, and a search for something specific. Whatever it was they were looking for it wasn't the usual loot. There was plenty of that left untouched. TV sets, cufflinks, silver-backed hairbrushes. All still there in the light of his torch.

On the ground floor the picture was the same. Or very nearly. All the rooms leading off the hall had heavy mahogany doors tidily closed. Through a glass door the letters he had seen from outside still lay undisturbed on the tiled floor of the porch and he left them as they were. When the local police investigated it wasn't his job to make their task more difficult.

He worked round the rooms methodically just as someone had done before him. Whatever they were looking for had been well hidden, but in every room they had taken time to clear up the mess near the windows. It argued that they were in no hurry, that they were not afraid of being disturbed. They? He? She?

When he opened the last door the stench hit him like a physical blow to the face. He tasted the sharp sting of the whisky at the back of his throat as his stomach heaved involuntarily.

The body lay face down on the carpet. Webber stood and forced himself to breathe knowing from experience that he could adjust and accept it. He had stood and looked down on many dead bodies in the course of his long career, but always with colleagues around him and the comforting presence of a police doctor or a pathologist from the Home Office. He didn't touch the body but used his torch and looked long and earnestly.

A wallet had been tossed on to the carpet and its contents scattered. There was money as well as a driving licence. They hadn't been disturbed but they were making sure they'd got the right man. It suggested that their victim's face was unknown to them. The driving licence would have told them, as it now told Webber, that the thing on the floor had once been Donald Walton.

There wasn't much left that was recognizable. In his early days he would have guessed that the putrefying body had been there for many weeks. Since then he had learned that maggots have astonishingly voracious appetites. They were everywhere, fat, gorged, and he guessed third-stage, but none of them yet in pupa cases. That would mean that Donald Walton had been felled, with a crushing blow on the back of his skull, only about nine or ten days earlier. Someone had struck him from behind as he walked into the room and then searched the place at leisure. There was no sure way of telling if they had found what they were looking for, but unless they had found it at the very end of the search it seemed possible that they were disappointed. Donald Walton was dead though, and they had come to do that too. Who? Someone bloody well had.

He closed the door thankfully and sat on a hard chair in the hall. The stench had probably gone right through the house but by comparison it was more bearable outside the room. He tried to think constructively but after his long day the shock defeated him. He needed sleep and caught himself seriously considering one of the comfortable beds upstairs. An hour would have revived him completely and he rejected it only because there were things he had to do. There were priorities.

The telephone in the hall was working. He had expected that it would be. A telephone repeatedly reported as out of order

164

would have drawn attention to the house more quickly than one which simply remained unanswered. He found the number he wanted in his diary and breathed a sigh of relief when eventually it was answered. He had some difficulty in making himself understood and only when he was satisfied did he put the receiver down and make another call to the Glockemara Hotel.

He found a woollen scarf on the hall stand and in it he carefully wrapped something he had seen in one of the first rooms he'd entered on the ground floor. His earlier good intentions of leaving the place as he'd found it were now abandoned. He hoped it wouldn't interfere with the police inquiry. He didn't think so and anyway, he told himself, he too had a job to do. And a long night ahead of him.

The road at the end of the drive was deserted as he edged the car quietly out on to it and headed back to London. Three or four miles down the road he found a telephone box and rang the local police. He made it short and hung up before they could put a trace on it. Once on the motorway he drove quickly but carefully until he came to a service station with a car park. He drank tea not coffee before dozing over the wheel for nearly an hour and waking stiff but refreshed to face the night ahead.

Mrs Thomas didn't stay long with her daughter and son-in-law after leaving the pub. Long enough to make a show of politeness and gratitude. Mother and daughter were not close, in many ways they were too alike, a condition which neither of them appreciated. Mrs Thomas got on much better with her daughter's husband, Jimmy Trottwood, and was one of a small circle of intimate friends privileged to call him Betsey. She was glad when she could decently plead tiredness after her journey and seek the comfort of her own cottage. She couldn't manage her luggage and the cat basket and gratefully accepted Betsey's offer to accompany her and see them both installed.

Released from his basket in the kitchen, which was the room in which he was most at home, Bunter selected a favourite vantage point on the Welsh dresser and reserved any display of affection until such time as he considered it appropriate or expedient.

"You look exhausted Lizzie."

"A bit of a day, travel takes it out of you."

"I'll leave you to unpack. You don't want visitors at this hour."

165

"Stay for a nightcap. I'm going to have one. I need something to get me off to sleep anyway."

She sat and listened. The nice thing about Betsey was that he didn't need any prompting. He knew all the things she wanted to hear and told her, sipping his nightcap with his red crew-cut wig sitting incongruously on the paler remnants of his own hair. A round face with the cherubic smile of a clown, beaming with love and goodwill, sad only when he was alone. He didn't like being alone. That was why he had married Doreen and he was happier than most.

"Mr Snow? Oh yes dear, settled in nicely, at least she and the children are. He's away most of the time, something in the City he's supposed to be, not that he fooled me dear, I've seen too many policemen in my day. My dear, such a shock! He'd left his wife and the children in the car and came to the shop alone. Well I ask you! A bowler hat, big feet and he tells me Mr Webber had spoken to him about the cottage. I nearly died! Innocent as the Festival of Light and face to face with Lily Law on the doorstep of my own shop! Luckily I kept my mouth shut, sheer instinct of course, and then I realized I'd gone chalk-white for nothing."

"He didn't say how long he'd be staying?"

"No, a bit of a rest for her and the children while he's busy. They're nice kids, the boy is very bright, he wants to feed all the stock in the shop into a computer. He says he could double my turnover. Where is John by the way?"

"He must be busy too. I've been trying to get him on the phone. Tomorrow I expect."

There were things she would dearly like to have talked to Betsey about but she held back. It was John she needed. Talk to Betsey and he'd talk to Doreen and you might as well talk to a newspaper as confide in her daughter. She couldn't tell him about France or that she was worried about Webber who should have been safely in bed and asleep at the Glockemara. She wouldn't admit, even to herself, that he might have discovered company more congenial than her own. She sought safer ground, nodding towards Bunter who had folded his paws and was feigning sleep.

"I saw tins of cat food in Doreen's kitchen," she said accusingly.

"Emergency rations dear, you said three meals a day and he told us he was used to five. I didn't believe him of course but anything for peace and quiet, remember I had to live with Doreen as well as Bunter."

166

"Lazy little madam, too much trouble to shop for fish I suppose." She eyed both Bunter and Betsey fiercely. "He's my cat, not hers. I hope this doesn't mean he'll be outside your kitchen with a begging bowl every day."

The attack didn't disturb him in the slightest, he understood her far too well for that. She had said she'd had food in The Bull, a packet of crisps probably, if that. Then Guinness and now whisky, and she was grey with tiredness. It was a situation in which he felt completely at ease. He ignored her protestations and carried her suitcase upstairs. He ran a bath for her and turned down the bed. He found fish in the freezer and prepared Bunter's sixth meal of the day, she wouldn't care to be woken too early by a hungry cat.

For hours she had talked and listened, unwilling to give in to sleep. He was shocked when he saw how late it was.

He put the cooked fish on the floor as Mrs Thomas descended in an old flannel dressing-gown and curlers to apologize and say goodnight. The doorbell rang at the same moment.

He opened the door to reveal a dishevelled Webber supporting a strange drunken woman with her arms round his neck. They were accompanied by a large dog which made a beeline for the fish and finished it with two flicks of its enormous tongue.

The outrage on Bunter's face was reflected in that of Mrs Thomas.

The woman disengaged her arms and surveyed the table with the whisky bottle and glasses.

"A party! How super. Mummy loves a party doesn't she Dahlia?"

"Lizzie dear," Webber said. "This is Mrs Motherwell. I'd like you to put her up for the night if you would. I'll explain in the morning."

"I think," murmured Betsey, "I think I'd better be getting back to Doreen."

167

❧TWENTY-FIVE❧

WEBBER SLEPT ON the sofa downstairs, Bunter retreated to the shed at the bottom of the garden. Molly Motherwell and Dahlia were allocated the spare bedroom and Mrs Thomas retired at long last to her own bed. Surprisingly, apart from Bunter whose eyes never left the house all night, they all slept well.

Webber was up before anyone and saw Snow before he left for London. They sat in Snow's car with the early morning sun slanting across the road. He watched Snow doing his best to overcome his breakfast. Mornings had never been a good time of the day for him and now he was depressed that Webber wasn't in his own home.

"Forget it," Webber said, "I shan't be down for long. Things to do."

There wasn't much time to talk. Snow had to be at the Old Bailey by ten o'clock and at his office before then. Webber was concise. First he told him about Arnold Swan, then the house in Solihull. Ted Snow woke up, became professional again. Webber felt almost guilty until he remembered the money. It was still after all a partnership, business. Snow thought of the money too and listened.

"No sweat John," he said, "the local troops up there may not even ask the Yard for help. If they do I'll make sure they know about his mother and father. I'll probably phone them anyway. They won't welcome it but it might save them an hour or two. It'll look better later on if I do. Don't worry, I shan't bring you into it. 'Information received' is good enough. I wonder what they were looking for at Solihull or did they just want to shut him up d'you think?"

"My guess is both. He'd have enough of that book in his head to make him dangerous to a lot of people. There might have been another copy of it too, a carbon perhaps. Then there must be

168

keys to that factory place of Walton's in the meadow, they could have been looking for those. A lot of people would like to see inside that, but it was intact."

"They could have burnt it down," Snow said.

Webber shook his head. "Too solid. It's cased in steel, you'd need the army to destroy a building like that. Not a chance." He saw Snow steal a glance at his watch and quickly produced the negatives and contact prints that Mrs Thomas had given him to pass on. "God knows where she got them, she was in no state for chatting last night. It's professional stuff anyway, beach snaps, can you cope? Detailed enlargements? Comments perhaps?"

"I'll farm them out to the lab boys," Snow said, "there's some notes for you in my office too, I'll bring them down. Try and let me know when you'll be here."

"And you," Webber said. "How is the Brixton case going Ted?"

"It should be all right this time, a nice clean jury, and well guarded thank God. It should be all right, a bit of a waster but there's no other way. No more frighteners through the post anyway, they seem to have lost us thanks to you, probably run out of money to pay for it too. You need money for the heavy mob."

Webber nodded. He was as relieved as Snow that Betty and the kids were safe. Marriage was a hazard for an active policeman.

Snow stowed Mrs Thomas's prints safely in his briefcase. "Lizzie all right? No trouble?"

"She's nesting," Webber said, "glad to be back. Lizzie's different. I'll let her breathe a bit, she goes her own way. A good night's rest and she'll chat a bit more."

Webber had never been one to rush things, some had seen it as a fault but Snow had envied him and still did. It was time for him to leave, he couldn't know that Webber envied him his day's routine. He waited briefly while Webber leaned in through the open window of the car before he could drive off.

"How is His Lordship behaving himself?"

"Patient," Snow grinned. "He's a wise old bird, seen it all in his day. He wants it to look right. If he gets the verdict he knows is right he'll put him inside for a long stretch to encourage the others. He manages to get the odd laugh too. I've had him before so I've heard most of the gags. It helps a bit, not as much as knowing Betty and the kids are safe." He paused with the car in gear, engine running. "Things are moving John. The Walton boy at Solihull and Lizzie seems to be on to something in Le Bosquet. Think back to the beginning old son. I told you I had a sniff of something." With a wave of his hand he moved off.

Webber stood and watched it disappear round the corner. No you didn't you crafty old bugger, he thought, you wouldn't bloody well commit yourself.

It took barely twenty-four hours to sort out the sleeping arrangements. Webber wisely left it all to Mrs Thomas. It showed the essential goodness of his nature that it never occurred to him that she had brought it all upon herself. He simply turned to her knowing that she would make the best possible arrangements for everyone and that they would work. Like dropping an Alka-Seltzer into a glass of warm water: after the fuss and fizz, the calm.

Indeed it turned out to be a curiously calm week and he was grateful; a time to listen and think as she brought the dormitory to order. Molly Motherwell was moved to join the other refugees in Webber's house. It meant that the children had to share a bedroom but they were careful not to complain because they were not being sent to school and inland at Flaxfield the weather was a minor spring miracle of warm sun under a great arch of East Anglian sky. The children would be good for her, Mrs Thomas explained, and so would Betty, she would need the comfort and companionship of another woman. Webber wondered why Lizzie had not included herself in that category but conceded that Bunter could hardly be expected to cohabit with a yeti. It was also true, he admitted, that he and Mrs Thomas had a lot to talk about. A more compelling reason was Lizzie's almost casual reference to Betty Snow's culinary ability. There were no arguments.

Molly Motherwell's reaction to the death of Donald Walton surprised Webber. On the journey down to Flaxfield he had told her nothing. In the half-drunken state in which he had found her waiting for him at the Glockemara she had simply accepted the journey as necessary for her safety and trusted him. Webber's second telephone call from Solihull had alerted the night porter at the hotel and, having been promised a good tip, the man had met her taxi and then opened the bar for her. She had slept nearly all the way down to Flaxfield and not until she and the dog were safely moved in with Betty and the children did he tell her, before she could read of it in the newspapers.

At first he thought that her muted reaction was due to shock but Mrs Thomas saw strength of character too.

"She's tough John, a survivor. In a way it's almost a relief for her. She was too old for him, she'd never have kept him. At least she knows where he is now. It's a comfort."

Webber's look told her that he thought her cynical.

"It's true," she said. "I remember neighbours in the war like that. 'Reported missing' was harder to bear than knowing. She's frightened too. She knows you wouldn't have pulled her out of it without good reason. And she's stopped drinking. It won't last."

It was true. She settled into Webber's cottage with Betty Snow who had the sense to tell her about Brixton. The children took to her too and delighted in the weather when they and the great lolloping dog took her for long walks on the common blazing with yellow gorse. She marvelled at the sophisticaton of the modern child, remembering her sister and herself at their age. She drank alone in her bedroom at night.

For Webber the days were a bonus he told himself, a gift and a luxury. In his days as a serving policeman he would have been running three or four cases at the same time, like poor Snow was now. Caught up every day in court perhaps and trying to make sense of all the other stuff on his desk.

Mrs Thomas was as good as her promise to herself. She needed time to recharge her batteries, she knew Webber wouldn't stop now. She wanted him to be in command. You pushed him so far and then he rolled forward on his own. They sat late into the nights, long after they had eaten and he had taken her through every hour of the time she had spent in France. When she told him about the blockhaus and the suicide of Paul Colbert she deliberately presented it as factually as she could. Making it sound as professional as she could, as professional as any report he might have received from a colleague in the days before he had retired. It didn't fool him but he paid her the compliment of accepting it like that. He was shaken and admired her. She had more than justified his trust. He longed to call her a meddling old

171

fool but said nothing. He repaid her faithfully with a detailed account of his own time in the Midlands. He didn't tell her about the woman in the pub. She did not hesitate to emphasize Father Bernard's gentle infatuation. Disappointingly it made not the slightest impression upon him that she could detect. What they both needed now was time to be on their own and to think. It suited her. She had got what she wanted, her own kitchen to herself, Bunter, and Webber under the same roof. It was more than enough. She was nesting. The week lay before him.

Early on he rang the Elbergs' number in Holland Park. He wanted to see her and give her some comfort for the death of her brother. It would break her husband's complacency too. A serious development; Webber needed to see them both. Eventually he got connected to Miss Evans, what did she call herself, computer expert? Secretary? He pictured her neat and tidy, efficient and distant in an air-conditioned subterranean office with no daylight.

"Inspector Webber, I had expected you to call. Yes of course, the local police came round shortly after all the fuss in the newspapers. I had to tell them that I just didn't know anything. Mr and Mrs Elberg had already left on business. He has many interests you know, all over the place, not only in Europe. What? No I had to tell them exactly the same thing, that I know nothing, I never do. He will be in touch when he needs to be. No I'm afraid I don't know where they are. I can only tell you that it is nothing unusual – for me here I mean. It may seem very odd but I am well used to it. Yes the news is indeed very shocking, Mrs Elberg will be deeply distressed, and it couldn't have come at a worse time for Mr Elberg too. I'm just waiting for the gutter Press to try and make something out of his problems. Not that Mr Elberg's own name has come into it so far. They're awful fools you know, the Press I mean. You have probably been following the take-over bids?"

"Yes of course," said Webber untruthfully. "Tell them I am at their disposal."

"Mr Elberg has instructed me to say that the original financial arrangement is to be extended as long as you may be in need of it. You will simply send your accounts in to me and your salary is to remain as long as you need it." The tone was efficient, impersonal.

"Thank you," said Webber. "I'll be in touch."

172

It was probably the standard brush-off, he thought as he put the phone down. The perfect secretary safeguarding her employer's movements. Putting Webber on the same level as the dozens of newspaper inquiries that reached her every day. The dragon guarding the lair. So far no one seemed to have linked the take-over dramas in the financial pages with the horrors which had fallen on the Waltons and the Elbergs. Boardroom battles were largely anonymous. Murder was more public.

He got Snow early at his office at the Yard.

"It's been mostly in the financial pages," Snow told him. "It's double Dutch to me. I've got to rely on the fraud boys for a breakdown. Don't worry they promise they'll keep me covered."

"Ted can you talk?"

"Yes, it's early, I'm alone."

"Your tame snout in the Foreign Office, have you been in touch?"

"John I've got three heavy cases apart from the court."

"I want him."

It broke all the rules. He would never have asked Ted if they had been still serving together. A policeman keeps his informers to himself. Snow hesitated. Webber told him that the money was to continue.

"Leave it with me," Snow said, "I'll fix it."

"Tell him to do some homework," Webber said. "I want the lot, anything he can get on the Waltons and on Elberg."

It was Wednesday. When he hung up he felt better. The village where he had been born closed about him like an old familiar coat, fitting every angle of his body. It was soothing and comforting and dangerous, it was too soon to slip into comfortable old clothes, there was too much to think about.

He walked around the village early and alone. He looked at his neglected garden and was glad when it failed to shame him. Later he walked in the High Street and bought tobacco and paid some bills. Coming out of the butcher's he met Mrs Thomas.

"Lizzie, I'm driving over to Dunwold, do you want to come?"

She knew he was being kind. If they hadn't happened to meet he would have gone on his own and been back as usual for his evening meal. He liked Dunwold and he liked the sea as long as he wasn't expected to sail on it or swim in it. He needn't, she thought, have looked so apprehensive.

173

"You go off on your own," she told him amiably. "I've got plenty to do."

"Shall we say about half past six then?"

"It'll do, dinner at seven. Don't go stuffing yourself with Mars Bars."

"Might I inquire . . .?"

"No, wait and see."

Like Pavlov's dog Webber salivated gently and watched her walk down the High Street until she disappeared into the fishmonger's and a world of her own. He considered checking on her purchases and dismissed the thought as being unnecessarily destructive of anticipation.

It was a short journey to Dunwold and the sea. He could be there in half an hour. For a small boy with his brother and his mother and his father driving the slow old family car the journey had been an adventure, planned and looked forward to for weeks. Now it was nothing. Only the road and Dunwold itself would be the same, and the sea, they never changed, that was why he wanted to go. The day stretched before him, marred only by the nagging and persistent thought that this was turning out to be a case, where, like too many in the past, he would fail. He told himself that he had had the same feeling before and that he had been wrong. The same doubts and yet sometimes – not always but sometimes – he had found a way through in the end.

Before he left for Dunwold he had one last call to make. Across the road was the familiar frontage of the antique shop owned by Mrs Thomas's daughter Doreen and her husband James Trottwood, Jimmy to Webber, he had never presumed to the intimacy of that inner circle which was allowed to call him Betsey. Jimmy Trottwood would have welcomed it, he was genuinely fond of Webber and in the course of his not uneventful life there had been very few policemen he had felt free to address as 'dear'.

"John dear! Come in do."

∾ TWENTY-SIX ❧

WEBBER CLOSED THE ill-fitting door behind him. He knew instinctively that Doreen was out. Her physical presence, like her mother's could be detected through walls. Not for the first time he reflected upon the unlikely nature of the Trottwood ménage. It never occurred to him that both Jimmy and Doreen frequently speculated on the precise nature of his own relationship with Mrs Thomas.

While Betsey was making coffee Webber glanced round at the stock in the shop. As far back as he could remember it had remained basically unchanged. The rocking horse, the walls warmly lined with the mahogany fittings from a Victorian chemist's shop; rubbed gold lettering on mellow wood softly proclaiming the virtues of Pot. Permang. and Nux Vomica to a shop full of comfortably padded chairs and bric-à-brac. It was not in Betsey's nature to sell anything if it could be avoided. He regarded the shop as being more in the nature of his private sitting-room and it was his good fortune that, although he kept very quiet about it, he had enough private capital to ignore the fierce forces of the market-place. He was not a dealer at heart. What he liked best was to welcome his friends and, in the times when he was alone, to browse in his books on antiques. His specialist library, built up through the years, would not have disgraced that of many a museum or expert London dealer. He looked upon it as an insurance for the time when, against all reason, his shares in Marks and Spencer might fail and throw him into the harsh world of the antique trade. He did not regard himself as an expert but privately conceded to himself that he had become knowledgeable.

"Doreen out shopping?"

"Stalking her mother," said Betsey, delicately removing the skin of milk from his coffee. "She likes to keep a line on her."

Webber nodded. Doreen liked to be privy to her mother's affairs. She would certainly have bitterly resented her mother's unexplained absence in France. Betsey too was curious although his approach was more subtle than his wife's. It faintly disturbed him that Webber's cottage should be full of strangers. Flaxfield was his own private refuge and he had no desire to see it disturbed.

"Lizzie's out shopping for tonight," said Webber. "It's no secret, except from me perhaps."

"I envy you, settling in with her?"

"She makes it easy." He was amused by Jimmy Trottwood's careful approach and was prepared for his next move.

"You've got a full house up at your place John?"

"A few friends, not a long visit, God willing. What do you know about Staffordshire pottery?"

"A bit, mostly from the books and the odd piece that comes in. Pugh is sound, and the two by the other man, the London dealer. They cover pretty well everything between them. Why?"

Webber grunted and drained his cup. "I'll leave this with you," he said, indicating the padded carrier bag he had brought in with him. "Have a look at it, I'd like to know what you think. Don't let anyone else see it. What time do you close?"

"I'm like the Windmill Theatre, John dear. I never close, not for you anyway."

At Dunwold the wind off the North Sea was cold. He had never known it when it wasn't. He parked the car near the Old Pier where some men and boys sat silently with fishing rods begging for answers in the swell of the sea below them. It was low tide and he walked along the beach below the line of the wooden breakwaters, sometimes with the rough shingle sounding out his steps until the stretches of soft wet sand let him walk silently into the distance where the wall of the harbour entrance was low and grey against the sky. The bright sunshine had lured only a few people on to the beach. They sat huddled behind canvas windshields, sipping hot drinks from thermos flasks, and watched him as he passed.

Webber barely noticed them. He was thinking of the mess in his mind and desperately willing it to make sense. Of all the attributes freely granted to detectives in fiction, he thought, omniscience was the one which made him angrier than any other.

Up on the promenade the severe outlines of the hotels and boarding houses were like cardboard cut-outs against the sky. He thought of another beach and of Julie Pichon watching it. The blockhaus and the boy Colbert. A young priest being engaged in polite conversation by the manager of a factory. Lizzie Thomas had frightened someone. He thought of the blockhaus again and shivered as though someone had walked over his grave. It was difficult to tell how much it had affected her. He ought never to have agreed to her going. Her rightful place was at home in Flaxfield, only of course she would not have agreed with him. He made himself angry by realizing that his thoughts had leapt ahead to the evening meal and wondering what she had planned for him. He walked on and thought of Spavin and Swan and Donald Walton with his head and his face crawling with maggots in his father's house in Solihull. There was a point at which coincidence had to be ruled out, it was always possible but at some point you ruled it out. People were knocked down and killed on badly lit roads at night. Thieves broke into houses and they killed in panic when they were disturbed. All boys were soldiers at heart, boy scouts – sometimes murderers. In the junk-pile of weapons and fancy-dress uniforms that was the blockhaus a boy might tip over the edge for half a second. He might, but what about all that rubbish he was yelling? Only it wasn't rubbish to Paul Colbert. He had been frightened of Lizzie and of the photographer. Webber thought he was probably frightened of his mother more than anyone, he wondered what she was like. It was Father Bernard's job not his; delegate, that was part of the game. You might explain those deaths on their own, any single one of them, but not together, not when you connected them however tenuously with David Walton and his wife lying burnt and blackened on a smooth stretch of yellow sand in France.

He paused and watched a grey-haired man with thin legs walk slowly into the sea and swim in the waves without any apparent sign of discomfort. He looked older than Webber, somehow it was a comfort to watch him, it gave Webber courage, made him feel younger. He walked on and thought of the house in Holland Crescent, and the woman who wanted to find out why her mother and father were dead, and her husband who was paying him to do it. He pictured Arnold Swan, frightened, driving his expensive car into the crowded safety of London and hiding in the anonymity of a small hotel. He thought of David Walton's book and his women and of James Spavin who had crucified him all those years ago. Spavin with his pride and his reputation, washing dishes in a concoction of ivy leaves. Webber turned his back to the wind and watched the grey-haired man bobbing in the waves with his slow breast-stroke. The wind snatched at some sparks from his pipe and Webber watched them fall on to the sand and die. Some children in swimming costumes threw pebbles into the sea but didn't swim.

At the harbour entrance he climbed up the steps and sat in a shelter looking back along the beach. He saw the dog first, its thick coat flying in the sea wind, bounding ahead and then skidding to a halt to make sure that Molly Motherwell was following safely. Her unsuitable shoes gave her an erratic walk on the sand and shingle. Sometimes she paused, shading the sun with her hands, and surveyed the people on the beach. It was unlikely to be a coincidence that they were both on the Dunwold beach, she must be looking for him, and her pleasure when he went down to meet her confirmed it. There was a touching old-world elegance about the way she allowed him to help her up the steps to the shelter, where she sat in a corner protected from the wind, the dog sitting protectively at her feet with its pink tongue lolling. The wind, he decided, charitably, had made her eyes water, probably the dog's too, only you couldn't see that behind the thick fur. Molly Motherwell looked at him earnestly, combing her own hair off her face with her fingers.

"I am not pissed," she announced firmly and clearly, "not properly pissed that is, but with those blue eyes of yours looking at me and wondering I will tell you that I have lined myself with exactly one large gin to face the morning and no more. I find it useful don't I pet?" She fondled Dahlia's head and waited.

"One gin seems very modest. I didn't think you were drunk."

"Truly?"

"I have seen you drunk you know, not now though."

"I'm tougher than you think. I can stop any time – just like that," she snapped her fingers. "How long am I to stay here?"

"You're not happy with Betty and the kids?"

"It's not that. I think I'm just panicking. Donald's death was a shock – is a shock."

"For me too," he said. "I remember years ago when I was a

178

very raw young policeman on my first messy case. Some madman, we never found out who, had mutilated a young girl with a knife. I'd never even seen a dead body before. I remember the old sergeant telling me that I'd soon get used to it. But I never did."

"I think I'm much harder than you," she said, "more sensible perhaps. I said Donald's death was a shock, so it was. Oh yes for all the obvious reasons, he was young and good to hold – young, yes that's it. It's easy to love youth, a sort of love anyway, a waste. But when I analyse it, I was really shocked at my bad luck. Like my first husband, the loss was just as complete. I must be basically a very selfish woman. Twice in my life, too late in my life, I've had luck, first the money from the pools and then meeting Donald and his father. Twice I had money and the chance to make more and both times it went wrong. I'm not a fool you know. I never made any money as a dancer, that was a wasted time if you like, but I was a good dealer. With Donald and his father I was on to a good thing. Now it's gone and I'm shit-scared into the bargain. Now *that* Johnny blue eyes is rotten bad luck. How's that for the truth?"

"There's nothing wrong in wanting money, stick to being frightened. When it's all straightened out the money won't seem so important."

"Will it straighten out?"

"Oh yes," he wondered whether his optimistic voice was to convince himself as much as Molly Motherwell.

She lit a cigarette and smoked it in silence while they watched the old man finish his swim and dry himself.

"Betty Snow is all right but I wish she had more guts. You know about Brixton I suppose?" she asked.

"Ted told me some of it. You mustn't be too hard on Betty, she's married to a career man, he's good too. It's just her bad luck. The force is full of them, you can't fight it. If you're like Betty you just accept. After all she's got the children, she's settled for that."

"She's a dreadful cook too."

"It's no secret, but she's a nice woman," Webber said mildly.

His reasonable tone seemed to irritate her. She swivelled round on the wooden seat so violently that she hit the dog with her knee, making her yelp. She glared belligerently at Webber. "Did you know that your little Welshwoman is in love with

179

you?" Oddly, instead of matching the fierceness of her face, the words sounded flat and unemotional, almost as if she was no longer interested in what his answer would be.

"Lizzie and I are old friends," Webber said, and then when she didn't say anything he felt awkward and angry that she had embarrassed him. "She's very fond of her cat too," he said.

This time there was genuine humour in her laugh, matching the delight in her face.

"Which is why," he continued firmly, "she asked you to move in with Betty Snow, she just didn't fancy coping with a cat and a dog in a small cottage. There was no deep-laid plot to get me to move in with her I promise you."

His sincerity made her laugh again until she saw that he wasn't joining in and she became contrite. "Dear John, I'm sorry. You have to make allowances. Come on, I'll buy you a drink and some lunch if you've got time, or do you want to be left alone with your Dunwold?"

"Lizzie told you where I was?"

"I went to see you this morning and she said I'd probably find you here. I caught the bus."

They went to the Dunwold Arms and he was grateful when she seemed happy to have sandwiches. He was concerned to keep his appetite for the evening and she was happy to concentrate on wine and nibble the food. If she had had some special reason for tracking him down that morning, he thought, then she had either forgotten it or decided against revealing it. This second possibility worried him. It was no part of his job to antagonize people, least of all someone who had been so closely connected with Donald Walton and his father. Somehow in the shelter he had got on the wrong footing with her. Now he set out to relax her and the wine was on his side. With one bottle he felt reasonably safe. It reminded him of the time he had first talked to her in the shop.

He judged his moment. "Do you remember telling me what Donald said to his father that first time you met him? Something like, 'What do you think Dad, shall we adopt her, will she do?', something like that?"

She nodded, a wisp of hair falling down beside the glass she was holding.

"What do you think he meant by that?"

"At first I thought it was Don's way of asking if his father

180

approved of me. I suppose a woman would think that. I was wrong of course, I see that now. I was just useful to his father. I'm sure I wasn't the only one either, in fact I know I wasn't. I could put the things he found into auction. It was a good way of laundering them. They came out with a good healthy provenance. That's what they wanted, not me. Well – a bit perhaps."

"You said that Donald told you about his father's book, that it was to be a sort of exposure of the antique business?"

She looked at Webber without expression. "In bed, yes he told me in bed, the big secret. He was fond of me you see."

"Did he tell you that his father made fakes, very clever fakes? That some of the things you put into auction might have been fakes too?"

She broke off some of the sandwich and gave it to the dog. "No he didn't tell me that but we knew didn't we petal? It was all in the book you see. They weren't always in the flat, the boys weren't, Donald and his father. They kept it in the chest of drawers but it wasn't even locked half the time."

"You read it? Before it was stolen?"

"Yes, certainly."

"Have you ever told anyone else you've read it?"

"No, no one knows that, or that I have a photostat copy of it."

❧ TWENTY-SEVEN ❧

IN FLAXFIELD MRS Thomas entertained her daughter to tea. Anyone seeing them sitting at the kitchen table together could have no doubt of their relationship. Doreen was a later edition of her mother. They shared the same features and colouring: dark-haired, sharp-eyed and inquisitive. Doreen lacked her mother's single-minded energy and she knew it, but in all other things they were very alike. Too alike for comfortable companionship. Mutual curiosity sometimes drew them together.

Doreen knew that her mother and Webber shared secrets to which she was not a party. Webber's house was full of strangers. She very much wanted to know what was going on and her mother liked to keep abreast of current opinion in the village. Crude direct questions would have been ignored by both of them and spoiled their enjoyment of a tea-time chat.

"John's very kind," Doreen ventured, "and with his own place so full of his friends, it's only natural he should move in with you for the time being. Staying long, are they?"

"I never like to bother him for details when he's busy."

"No, of course not. Better food for him with you too. She's not much of a cook that Mrs Snow, all frozen and fried."

"I have heard."

"Blue smoke the moment she sets foot in the kitchen. Black sometimes," Doreen added.

"Cooking doesn't come easy to everyone," her mother said virtuously, adding as she topped up Doreen's cup, "What are you giving Betsey tonight?"

Doreen ignored the question. They both knew perfectly well that Betsey did the cooking at Trottwood Antiques. Doreen had not inherited her mother's culinary gifts.

"That Mrs Motherwell drinks," Doreen volunteered. "Gin mostly. She gets it in half-bottles from the Co-op."

182

Mrs Thomas had already checked at The Bull but hadn't yet investigated the other outlets. She imagined that Molly Motherwell was getting her supply from somewhere in the village but it was pleasant to have confirmation. She also wondered what the woman had had in the parcel she was carrying and whether she had taken it with her to Dunwold. From Doreen she learned that Molly Motherwell had been seen entering the bank with the parcel and had emerged some time later without it.

In the following hour of skirmishing neither of them gained any solid information. Mrs Thomas congratulated herself on successfully leaving Doreen as ignorant as she was before while at the same time reassuring herself that neither Betty Snow nor the Motherwell woman had indulged in unwise chatter with her daughter. Doreen accepted defeat and rose to go. She surveyed the meal-preparation she had interrupted.

"John looks tired, he needs a good dinner, fish is it?"

"Steak and kidney pudding."

"I only wondered," said Doreen, "I happened to see you come out of the fishmonger's."

"Half a dozen oysters I ordered from Orford. I put them in the pudding last thing, makes it special."

For a brief moment Doreen considered abandoning the set rules of the game and asking her mother some direct questions. Only the certainty that the effort would be wasted prevented her. She gave up and prepared to go. Her mother saw her standing there and remembered her looking irresolute like that as a little girl; the face that wanted to ask her something. It was no use being weak and sentimental. Doreen was no more to be trusted now than in the days when she had stolen the Christmas savings to buy a new tyre for her boyfriend's motorbike. Always boyfriends, that thank God seemed to be safely in the past.

"There's nothing wrong is there—with you and Betsey I mean?"

"No, nothing. It's a bit dull sometimes. He just sits in the shop all day. I expect it's my fault, I should push him a bit more, get him moving, get him out and about a bit."

"He's happy where he is," her mother said. "Don't fuss him." She saw nothing incongruous in that advice.

Doreen opened her mouth to reply but changed her mind and left it. Lonely and unfulfilled in her marriage, she envied her mother's relationship with John Webber, the more so because she wasn't sure what sort of a relationship it was. Sometimes, as now, she wished she could tell her mother that she loved her.

"What do you think?" Webber asked.

Jimmy Trottwood sipped his tea and they both looked at the equestrian Staffordshire figure of Sir Robert Peel that Webber had left with him that morning.

"Where did you say you got it?"

"I didn't say, just tell me what you think."

"It's rare, must be, Victorian of course. It's not in any of the books. There are some equestrian figures of Peel, they're rare too, but I don't think this has ever turned up before. The style is quite definite though, it looks as though it was made by a man called Thomas Parr of Burslem, everything points to it. The printed title and the modelling, everything."

"Anything else?"

"It's a very complicated mould, do you see how the horse leans a bit? That happened in the firing I should think. It doesn't matter, it's very beautiful."

"Go on."

"My guess is that Parr saw his chance to make a really superb figure when Peel was thrown from his horse and killed, in 1850. A big market—a sure winner. I think he overreached himself and found he couldn't make enough of them to sell at a profit—too complicated. It's only a guess but it would explain why this is the only one to turn up."

Webber nodded, he saw David Walton facing the same challenge, failing at first with this one before succeeding with the one in Elberg's collection. He couldn't bring himself to throw his first trial away and kept it. Then Webber had seen it and brought it away from the house in Solihull.

"And it's quite genuine? Nothing suspicious about it?" he asked. "I mean you'd buy it yourself—if you had the chance?"

"I couldn't afford it John dear, out of my class. Yes, it's genuine all right."

It was what Webber had to be sure of. If David Walton's work could fool Jimmy then it would fool anyone.

If Doreen thought her mother had missed the significance of her

184

apparently incongruous advice she was mistaken. Betsey was a nice gentle soul and if he wanted to vegetate quietly in Flaxfield then Mrs Thomas truly believed that he should be left to do as he wished. John Webber was her own preserve, and he was different. She would cook and care for him when she could and let him stretch himself.

In the few days left before Snow came down for the weekend Webber read the photostat of David Walton's book and then thankfully let Molly Motherwell replace it in her safe-deposit box in the bank.

"It's dynamite," he told Mrs Thomas. "No wonder someone wanted to shut him up. If he wanted to throw a spanner into the international market for English pottery then he's done it. The man had a grievance, against critics, salerooms, collectors; he made up his mind to make them look fools and he's succeeded. He describes how he worked but doesn't say enough for anyone else to try it themselves. Then comes the crunch, and he knew it. He gives only about ten concrete examples, all Staffordshire, all rare, or they would have been if he hadn't made them himself. There are photographs and then the details from the saleroom catalogues and the prices they fetched; eighteenth-century, nineteenth-century, the lot, the man could do anything and did. That's what he wanted of course, people to know: he wanted the publicity, he needed it, you can see it in every line he wrote. Ten examples only! Jesus, what about all the others! He just says calmly that it had been going on for years. Every single one of them with his fingerprints on it somewhere, baked into the clay, and just for good measure a complete set of his own prints to compare them with; you can't argue with it. Imagine the art world sorting out that mess!"

"The photostats I saw you looking at didn't seem very clear, not the photographs anyway," she said.

"The one of his fingerprints was. That's the only one that matters."

"What about the original typescript, the one that was stolen?"

"Burnt I should think, I imagine that's what they wanted. I think Molly's is the only concrete proof left."

"I never took her for a fool," Mrs Thomas said.

"No, no she's not a fool, only to herself perhaps."

"Nobody knows she's got it," he said, "apart from us. She's had enough sense to keep her mouth shut, thank God. I shan't tell Ted yet either. He's got enough on his plate. I know Ted, he'll start asking questions for me at the Yard, getting the Fine Arts Squad in a corner and pestering them. It won't help me and it's risky for him, he's done enough. Too many questions and he could be out on his neck."

Webber's loyalty to his friends was only one of the reasons that she loved him. She planted a kiss casually on his head as she passed his chair and got on with her work.

Webber watched her with affection as she moved round the kitchen, the picture of quiet domesticity, talking both to him and to Bunter the cat impartially. With her face red and glistening from the oven and her hands rough and clean from the cooking and scrubbing, it was difficult to imagine her in France. Impossible to imagine her in the horror of that blockhaus. She was glad to be back, it had been a shock and she was mercifully recovering. It was, he knew, the reason why she was so subdued. Well, she'd done enough. Now it was up to him. It didn't occur to him, but he felt and looked better than he had for years. It occurred to her.

When Snow arrived at the weekend Mrs Thomas had organized everything. She knew that he and Webber would want to talk alone. They were to have that time privately together in her cottage while she prepared an evening meal at Webber's house.

"Monday or Tuesday," Snow told him, in the kitchen, "and that'll be it. I can't see anything else but a guilty verdict thank God, then I can get Betty and the kids back to Finchley and you can have your place to yourself again."

"Best give it a day or so – I shan't want it. I'm going to be busy next week. What have you got for me?"

"Not much, I don't envy you," Snow said.

"I don't envy myself but at least I've got more time than you have. I don't have to listen to His Lordship's jokes all day."

"I've got the lab and pathologist's report on the photographs Lizzie brought back. Nice clear enlargements, quality stuff." Snow spread them out over the kitchen table. "Like old times John?"

"Yes."

"Where did Lizzie get these?" Snow asked.

Webber told him, his memory of Mrs Thomas's story was sharp and clear.

"She was lucky, you shouldn't have let her go over there."

"You can't stop her," Webber said. He wasn't going to try and explain her character in depth and he contented himself with: "She's got the language and she doesn't look like a copper."

"I'll give you the pathologist's comment," Snow said, "it's unofficial so he wouldn't write it down. It's only useful in a negative way. Death by burning – without the bodies there for a post-mortem that's all he would say. Fire has often been used to cover up the original cause of death, he said. Well we could have told him that, but without the bodies he settled for burning, unless there's any other evidence."

Webber picked up a photograph which showed the bodies at a distance. In the foreground was the fire-engine, its wheels stuck in the loose sand. Further out, where some firemen stood impotently by the charred bodies, the sand was firmer. Apart from the tracks of the firemen's boots and the footsteps of David Walton and his wife the sand was unblemished. Far out in the distance the film caught the sun sparkling on the sea. A light plume of dirty smoke rose gently from the bodies and drifted away from the scene. So it was only a breeze then, that morning, and no sign that anybody or anything had approached them on that fatal walk. Apart from the tracks of the firemen there was only the pathetic line of the Waltons' own footprints. Micky Marks, Webber thought, must have taken that photograph first, before the crowds and the police had arrived and churned everything up or taken anything away. He told Snow about the nurse's evidence and what Julie Pichon had said before she died.

"A motorbike?" Snow said thoughtfully. "Well, she was obviously talking about herself, poor woman. Certainly it couldn't have been anything she saw here on the beach, motorbikes leave tracks."

"The hospital thought her injuries were too much for a bike, more like a heavy car they thought."

"There could have been a bike travelling behind a car," said Snow, "she could have heard that and assumed that was what hit her."

"And no one stopped?"

"It wouldn't be the first time John. People don't like getting involved."

Webber grunted, turning over the photographs without emotion, like exhibits in a trial; like Snow he had spent long hours in witness boxes. Marks had done his job well, covering the charred and blackened bodies from different angles. The things on the sand bore little resemblance to human beings, puppets made of charcoal, the burnt muscles and tendons had pulled their arms up into a parody of boxers sparring with each other. It was a phenomenon well known to policemen and pathologists; it even had a name, 'The pugilistic attitude'.

"Marks thought they had been fighting," Webber said. "You'd think he'd have known, wouldn't you."

"Press photographers don't see people," Snow said. "They only see news."

Webber picked up another photograph, an enlargement of something on its own.

"The lab boys saw something else," Snow explained, "something lying on the sand near the bodies, something metallic it looks like. They've enlarged as much as they could, looks like a bit of twisted metal. Could be anything, they couldn't say, a bit of a handbag frame, something like that. Any ideas?"

Webber shook his head, and tidied the photographs into a pile. "I'll look at them later. Anything else?"

"I've had a phone chat with the West Midlands sergeant in charge of the Donald Walton case, they knew about his mother and father but they're treating it as a casual break-in, a disturbed robbery, a coincidence they reckon. You could say they were polite but distant. Two things he told me were interesting though. They managed to open up the barn in the meadow, Walton's workshop. Nice clean place he said, tidy benches and not a piece of pottery in sight. Walton didn't believe in revealing anything before he was ready."

"You said two things," Webber said.

"There were no prints anywhere. I can understand the house perhaps but there were none in the barn either."

There was a tentative tap on the kitchen door and Snow opened it to admit his son.

"We're busy Alan," his father said, "I'm afraid you can't stay."

"I know, I'm sorry, I won't be a second."

"Too many women for you?" Webber said sympathetically.

188

"They're all talking about cooking. Mrs Thomas said I might borrow her library ticket. It's on the mantelpiece. You have to be a resident," he explained, retrieving the ticket apologetically.

Webber saw the boy's eyes fixed on the top photograph, unable to conceal his curiosity. On an impulse Webber handed it to him.

"It's an enlargement," he said. "A puzzle, a bit of twisted metal of some sort, it was burnt. Your father and I don't know what it is."

The boy studied the photograph with interest, turning it in his hands, his face bright with shy intelligence.

"I think I know what it is," he said.

❧ TWENTY-EIGHT ❧

IT WAS GOING to be a busy time for Webber and he tried not to show his relief when Mrs Thomas elected to stay quietly at home in Flaxfield and not come up to London with him. It showed, he thought, an unexpected feminine aspect of her nature that became her. She ignored all the advice that any doctor had ever given Webber about his diet and gave him the sort of breakfast that would make up for all the rushed sandwiches she suspected would be his main food in the days ahead.

"It's not much is it?" she said, watching him butter his toast for her homemade marmalade. "I mean what Alan said. All right it suggests how it could have been done, and it ties up with what Julie Pichon said. All that makes sense for the first time, but it doesn't prove who did it – or had it done. It still leaves a lot of loose ends."

"Real cases very often do. You do your best and perhaps you can make it stick. Ask Ted, he'll tell you the same. I know this," he said thoughtfully, "if someone threw this lot up in my face and put me in court for it, I wouldn't give much for their chances. A lot of murder cases are nice simple family affairs, no trouble at all. You and Ted would have to go and pick this one for me. Not that I'm not grateful for the money. But then apart from that," he added grinning at her, "I'm rather enjoying myself."

Snow wasn't due in court until later that day. He could have found a hundred things to do at the Yard but he phoned his office and delegated as much of it as he could. The children couldn't believe their luck. Webber envied him their excitement and affection. He and Snow drove them over to the huge wool church at Blythburgh which they wanted to see, or Alan did; his sister was happy to be anywhere with them.

"Cromwell's men used it for stables Dad, you can still see the iron rings on the pillars where they used to tether their horses."

190

Webber and Snow sat in the churchyard while the children were inside.

"Don't take too many risks at the Yard Ted, I never fancied turning my back on my lot for long—not when I was up to something anyway."

"I remember. Don't worry John, you can't get anything without risk. I think of the kids and everything's worth it. Anyway I've done all I can for you for a bit, have you read all the notes I knocked out for you?"

"Yes everything, phone numbers, the lot. I haven't decided where to start yet but I'll play it by ear as I go along. I hope you're right about risks. Not much point in getting the kids educated and then finding yourself on the dole. You've done well for me Ted," he added, seeing Snow's face cloud over for a moment. "Cost much?"

"I cashed in a few favours at the Yard and I paid for a bit too now and then. It's surprising how few scruples people have about taking money. Nice to have a bit of cash John."

"There's not much you can't buy," Webber said. "A bit—but not much."

Soon it would be time for both of them to go, Snow to drive the children back to their mother and then to face his London routine again. Webber had already said goodbye to Mrs Thomas. While Alice walked with her father and collected wild flowers in the overgrown grass between the gravestones Webber talked to Alan.

"You like churches Alan?"

"Oh yes, I like them, they're interesting. Not just the buildings, I'm interested in what they say in them too, some of it's very difficult though."

"Not like computers, you don't find them difficult?"

"No, useful but not so difficult."

The boy sat on the churchyard bench swinging his legs and watching his father and sister in the distance. "You don't have to answer," he said, "but that problem Dad set me, you know, the two people who were burned to death on the beach with no one near them. That was real wasn't it sir?"

Webber had no desire to usurp Ted Snow's parental authority.

"You'd better ask your father Alan."

"I guessed it was, don't worry I shan't say anything unless he

191

does. Have you still got the printout I made from that Falklands program Mr Webber?"

"Yes, I've still got it."

"It wasn't far wrong was it?" Snow and the girl had started to walk towards them. "I think that was really what I meant just now," Alan said. "Computers can be jolly useful but they're very limited aren't they? I mean, sometimes they might suggest how, but they're not much good when you start asking why, especially when you've only got a limited program."

The boy, Webber thought, was well worth spending money on, but he was quite relieved when the others rejoined them. He had been about to ask him what a computer would make of the Ten Commandments and on reflection he was glad he hadn't done so.

In London he settled into the Glockemara, carefully re-read all the information Snow had found for him and made some arrangements for the next day. He found Mrs Thomas's fish and chip restaurant and ate early before settling down in his room to watch the black-and-white television which the hotel provided for its guests. He switched on the evening news bulletin to find bulldozers tidying up a massacre in Lebanon and covering the bodies with sand and rubble. Some bombs had gone off in Belfast, there'd been a pile-up on a motorway, a woman's body had been found in a ditch and a young man had been stabbed to death at a football game. Webber watched with admiration as the Queen was shown being polite to people with whom she had little in common and then heard that a little-known art connoisseur and businessman called Elberg had lost his battle to control International Enterprises. There was a shot of the house in Holland Crescent and a reporter outside the gates explaining that Mr Elberg was not available for comment. Webber sat through some golf results and wondered if Elberg would have enough money to honour his promise to continue paying him.

There was nothing he could do that evening and he didn't want to try and speak to Ted Snow or even Mrs Thomas, he hoped they had missed it and wouldn't ring him up. The phone stayed mercifully quiet and he poured himself a second glass of whisky to watch an ingenious murder play with a dozen likely suspects. He failed to guess that the murderer was the kind old woman with white hair who made tea for everyone and was so

192

helpful to the detective. As he undressed he thought it served him right for letting his thoughts wander. They wandered again as he drifted into a sound sleep. He dreamt that the Walton case was neat and tidy, like a play on a black-and-white screen, with no loose ends. He saw himself explaining this to Mrs Thomas and she told him not to be a fool. Even in his dream he had the grace to agree with her.

He woke to hear rain drumming on his window and groaned. It was bad enough having to traipse round tying up boring loose ends without getting wet. In spite of the damp in the room he was encouraged to find that his arthritis wasn't bad and he dressed fairly easily and set off in his car for Putney and his appointment with Trina Murphy, the girl who had been living with the Elbergs' chauffeur until she'had been rudely supplanted by her lover's change of heart.

He found the place easily enough, a dingy flat off Putney Hill.

"It was good of you to see me," he said when she sat opposite him in a communal sitting-room, smelling of dead flowers and wet underwear, which he suspected had only recently been taken out. The single bar of the electric fire served only to emphasize the gloom of the room. "How do you like the job in the supermarket?" Webber asked her, smiling encouragement.

"I'm not Irish you know." Her voice couldn't have been more cockney. She looked frightened and defiant. "I've never even been there," she said. "Me Dad was Irish but he's been dead for years, my Mum came from Lambeth and she brought me up, I told the other lot all that before."

Webber felt sorry for her, it couldn't have been pleasant for her having Snow's men finding out if she had any strong Irish feelings.

"I'm sorry Trina, can I call you Trina? No, I know all that. The police can be very upsetting I know, it's just a job. I told you that my inquiries are quite private didn't I? Nothing official, and you don't have to talk to me at all if you'd rather not."

She lost the defiant look. Unsure of herself she looked sulky and stayed silent.

"I can promise you," he said gently, "that you won't have any more questions about Ireland. I wonder if you'd mind telling me what happened at Holland Crescent when you were living with Mr Dunning, the chauffeur?"

It took longer than he thought. Underneath the facade of the brash London shop-girl she was not only frightened, he thought, but possibly even ashamed of herself too. It took him nearly an hour and he resorted to tricks and encouragements he hadn't used for years. David Walton must have seen her around the place on one of his many visits. One day, she said, when Walton had seen Dunning drive off in the car he had talked his way into the mews flat. She described what happened next with perfect candour and without a trace of embarrassment. Dunning hadn't quite caught them in the act when he returned unexpectedly but she hadn't denied it.

"And that finished it. That's why you left?"

"It was finished anyway. John had another girl, I knew that. I think that's why I . . . He was glad of the excuse. I wouldn't have minded would I, only the silly slut turned up in the middle of the night and created something awful. Common little cat. I was glad to get shot of the place, gave me the creeps, I'm not kidding."

"Did you ever see David Walton again?"

"Nah! Randy sod, old enough to know better, you couldn't help liking him though. I didn't care a monkey's. I read about him and his wife in the paper, that was awful wasn't it?"

"Yes, a terrible accident. Did you ever see his wife? I mean did she come to Holland Crescent with him?"

"She might have done, I never saw her. She certainly wasn't with him that day. I'd never have let him near me!"

Whatever her morals were, thought Webber, you could trust her, he knew the truth when he heard it. It would have been a mistake to offer the girl money earlier, now that she was talking and more relaxed he made her take a £20 note. She took it without comment or fuss and he liked that. He got her talking again, more easily now that she had accepted him. He didn't expect to get any more out of her, she was simply part of the chain, someone that he had to see, a loose end to be tidied up. She had moved around on the edge of life at Holland Crescent and he didn't think she could tell any more. She recognized Spavin from Webber's description but apart from the chauffeur's opinion that he was "A bit of an old woman" she had no personal knowledge of him. Once while they were talking a girl came in looking for a pair of tights and was told that she should look for them in the kitchen. Webber made the interruption the excuse to thank her and prepared to leave.

"You said the place gave you the creeps, why was that Trina?"

"I don't know really. It was weird, that Chinese pair padding about and never a word of English, only grins, and all the stuff under the garden, I never saw it but John used to tell me, it's not natural is it, a place like that? Then John was out at all hours driving him to London Airport and places, at least that's what he used to tell me."

Webber picked up his hat. "Yes," he said, "a funny sort of place, I see that."

"I only saw Mrs Elberg once," the girl said. "She said good morning to me, not like that snooty Miss Evans, rude old cow. John reckoned she was sweet on the Boss."

"On Mr Elberg?"

"Yes, silly bitch, some hope John said. The Boss never thought about anything except his wife and his money, and he had plenty of that."

Trina Murphy didn't always read the newspapers, Webber thought, or watch television news. All the same he was pleased, the morning hadn't been a complete waste of time. It was a pity it was still raining, his shoes leaked.

He looked at his watch and decided that he wouldn't have time to go back to the Glockemara and change them before he was due to meet Snow in the pub at Strutton Ground. He had a brainwave and found a shoe shop where he bought a new pair and some dry socks. No, he thought as he sat in the shop, not a complete waste of time. He thought back on the things Trina Murphy had told him. She wasn't an Irish sleeper she'd said and he believed her. The sex episode with the randy Walton? Well that seemed of little consequence knowing Walton's past history with women. But that wasn't why she had left. It was finished anyway, she had said. John had another girl.

Webber wriggled his toes experimentally in his shiny new shoes. Another girl who had been so anxious to replace Trina Murphy that she had turned up at two o'clock in the morning and created an unpleasant scene. Something didn't fit, it was odd, that and Miss Evans being sweet on Elberg. He had seen them together and couldn't believe it. The calm efficient computer expert had about as much red blood in her as the machines she tended and controlled. Household gossip he decided, they were so jealous of this new type of servant whose work they didn't understand and which brought her so close to Elberg that they had chosen to call it love. All the same that was

195

odd too. Those two facts then. The chauffeur's new girlfriend and the dislike of Miss Evans. His professional instinct told Webber that they were important. But why?

Snow was depressed too, he had hoped to be finished with the Old Bailey but the jury were still out and he had to be there when they came back. They settled for a quick lunch of hot pies and cheese.

"You've seen the papers about Elberg?" he asked Webber.

"I caught it on the news last night. I've tried to get a meet with him but his secretary says she can't contact him, he might be out of the country she says."

"Looks like the end of the money John."

"It could be. Mind you I'll be surprised if he hasn't taken care of himself."

"Pity it's turned out such a mess," Snow said. "We could have had a bit of luck couldn't we? I thought that with that kind of money and with you . . ." He left the sentence unfinished and looked despondently at the anonymous brown purée that oozed from his pie.

Webber forced his mind away from Mrs Thomas's version of steak and kidney pie but with dry feet was disposed to be cheerful. Snow's immediate destiny was to be involved with security-van robberies and an unsavoury case of sexual blackmail. He didn't envy him. It wouldn't help if he appeared disheartened too.

"Early days yet Ted; yes it is a mess, but you know, I'm rather enjoying it. I might as well tie up all the loose ends even if we finish up with nothing in the parcel."

Even Webber's cheerfulness was in danger of being defeated by the pie and he concentrated on the cheese and the beer, which was at least real ale drawn from the wood. He offered the remainder of the pie to the ginger cat who had walked across from the gas fire more out of politeness than hunger.

"I spoke to Sergeant Cooper in the West Midlands again," Snow said. "They've settled for routine robbery, lazy sods. The theory is that they were after cash and probably got it. The car in the garage was clean by the way, not a print anywhere, a good thorough wipe, the same as the house and the workshop. Not amateurs, very professional."

The cat completed its careful examination of the pie and returned to the fire, pausing on the way to shake each of its feet in a gesture of contempt.

196

Snow looked at his watch and stood up. "I must get back, I reckon that Her Majesty's subjects might have well and truly tried the case before them. They should bring in a verdict after lunch. Are you sure that Betty and the kids are no trouble at your place for a day or so?"

Webber spread his hands and beamed amiably behind his beer. He wouldn't delay Ted and keep him from the court. Trina Murphy's chatter could wait, and the others too. He hadn't seen half of them yet.

"I told you, I don't need it. I'm going to be busy. Be my guest. Cheer up old son, you never know. Perhaps the parcel isn't empty after all. Don't tell me you don't believe in Father Christmas?"

✌ TWENTY-NINE ✌

WEBBER FINISHED HIS beer slowly and read through everything in his briefcase again, right back to the earliest notes Snow had made for him. He read the account that he had painstakingly compiled for himself, something he had always done, a way of clarifying his thoughts. Sometimes, in the past, when a case was over and done with he had looked back on his notes and been horribly embarrassed to read of the blind alleys he had blundered down with such hope and confidence and to read of the number of times he had been wrong. Then he had comforted himself by remembering all the times when his instinct had been right. Those were the times, he reminded himself, when he had hung on even against the weight of evidence and common sense.

He tidied the papers and returned them to the briefcase. The ginger cat turned its head from the fire to see if he might be unwrapping some more acceptable delicacy.

"You may well blink," Webber informed it. "But that is what I believe. Mice have to be caught you know, you mustn't expect everything to be handed to you on a plate."

It was still raining. His car was parked comfortably in the private yard of the pub. He didn't like the idea of searching for a parking meter in Pall Mall. It wasn't far and he decided to walk. In fifteen minutes, wetter than he liked, he went through the revolving doors of the Royal Automobile Club and gave his name to the man at the reception desk. He was joined almost immediately by a youngish man who must have been waiting for him. The man introduced himself and when he had shown Webber where to leave his hat and raincoat led him into a vast smoking-room with an encouraging fire and huge oil paintings of solemn birds with impossible plumage. Webber accepted a low leather armchair and wished it had been higher. He admired the ease with which the younger man sank into his own chair and managed to look both elegant and comfortable. It was probably something, he decided, to do with his well-cut suit and with the thin gold watch-chain on the flat stomach. Webber instinctively disliked him in spite of the smile. The man looked as though he could smell something unpleasant and was doing his best to ignore it.

"Yes of course," he was saying, "I quite agree, telephone conversations are so unsatisfactory. I hope this place isn't inconvenient for you? I had to lunch here today and I have to fit things in as I can, it's a boring question of time I'm afraid."

"Yes of course, I don't think I need keep you long," Webber said.

"I must tell you that I appreciate your taking the trouble to tell us about your – research work. As I said, phone calls are a bit impersonal, perhaps you'd care to elaborate?"

Webber recognized the faintly patronizing tone with professional interest, he had interviewed too many people himself to mistake it. The expert from the saleroom thought that at best he was a harmless old fool with a bee in his bonnet. Someone to be humoured politely for half an hour in case he turned out not to be a nutcase but someone with something important to say. It was quite interesting to find himself on the other side of the fence.

"My position," Webber said, trying to match the man's reclining elegance and not succeeding, "is quite unofficial. I'm sure I explained that."

"Yes you did." The smile was still firmly in place but the smell under the nose seemed to have grown stronger.

Oh dear, why did he have to pick this one, he simply wanted to do his good deed for the day; and, well, yes, be honest, to see what reception his news would have.

"You also said," the man continued, "that you thought that the market for English pottery might be – how did you put it? Ah yes, 'In some danger'. At least I took that to be the gist of what you were saying."

"You could say gist," said Webber evenly. It was a pity that the man seemed determined to be tiresome. It was a bit late but he tried to establish a happier and more relaxed atmosphere. "You'll forgive me for saying so," he said, "but you are a younger man than I had imagined. I had expected to be talking to someone rather older." Before he had time to make it clear that he intended this to be a compliment from an older man he was interrupted.

"Mr Webber – it is Mr Webber isn't it? We are, as I'm sure you know, a very old-established firm, world leaders we like to think, especially in the field of English ceramics. Mercifully—" the smile and the tone of voice could have been used to a dull child—"our policy has always been to employ the best people in their field. I did of course discuss your telephone call with my directors. They seemed to think that as head of our ceramic department I was fully qualified to talk to you and to hear what you had to say. I also passed on your solemn assurance that you had no connection with the Press."

It was worth another try, perhaps it hadn't been a very good lunch, perhaps he wasn't as unpleasant as he seemed. Webber produced one of his best smiles. "I'm sorry if I gave you the wrong impression, experts get younger-looking every day." He allowed himself a more serious tone. "I'm not a nutcase you know. I'm a private investigator now, but I was a police officer for many years, an inspector, so I do understand that you have to establish credibility. I can also repeat that I am not in any way a newspaper reporter." A little sign of encouragement would have been nice, Webber thought, a nod or even a grunt, but the elegant dark suit was not disposed to make his task easier and remained silent. It was bad luck, another of those unforeseen things that could hold you up for hours and make the job more uncomfortable than it need be, like wet feet. He wished he had chosen to speak to one of the directors and not this supercilious little runt with illusions of grandeur. No, he didn't wish that at all. It was the right choice, he'd picked this man because he was in charge of the auction-room ceramics, not only an expert but a man who personally conducted most of the important sales. It shouldn't be too difficult, he told himself, all he had to do was to inform this expert, this world leader, that he might have been selling fakes. It wouldn't improve the smell but when it faded a bit he could try pumping him about David Walton or anything else he could usefully extract from the bomb damage.

"I think that someone has been making very good fakes of antique English pottery and I think that some of them may have been sold through the auction rooms."

" 'Think' is rather a weak word Mr Webber, surely?"

200

"It's something I heard when I was working on another inquiry, something quite different. I thought you'd like to know. That's why I asked to see you. I believe in going to the top."

The open flattery might have made him more amenable but it didn't.

"I suppose you realize that what you have said is serious in the extreme? People – let me be specific – I mean dealers, collectors and museums, indeed anybody who buys from us, all rely on our judgement, our expertise if you like, that what we sell is genuine. If anyone – anyone Mr Webber – should be unwise enough to repeat in public what you have just said to me in private and then merely said that he *thought* so without any proof that would stand up in a court of law, I can only say that he might well find himself facing serious charges in another court."

Webber disliked being threatened. He had been wrong, the man was just as unpleasant as he seemed, but he wouldn't gain anything by allowing himself to get angry however justified it might be.

"I can promise you," he said, "that I have no intention of repeating in public anything I am telling you in confidence. It just so happens that some inquiries overlap. We seem to have got off on the wrong foot. I'm sorry. I'm only trying to be helpful. Perhaps you could tell me if you've heard of a man called David Walton?"

This time the smile seemed genuine, perhaps, Webber thought, because it was prompted by relief, not goodwill or humour.

"Mr Webber, I don't know what case you've been working on but I think I begin to see what kind of rumour you've got hold of. The world of antiques is very small you know, there's not much that we don't hear of one way or another. Walton – yes, I recall the name. Perhaps I can explain. Some time ago a woman brought some pieces in and asked us to sell them, they were English Staffordshire, both eighteenth- and nineteenth-century I recall, good and quite genuine. So good in fact that we made some very discreet inquiries. The woman herself, I may say, was far from discreet, we soon found out that she owned a very third-rate antique shop, I forget where now. The point is, that we do our best to establish that goods of such rarity – how shall I put it – have not been stolen, it's a problem that we have come up against in the past and we have our reputation to consider."

"World leaders," murmured Webber. "Quite, and?"

"Oh they were clean enough, we found out that the woman was selling them for a man called Walton – David Walton. It wasn't difficult, the woman was a notorious chatterbox, she was often the worse for drink and often hanging about the saleroom on viewing days. Quite frankly she was a very boring woman. It didn't surprise me at all to hear that she was spreading the sort of rumour that you have repeated to me just now, out of pique I imagine. Walton's motives for using her didn't concern us, the pieces were quite genuine and some collectors don't want it known that they are selling, that's their private business."

"Did you speak to this woman yourself?"

"Frankly I always did my best to avoid her. She was quite well known in the ceramic department. In the end she stopped coming in, perhaps someone tactfully suggested it, I really don't know, I remember feeling quite relieved. She was not the sort of person we like to do business with. I can only imagine that she started the rumour as a form of revenge. I seem to remember that the last I heard of it was some cock-and-bull story that she had lost her evidence in a burglary. I was glad to see the back of her. It was a very silly thing to do. A stupid woman."

"You know the Elberg collection of course?"

"Certainly, quite a large part of it came through us, in fact we have valued it for him several times."

"A man of some considerable knowledge," said Webber.

"He is a collector who has always taken the best advice, I don't think that is any secret. The collection is probably the best in the world, better even than the Burnap in America or even the Fitzwilliam. The Fitzwilliam," he added helpfully, "is a museum in Cambridge."

"Priceless would you say?" Webber asked, realizing even as he spoke that it was a silly question to ask an auctioneer.

"Everything has a price Mr Webber."

"Yes of course." The man was right. Everything and everyone. Afterwards Webber considered the ethics of not taking the wind out of the man's sails and giving him the news of David Walton's book. As a serving policeman it would have been his duty however much he disliked him. As a private citizen he had the luxury of keeping his mouth shut and his own council.

One way or another it was coming to an end, probably not the nice copybook ending that he had hoped for. There might yet be cards stacked up against him that would take him by surprise, even rob him of the game altogether. Perhaps even Walton's book wouldn't swing it in his favour. Meanwhile it was a good card and he had no intention of throwing it away in the privacy of a club smoking-room, not to a shit like that.

A pang of conscience struck him when he realized how long it had been since he had tried to telephone Mrs Thomas. Armed with a pocketful of coins he tried her number and got no reply. He tried for a quarter of an hour and then gave way to the vicious glare of the people waiting outside the telephone box. He failed with Snow too, he was in court his office said. Webber told them it wasn't important, he was speaking from the country about some roses for Mr Snow's garden, he'd speak to him when he could get down. Ted would understand. No point in giving them his name to leave lying around.

He sat in a tiny Italian sandwich bar catering for office workers and drank coffee at a dull plastic-topped table. He stayed for some time, going over a list of things he still hoped to do. Regretfully he drew a line through the name of Sir Michael Humper. He'd tried to get an appointment to see him and failed, even mentioning that he was acting on behalf of Hans Elberg hadn't made any impression. The secretary had been quite firm. Sir Michael never discussed his patients either with or without their consent. Since Webber couldn't contact either Hans Elberg or his wife there seemed no hope of making the man change his mind. It wasn't vital, it was simply that he had always believed in following up every possible source of information. It was a curious relationship that Elberg seemed to have with his wife and Humper might have thrown some light on it. He might even at some point have known or met Spavin or Walton himself. You couldn't do much with a man who threw his profession at you, Lizzie Thomas had done better with her Catholic priests. He phoned her again without any luck. It was going to be one of those days. Eventually he phoned Doreen at the antique shop.

"What do you mean gone?" he said.

"Just gone, like she does. I'm only her daughter, how should I know? She never tells me anything. I thought she was with you."

"Well she isn't. When did she go?"

"Early yesterday morning, in her pink – her travelling pink." Doreen let it sink in, she disapproved of Webber's influence on her mother, most of all when she didn't know what was going on. "If my mother gets into any trouble . . ." she said ominously.

"No one's going to get into any trouble," Webber said. "I'll try later on, she'll probably be back by then."

"I doubt it, she's left the cat with us again."

Outside the telephone box the rain had stopped, the sky hadn't cleared but the clouds were thinner, letting the sun show through them as pale as the moon. At least, he thought, I can walk back to the car without getting wet again. He stood and checked his appointment and the address of Snow's Foreign Office informant. Eight o'clock, that would give him time to get back to the hotel and have a bath and change. The offices weren't out yet and the street was relatively quiet. Ahead on the left was an ancient bomb-site long since turned into a car-park surrounded by gaudy advertising placards. Beyond it an even quieter street led off in the direction his senses told him he must take to get back to the car. It was no good letting himself be disturbed by Lizzie, she would work in her own way. Indeed she might be waiting for him at the Glockemara, she was quite capable of turning up without bothering to phone first. Leaving the cat with Doreen didn't sound like it, it sounded more like a serious safari. All the same it would have been nice to have a quiet meal with her, nice just to see her again, even in travelling pink. Well he couldn't anyway, he was meeting Snow's Foreign Office mole. He wondered how much the man had found for him, he'd sounded reasonable on the phone, apprehensive but reasonable.

A slight breeze had thinned the clouds even more and now the sun made a serious effort to shine, making the advertisement hoarding look cheerful and gaudy, with its orange-haired rock stars and a familiar woman's face inviting him to see Noël Coward's *Hay Fever*. His clothes were drier but the rain made the arthritis in his hip ache. He heard the car behind him slow down. At first he thought it had slowed to turn into the car-park but the entrance to that was much further back and he was alone in the street. He didn't look back, if he made a fool of himself it wouldn't matter, better an instinctive live fool than a dead one. Two yards ahead of him on the pavement was a solid metal container holding sand to spread on icy winter streets. He made a dive for the safety of the far side of it. He realized an instant later that he would never have made it. A combination of his arthritic hip and his new shoes on the wet pavement flung him to the ground more quickly than any professional stunt man. He heard the bullets bark and slam harmlessly into the hoarding above him and the scream of the tyres as the car turned the corner and vanished. He was unhurt but the woman in *Hay Fever* was a mess.

⳩ THIRTY ⳩

AFTER LEAVING HIS Foreign Office contact Webber drove back to the Glockemara and parked his car some streets away before entering the hotel by the kitchen entrance. It was nearly eleven o'clock. He spent some time leaving instructions at the reception desk. The residents' lounge was packed with foreign tourists disgorged from their buses after an evening at the theatre. It took him some moments to push through the chattering crowd before he found Mrs Thomas seated in a corner drinking Guinness.

"They told me at the desk you were here," he said.

"My God you look a mess, what happened to your suit?"

He could have told her the same thing, the pink coat with the astrakhan trimming had not travelled well.

"A lady from Harrow-on-the-Hill was sick on my lap in the Hovercraft," she told him. "Nice little thing, I felt sorry for her."

"A gentleman shot at me from a car," Webber said. "I shouldn't think he was very nice and I never found out where he came from."

Old George, the Glockemara's receptionist. who knew them well and was surprised by nothing they did, came in and told them he'd used his influence and found accommodation for them round the corner at the Newport Palace.

"It's not much of a palace," he confided, "we use it as an overflow, but you've left it a bit late. One of the girls has packed your case Mr Webber, I've got it behind my desk."

"I might be fussy," Webber said when old George had shuffled off, "but you never know, I don't fancy being a target twice in one day. I wonder if he managed to get one room or two."

"It doesn't matter," she said, "last night I had to share a room with a nun."

206

"You've been to Calais to see Father Bernard."

"Yes, where else? Shall we go out the back way? I don't like this corner by the window very much."

It was a single room. The twin beds hard and stark against gloomy walls.

"We'll be all right," he told her, "I don't see anyone climbing a drainpipe up to the sixth floor at this time of night. Come to think of it, the last sight they had of me was lying flat on my face, they probably think I'm dead."

It was still early enough for them to have gone out for a meal but they weren't hungry. They sat on the beds and drank some of the malt whisky she'd bought on the hovercraft, and she told him about the Hospice Ecclésiastique and the things that Father Bernard had found out for them.

"I'm sorry John, I didn't think it would be like this, I only wanted something to cheer you up and keep you busy."

"Funnily enough I am quite cheerful but that may be the whisky. It's nearly over Lizzie. Go and see if the bathroom works, I'm going to try and get Ted at the Section House."

It took him a long time to get through and he guessed that poor Snow was being fetched from his bed.

"Sorry Ted, early night?"

"I wasn't asleep, it's a bloody hard bed."

"Who'd be a copper. I take it your Bailey case is over?"

"Guilty on all charges. When I read out the poison and all the previous convictions His Lordship sent him down for twenty years."

"Very satisfactory, bugger the bed, you'll sleep well son."

"I know that tone of voice, you didn't phone me up to say goodnight. Is it what you thought?"

"Best not on the phone, not in detail anyway. Let's just say there's something in that parcel but it's still badly tied. I'm working on it. Are you going down to Flaxfield for the weekend?"

"Yes, don't worry I'll get Betty and the kids up soon."

"No hurry, I didn't mean that. I want to see you there, that's all. Tell Betty not to shop for food, Lizzie can cope. Now listen, do something for me before you go down. Get hold of Swan and Spavin, you've got the addresses. Shift Swan and remember where you put him, he won't be any trouble. Spavin might be, get him in the country before he comes up to work, put out a shout for him, any excuse, just tell the local lads to keep him there, they can talk compost heaps to him, that'll keep him quiet. Book a room at The Bull in Flaxfield, I may need it for a woman, save me the sweat; I'm going to be busy."

"No problem."

"I wish I could say the same. It's getting a bit gutty, you could say naughty."

"Need any help? I can dress."

"Don't worry, I'm safe enough, I've got Lizzie with me."

Snow struggled with an irreverent response and wisely decided to leave it.

"Sleep well John."

"And you old son."

The sound of the bath water emptying heralded the appearance of Mrs Thomas in the doorway. She wore a bath towel emblazoned with the words Newport Palace as a turban, and a brightly coloured petticoat.

"Forgot to bring pyjamas," she said, "best I can do."

"You look very nice," Webber told her, "pink suits you."

❦ THIRTY-ONE ❧

THAT WEEKEND THE weather at Flaxfield was not just good, it was wonderful, with only a handful of white clouds drifting across the huge dome of the East Anglian sky. It was even warm. May, thought Webber, could be a tricky month, he had known it as cold as winter but now the trees in his garden wore their fresh green with an assurance that suggested there was no going back, summer really would come again. He sat in his favourite chair in his own sitting-room and allowed himself the luxury of mentally planting the garden, with a hired man, perhaps to do the heavy digging. From the kitchen came the comfortable clatter of saucepans and the voices of Mrs Thomas and Betty Snow busy preparing the evening meal. He stretched his legs to the log fire in comfort and gratitude. Lizzie must be mellowing, she usually liked to have a kitchen to herself. The fire made its own private noises and filled the room with the sweet pungency of applewood; it was all very much better than getting soaked to the skin and being shot at. Ted had phoned from London to say that he was held up at the Yard but he would be with them in time for the meal.

The Snow children were busy, Alice visiting a friend who was deep into the mystery of the local flora and Alan supervising a bonfire of winter debris at the bottom of the garden. Meanwhile he could close his eyes and imagine that things were back to normal and that he was once more alone in his home.

"I think I'm really more of a hindrance than a help," Betty's voice said, "I'm not very good in kitchens."

"Lizzie is very active with food," he said, hoping she hadn't seen him wake. "Best leave her, she gets very single-minded. You look like you used to when I first knew you," he told her.

"It's the relief. Twenty years is a long time but I can't feel sorry for him. If you can imagine what it's been like, even down

209

here, bless you. It's been wonderful not to worry every second the children are out of my sight. You too John, you're relaxed."

"Yes I suppose so, a bit of a mess but it's all there. Lizzie's told you?"

"Yes, in between cookery classes. I'd no idea puff pastry could be so complicated, I buy mine deep frozen from the shops. Ted's told me some too, but Brixton has rather taken first place I'm afraid. Your man – will they get him too?"

"I don't know, he's a cut above average," he smiled at her. "It's a bit like cooking I suppose, you've got to have a talent for it. You get all the bits and pieces together and serve them up to the Director of Public Prosecutions. He might turn his nose up and say he doesn't like the taste of it."

"Will he?"

"He can be difficult, you'd be surprised how many people get away with murder through lack of evidence or evidence that won't stick. You can sweat your guts out and then find yourself facing a clever counsel in court, cleverer than you are and tying you up in knots, making you look a fool – or worse a liar too sometimes. In the end it all comes down to the jury and even they can be got at."

"Yes I know," Betty said ruefully.

They listened to the fire and watched it in silence, then she said: "Ted says you're good John, he says you'll make it stick."

"I hope so." He thought of the woman he and Mrs Thomas had spoken to and her promise to them. He looked at the nice face on the other side of the fire, the green eyes that were as bright as they had been in the days when they were all young together. Now that her nightmare had lifted she was human again. You had to be a special breed to be a copper's wife and he loved seeing her restored and relaxed.

"Does Ted still tell you everything?"

"Oh yes, he needs to you see. Ted's not like you John, he's the real plodder and he knows it. It helps him to share things. Sometimes I think he deserves someone better for a wife."

"I shouldn't tell him that if I were you, Ted is lucky and he knows it. If you love each other like you two do nothing else is very important."

He had surprised himself. Betty had always had a way of guiding the conversation round to intimacies. He was fond of her but had no wish to be drawn any further. In the kitchen Mrs

Thomas had chosen to start singing to herself. If he wasn't careful Betty would bring Lizzie into the discussion and he had no intention of allowing Betty to indulge herself. To his relief he was saved by the entrance of Molly Motherwell and Dahlia which effectively and efficiently introduced a new atmosphere, with a scent of gorse from the common and a strong smell of dog.

"No don't move please! I'll sit here, no here or Dahlia will be too near the fire and it brings out the pong, doesn't it darling? Poor girl, I keep meaning to bath her but you really shouldn't dominate the bathroom in other people's homes, not with children and everything."

Betty Snow's face flushed red before she answered. "Molly you know perfectly well the times when the children might be using the bathroom, not nearly enough goodness knows, you can hardly say they stop you bathing the dog. You've never mentioned it once and in any case it's not even my bathroom! Oh dear how difficult everything is, I really ought to go and help Lizzie or at least offer."

"I've been thinking how well you've all adapted," said Webber amiably. "It can't have been easy, the bath's no problem, I'm sure you'll work it out all right. Betty, I'm not asking you to give away state secrets but puff pastry sounds very promising. Lizzie does something rather special with chicken breasts, I just wondered . . .?"

"I wouldn't dream of giving away Lizzie's menu. Secrets are strictly to be kept, you should know that."

"Getting fed up?" he asked Molly when they were alone.

"Not really, she's very nice, panics a bit about the kids, you can hardly blame her. She adores them, especially Alan, they're very close. I think he gets lonely down here, he's a very clever child and doesn't miss much. He should be back at school, he needs stretching. Alice is the shy one, I long to buy pretty clothes for her. Perhaps I will one day when I'm rich."

"And will you be rich?"

"Well dear, I've missed out twice in my life with money. I'd be a fool if I let this one go wouldn't I?"

"The book? Has it occurred to you that in law it probably doesn't belong to you at all?"

"David Walton's next of kin you mean? Yes of course it has, Molly's not that stupid, well they're welcome to it Johnny. They can even publish it if they want to, the more publicity it gets the

211

better. It's quite safe in the bank, the complete manuscript, well almost complete."

"Almost?"

"Somehow that nice sharp illustration of David Walton's fingerprints seems to be missing. Naughty Molly. Mind you the book still makes fascinating reading without them – except perhaps for a few special people."

"Like say, collectors, experts, museums and of course salerooms?"

You had to admire her, Webber thought. All over the world there were examples of his work; David Walton, master potter. His figures had fooled the lot of them. Sold and guaranteed genuine by the finest London auction houses with all their authority and prestige, bought eagerly and trustingly by collectors and museums all over Europe and America. Superb fakes and yet each one of them signed clearly and unarguably with his fingerprints baked into the clay. All examples of David Walton's fingerprints seemed to have disappeared. Unless of course you had a photograph of them signed and authenticated by him. Like Molly had. Then you were a great expert, people would be unlikely to dismiss you as a stupid woman. They would be eager to seek your advice – and pay highly for it too. He had a mental picture of the man's face talking to him in the smoking-room of the RAC club and the superior sneer on his face when he'd passed judgement on Molly Motherwell. It wasn't safe to judge people without taking the trouble to know them. Whatever else she might be she wasn't stupid. You could describe her as extremely knowledgeable.

"Did you know that you can memorize fingerprints Johnny? You can you know, it's no different from learning dance steps if you put your mind to it."

"Molly you're a lovely, clever, wicked woman."

"Yes I know dear, it's well worth keeping sober for, gives you something to aim at doesn't it? Had you noticed I'm off the bottle? Aren't you pleased with me?"

"You're very much nicer sober, you'll need to be if you want to be rich. You know that you'll have to keep quiet until it's all settled?"

"Yes I know. And you Johnny, dear Johnny blue-eyes, don't you want to be rich? Just a bit rich?"

"No – not really Molly – I don't mind you using the bath for Dahlia you know, as long as she doesn't block the pipes with fur."

212

For a moment he wondered if perhaps he had changed the subject too abruptly, but her voice when she rose and addressed the dog was sweet and unchanged.

"Bath-time darling, Mummy doesn't like to see that face, you know you enjoy it really. Oh do get up Dahlia or you'll take root and never move again. You don't want to get fat and lazy at your age, do you? That's better! Come and let Mummy wash hell out of you." From the kitchen Mrs Thomas's voice was heard issuing instructions to a silent Betty. At the door Molly Motherwell suddenly said quite fiercely, "Onion soup and chicken breasts stuffed with a puree of ham in puff pastry." She closed the door firmly without waiting for his reaction. Webber knew that she was angry with him. It would be wise, he thought, to pretend that he had noticed no such thing.

The late afternoon sky was clear and the smoke from the bonfire at the bottom of the garden rose up straight until it was caught by a high current of air and carried out over the village to the flat fields beyond. The flames had died down, leaving a glowing patch surrounded by the white ash of twigs and the winter's leaves. As he walked towards Alan, Webber was reminded dimly of a reproduction of a painting on a schoolroom wall. A peasant boy with a red pullover, old beyond his years, leaning on a rake and burning autumn leaves. Alan was like that, wise like a young man, no longer a child.

"I think it's a quotation," Webber said, "but I am fleeing from a monstrous army of women. Will you be pleased to go back to London?"

"Oh yes I think so sir," he grinned, a boy again. "I know what you mean about getting out of the house for a bit though."

"Do you now?"

"Oh they're all very nice. I don't really know Mrs Thomas of course but the others can be a bit confusing sometimes, even Mummy, and Alice is quite dreadful, you think she's listening to you but all the time she's only thinking what she's going to say next. It can be very frustrating."

"Sisters aren't the same as computers," Webber agreed gravely. "Very few women are – some, but it's rare. You'll adjust as you get older. Some of them are very bright indeed. Living with them is quite another matter."

213

"Mummy tells me quite a lot," Alan said, "but I think she gets muddled sometimes. She's been very worried of course, but so much of it doesn't make sense."

Webber nodded. "I don't think we shall get into the bathroom for some time and your father's not due for a while. We might walk a bit if you'd like that?"

"Thank you, yes I would like that very much." He put the rake tidily against a tree.

They walked slowly down the High Street where some of the shops had already closed. Outside the shuttered bookshop stood a deep trestle tray filled with second-hand books and old Penguins all priced at ten pence, a cardboard notice invited you to put the money through the letter box. It had been there ever since he could remember, right back to when he had been a schoolboy himself. Somehow it made an even stronger link and the years between them seemed unimportant. Alan found a book about wild flowers and bought it for his sister. The shops and houses thinned out until they reached the common and there was only yellow gorse and the cry of birds high in the sky above them.

"I'm not sure where it comes," Alan said, "in St Matthew I think, yes in Matthew: 'Thou shalt not kill and if you do you'll be found out and judged' – something like that. Is that what you felt when you knew, Mr Webber?"

"No, not like that. If you've remembered it right then the judgement part doesn't come into it for a policeman. You just feel glad that you haven't made a fool of yourself. You leave the judgement bit to others."

"Was it easy – did you know straightaway when you talked to him?"

"No, I didn't even know if it was a him. You have to be careful and think of everyone. It could have been Mrs Walton. I had to think of that, she wouldn't be the first jealous wife who killed her husband even if she had to kill herself too."

"I've just remembered what you said earlier," Alan said, "you know, about a monstrous army of women. You were quite right, it is a quotation, only I think it's regiment of women, not army. It's something John Knox said, I can remember it up on the left-hand side of a page somewhere. Sorry, I just thought of it. I think army is better anyway. Poor Mrs Walton."

"Yes, poor both of them. Did you think of them when you were watching the bonfire just now?"

214

"Yes I did. I often think of them."

"So do I. A man called Arnold Swan was his business partner you know, he inherited it when the Waltons died. And then when Mr Swan died it would have gone to Mr Walton's son, Donald."

"Yes I see – only someone killed him."

"Yes, someone killed him. So I had to think of Mr Swan. It's a good motive. David Walton was a very clever potter and he made some very clever fakes, he even wrote a book about it. In a way he was a very proud man, that's why he wanted people to know what he'd done, his son Donald knew all about it too. Mr Swan wouldn't have liked all that. You could say that all he wanted was to be left alone – alone with his nice respectable inherited factory making nice respectable pottery. That's what he told me when I talked to him. That's what he desperately wanted me to believe."

"And you did believe him."

"Yes, you've got to believe people sometimes and you've got to try and decide when. A policeman gets an awful lot of practice; it's about the most important part of his job, much more important than buttons and clues like that."

"But they can be useful too?"

"Oh yes, they can, and I was very grateful to you."

Webber watched the boy's face in the silence which followed. Most children of his age, he thought, would have been proud of the compliment, but he saw nothing on Alan's face except interest and concentration.

St Peter's, the village church of Flaxfield, was not as grand and imposing as the great wool church of Blythburgh; Cromwell's soldiers had passed by and left it in peace. It was still early and the two of them sat on a seat donated by the worthy citizens of a far distant and unknown Flaxfield in America. Webber was grateful to them and lit his pipe.

"I can understand about Mr Swan," Alan said. "Yes it was a good motive but I can see that you believed him, yes one accepts that. And so it was then you thought of Mr . . . what was his name? The one who was the expert on pottery and wrote articles and advised the museums sometimes?"

"Spavin," Webber said. "James Spavin, now that really was a motive."

"Daddy told Mummy that you thought he was a bit of an old woman."

215

Webber nodded. "Hell hath no fury like a woman scorned," he said, "an expert scorned if you like. He wouldn't have liked that. He didn't like Mr Walton either, and he certainly wouldn't have liked his book. He thought Mr Walton was a man with no principles and I suppose he was right. He also thought he was a man with no artistry or skill and there he was wrong. Just the same I couldn't see him as a murderer."

"I read somewhere," the boy said, "that all murderers are conceited. Mr Spavin was conceited wasn't he?"

"Yes very conceited but not nearly so much as the real killer."

Alan nodded earnestly. "Yes I see, he must have been very sure of himself."

✣ THIRTY-TWO ✣

THE SHADOWS OF the tombstones were now dark and long and soon it would be time to go. Webber chose his words carefully before he spoke. It was difficult not to think of the boy as anything but grown-up and responsible.

"Does your father warn you not to discuss things outside the family?" He smiled at the expression of genuine shock on Alan's face.

"Oh golly! Yes of course, not even in the family really, not Alice I mean, you couldn't. I don't think she would be very interested anyway, she's rather young you know."

"Ah yes," Webber said gravely.

"It's very difficult for parents with children," Alan said. "I see that, you can't keep sending them out of the room. Mostly they wait until it's her bedtime. Actually that's why I bought her the book, she tends to make less fuss if she wants to read in bed."

His eventual choice of career would be interesting, Webber thought, if he decided against the Church or the police he might make his mark in politics.

"I know about slander and that you mustn't ever accuse someone, not unless there's enough proof to arrest them anyway," Alan said.

"That is exactly what I meant, thank you," Webber said. "Ah, I see your father's back."

Snow was standing beside his car waiting for them. "Alan go inside and help your mother, I want to talk to Mr Webber." Left alone they sat in the car. Snow's face was grey and drawn. "I'm sorry John, I should have listened to you. I must have stepped out of line quite seriously somewhere. I can't find out what's happening. All I know is that they know at the Yard that I've been feeding you."

"Your Super sent for you and you've been sacked?"

217

"No, not the Super nor the Chief, I was shunted up to the Commissioner himself and I wasn't sacked. At least I don't think so."

"Tell me."

"He said he didn't want to discuss details with me, only to give me an order, otherwise there was a complete block. I was to tell you that myself."

To a policeman, a block was final. An embargo on all information, imposed from above.

"You wouldn't think there was anyone above the Commissioner would you?" Webber said cheerfully.

"There bloody well is you know – outside the Yard there is."

"No wonder you look terrible, what was the order? No don't tell me – you've got to report to Maggie at No. 10."

Snow didn't even try to smile. "Not No. 10 and not me – you."

It wasn't the most successful of Mrs Thomas's meals. It wasn't the food, which was as good as anything she had ever done. It was the atmosphere of blight which Snow had brought with him and his refusal to discuss it. Even Alan didn't press his luck and went to bed quietly at the same time as his sister without a protest. Only Webber was determined not to let the gloom envelop him.

"They can hardly send me to the Tower," he told Mrs Thomas, when they were alone later in her cottage, "or to a psychiatric hospital. We haven't reached that stage yet, thank God. We'll go up together tomorrow."

"Will they sack Ted?"

"They might, although I'm hoping not. The Commissioner didn't offer him a drink. I'm told it's always a bad sign if he does."

"You're not frightened?"

"A bit. I don't suppose they'll shoot me. Now that was really nasty."

"I wish I'd never started all this." She looked frightened and near to tears.

"Oh come on Lizzie love! I haven't done anything to be ashamed of. A nice quiet civilized talk in someone's office. You know, I'm quite looking forward to it, whoever it is."

He made himself sound more cheerful than he felt.

218

At six o'clock the next morning Mrs Thomas telephoned her daughter and son-in-law and arranged for them to feed Bunter during the day. The call woke them from a deep sleep but it meant, as she explained to Webber, that she could accompany him to London with a clear conscience. At ten past eight he dropped her at the Glockemara Hotel and arranged to keep in touch through the telephone at the reception desk.

"It should be safe enough now," he told her, "but you can always phone in for any message I leave."

There was plenty she could do, she assured him. She could shop in Marks and Spencer and Barkers. "I can get some Christmas shopping done." It would be something to occupy her mind.

"In May?"

"I always leave it too late. It'll make a change. Cheaper too in the sale. There's always a sale at Barkers."

He left her standing outside on the pavement, a fierce dumpy figure dressed in kingfisher blue. She was, he thought, oddly comforting. The address in Queen Anne's Gate was not far from Snow's pub in Strutton Ground and he parked the car gratefully in the yard at the back and walked. Across Victoria Street he knew that Broadway would lead him to Carteret Street and into Queen Anne's Gate. It was a fine day, sunny but not warm. The eighteenth-century houses, once grand private homes, had long since become the rabbit warrens of government offices, bare oak floors and draughty sash windows looking out over St James's Park to the traffic moving along The Mall in the distance.

He gave his name to the uniformed porter on the ground floor who announced his presence into an ancient internal telephone before escorting him up four flights of noisy wooden stairs and leaving him outside a door marked 'Forestry Commission'.

"Come in Mr Webber, come in." The voice which responded to his knock was pleasant, educated and welcoming, as was the man himself, advancing to meet him with his hand outstretched. If his object was to put Webber at ease then he had succeeded within two seconds. Dressed in grey flannel trousers and an ancient but beautifully cut sports coat, the general impression he gave was both elegant and shabby. He was about Webber's age with a mop of untidy grey hair, an intelligent face, pink and healthy, his brown spaniel eyes beaming at Webber with no sign of guile or overbearing authority. Webber had seen thousands

219

like him in pubs where retired English gentlemen were always happy to discuss the weather and their gardens.

"Do sit please," he waved Webber into a comfortable chair and sat himself at an untidy desk with his back to a spluttering gas fire. His voice was mild but businesslike, as though there was a lot on the agenda which he wanted to get through as efficiently as possible.

"I do thank you for being on time. Now then, I am going to talk first, and I hope that I can explain why you are here, indeed why we are both here. If I'm clever I hope to answer many of your questions before you ask them but please butt in if there is anything you want to know. Oh dear I'm sorry, there goes my efficiency far too soon. I do beg your pardon. My name is Smith, Rudyard Smith and that is mercifully my real name. R. A. Smith is useful in my job, it tends to be forgotten easily." He cleared a space for his elbows in the papers on his desk but continued speaking through the motion as if to forestall Webber's unspoken question. "And my job has nothing to do with forests. I don't really know why they put that on the door, unless the Holy Powers think it might suggest that we do not always see the wood for the trees, in which case they would be dead right."

He beamed and Webber smiled to acknowledge a joke that he thought had been used in the room many times before.

"By the way do smoke Mr Webber, you're a pipe smoker I know." He moved a file of papers closer and read from it aloud and rapidly a precise and accurate account of Webber's official history, from the date when he had joined the police force as a young constable to his premature retirement for medical reasons. "It was your friendship with the Welsh lady in Flaxfield, Mrs Elizabeth Thomas, that led you to renew your old association with Inspector Snow and thus indirectly to your subsequent employment as a private investigator with Mr and Mrs Elberg. Am I going too quickly for you?"

"I'm ashamed to say that I have always confused MI5 and MI6," Webber said, "but you are one or the other?"

"Gracious yes, I'm sorry, I do try and sound professional and always leave something vital out. Yes, certainly MI5 and MI6, that sort of thing, Secret Service always sounds so cloak-and-dagger doesn't it? Intelligence will do, and my authority you can check of course with the Commissioner at Scotland Yard. I do apologize if all this smacks of omniscience. Reports come in, you see, and land up on someone's desk." He waved his hand over the papers. "You are being very co-operative. I always prefer to deal with professionals. Unfortunately, through no fault of yours or I may add of ours, we seem to have got our lines crossed – a bit of a mess. Our task now," he said gently, "is to try and sort them out. I'm sorry, there should be an ashtray somewhere, ah yes here it is. Can I offer you some coffee? Good, let's be cosy." He crossed to an electric kettle in the grate. "I have to make my own. I never know whether it's for security reasons or because the tea ladies can't face the stairs."

"A remarkable man, Elberg," he said as he handed Webber a coffee mug with Miss Piggy's simpering face on the side of it and then pulled another file of papers towards him on the desk. "Dutch ancestry but British by birth. I see he first came to our notice officially quite some time ago and in a perfectly routine way. He was well established in business by then, nothing remarkable but he already had a small chain of supermarkets and was very well thought of. He was generating quite a lot of employment for British manufacturers, your Mr Walton's pottery for one, that sort of thing, nothing stupendous but he was growing all the time. There was talk of a suitable honour, a CBE or something like that and we were asked to do a routine check on him just in case. After all, he travelled around a good deal in Europe and South America and his business connections in this country were really quite impressive. You can't have Her Majesty dishing out honours to someone with the wrong set of friends, at least we thought you couldn't in those days."

"I didn't realize he was a CBE," Webber said.

"He didn't get it. No thanks to us I'm ashamed to say." Smith read from the file in front of him: " 'Hans Elberg is a hard-working business executive whose enterprises both in England and abroad seem beyond political reproach and his remarkable energy has been of considerable value to British industry and our prestige abroad'. I regret to say," he added ruefully, "that we gave him a clean bill. We should have looked further."

"Are you telling me," Webber said with genuine astonishment, "that Hans Elberg is a spy?"

"No, at least not in the sense that weak pathetic creatures like Blunt and his cronies were spies. Elberg has only one loyalty and that is to himself and his money. When that was in danger he was ruthless. He would sacrifice anyone for it as you seem to have

221

discovered for yourself." Smith pushed the file away from him. "It is a rather galling thing to admit Mr Webber, but you seem to have done your job better than we have. You found out that he would use his money to sacrifice people. It has taken us a good deal longer to realize that he would sacrifice his country too. Oh dear, I'm afraid your coffee is getting cold, would you like another? That at least should not be beyond us."

❧ THIRTY-THREE ❧

"THANK YOU," WEBBER said, "I don't mind cold coffee. You're generous Mr Smith, but you must remember that I had considerable help."

"Yes you did, and do let me assure you that I don't give a rap about the – somewhat unorthodox nature of Inspector Snow's help." His brown eyes sought Webber's earnestly. "My brief is far more important than that."

Webber said: "You were good enough just now to say that I was co-operative. I never had any intention of being anything else, but before we go any further can I just say that I hope Ted Snow will not be disciplined in any way? It's not a condition you understand," he added evenly, "simply an observation."

"I think I can guarantee that."

"Thank you."

"After all we both of us have good reason to be grateful to Scotland Yard, you to Inspector Snow and my lot to the Special Branch." Smith's finger searched down a page of Hans Elberg's file and read without irony: " 'Having noted your approval of Mr Elberg as a suitable recipient for an honour to be conferred by Her Majesty we hope you will find time to read the enclosed report from C6 – ' that by the way was the first time we became aware of your own inquiries, when Inspector Snow obtained several reports for you from C6, the City and Metropolitan Police Fraud Squad. It goes on. 'You will note that although they have not yet been able to prove it, it seems certain that Hans Elberg is, and has been for some time, deeply involved in a series of complicated company frauds to deprive, illegally, shareholders in his businesses of their money. The fact that many of his City associates seem to have been as unscrupulous as he is himself and appear to have discovered his intentions and outwitted him does little in our opinion to warrant his inclusion in an honours list.' "

Smith sighed sadly. "I recognize the style I'm afraid. I go back a long way Mr Webber. It's not the only time we've backed the wrong horse. I'm sure I don't need to detail some of our more notorious misjudgements in the past?"

Webber nodded and in the silence of the little room the names of Burgess, Maclean, Fuchs, Pontecorvo, Blunt and Philby filled their minds but remained unspoken.

"If his fellow directors were on to him," Webber said, "why didn't they simply come out with it and denounce him as a crook?"

"Lordy me! They wouldn't do that, not the City way you know. Most of them wouldn't have cared to have the thing too closely examined. The poor old Fraud Squad is not, I'm afraid, a popular topic in a boardroom. No, far better to get rid of Elberg legitimately. Outvote him by all means, but arrest him and what happens to the value of your shares, eh? Quite! No, they were glad to get out of it as well as they did. We don't know what Elberg got away with. Not all that much I suspect. He salted away as much as he could in his pottery collection as you know, and by now thoroughly nervous, he made sure that everything was in his wife's name." He spread his hands, palms upward, over the papers on his desk.

"So there we were. The Department had had a nasty shock, we had almost recommended a crooked businessman for an honour and this time the Holy Powers were determined not to appear – shall we say – gauche? The man to whom I am immediately answerable put it rather well I thought: 'It would be nice, he said, if in the event of any more dirty washing coming out we should appear to be at least as knowledgeable as the Fraud Squad and the Special Branch.' This lot – " he waved at the papers on the desk top again – "is the result."

Smith glanced at his wristwatch. "I suppose it's not too early to offer you a drink?" Without waiting for an answer he crossed to a corner cupboard and returned with a bottle and two glasses. "My little contribution to the department folklore. Most people serve sherry, I hate the stuff, I think a little whisky is far more civilized, a small glass, not a great slug in the morning, and I know you prefer malt. Oh dear it's all rather pathetic isn't it? This silly wish to impress. Malt? You are supposed to think, now how on earth does he know that I drink malt? He must be very clever. Well I'm not at all, there we are, not too full. Cheers."

Webber lifted the glass in salute and sipped. "So far," he said, "you have only saved yourself an embarrassment, not a disaster. A comparatively minor crook but still a loyal one?"

"How did he strike you, when you met him?" Smith asked with genuine curiosity.

"I liked him," Webber said. "Perhaps it was the Scots accent and his enthusiasm for his pottery collection, but yes I liked him. It was later that I had to consider him as a man who would not hesitate to kill. I could have been wrong, it wouldn't be the first time, but I didn't think I was, proving it was another matter, he's not a fool."

"No, you have to be bright to take on the City, that he failed doesn't alter the fact that he jolly nearly succeeded. I confess that I read the Fraud Squad report with admiration."

"I found most of it difficult to follow," Webber said.

"So did I, the technical aspects anyway, finance has never been my strong suit I'm afraid and I was hardly likely to succeed where the Fraud Squad had failed. However the Department's blood was up, wounded pride you could say I suppose. It's true he never got to Buckingham Palace and although I was grateful to the Special Branch there are few things more tiresome than being rescued by friends. They will keep reminding you I find." Smith's face brightened and he smiled at Webber with genuine satisfaction as he returned to the papers before him. "However, the breaks started coming for us, not before time, but there they were. Each to his own, figures for the fraud boys and names for me."

"Names you knew?"

"Yes, I knew them," he nodded at Elberg's files. "Company reports. France, Liechtenstein, all over Europe, and as if that wasn't enough for him, South America as well. Mr Webber I shall not confuse you with details even if I were at liberty to reveal them." Without offering Webber another whisky he returned the bottle to the cupboard in the corner and washed their glasses in a wash-basin near the window. He smiled at Webber over his shoulder. "It was suggested to me," he said cheerfully, drying his hands and returning to the desk, "that I might ask you to sign the Official Secrets Act."

"The answer," Webber said at once, "would be yes."

"Quite, that is why I have no intention of doing so. Your personal record is quite good enough for me."

"Thank you."

"Not at all, you would be naïve in the extreme if you didn't realize that this country, like every other, has agents looking after its interest, our ladies and gentlemen in the field. Incidentally while I think of it, your lady partner, Mrs Thomas, did she travel up to London with you?"

Webber hoped very much that the question was indeed incidental. He didn't underestimate Rudyard Smith and he had no desire to see Mrs Thomas with her fluent French being offered interesting errands or assignments as one of his 'ladies in the field'. He explained about their arrangement for messages at the Glockemara. "She's probably resting in her room, she gets very tired," he lied. At that moment, Webber thought, she was probably playing hell with the salesladies in Barkers' bargain basement. He hoped Mr Smith's omniscience didn't extend as far as Kensington High Street.

"A remarkable woman," Smith said.

"You had Elberg's factories investigated?"

"The names on their boards of directors could only mean one thing. They were all deep into the arms business, guns, ammunition, spare parts for tanks, that sort of thing. Look at any television news and you'll see that it's a very profitable market, quite legitimate of course, however distasteful. At the time of our first investigations Elberg was still important. He hadn't lost the take-over battle, he was very much still a force to be reckoned with, he still had power and as you and Mrs Thomas discovered he was prepared to use it. The Department didn't know that side of it of course, our concern was simply to learn the business facts. We'd made too many mistakes in the past, the arms business is potentially embarrassing. If something awkward happened we didn't want Ministers trying to answer questions stark naked on 'Panorama'."

A twinge of pain shot across Smith's face as he moved in his chair.

"Sorry, nothing serious, I get a little back trouble. I've been digging manure into my roses rather ambitiously I'm afraid."

"Shove it on the surface," Webber said, "let the rain do the work."

"Really? I was going to ask you about roses. Later perhaps."

"Yes later. And something awkward did happen?"

"An Englishman and his wife burnt to death on a beach in France? Yes that was awkward."

226

"It was murder," Webber said. "Why did you cover it up?"

"We didn't, at least not to begin with. Remember it was on French soil. By the time we heard about it the Foreign Office had got the bodies back and they were cremated." He grimaced. "As if once wasn't enough. By the time our Press got on to it, it was all over and done with. The verdict as you know was accidental death and we had to go along with it. I confess I'm surprised that the French acted so quickly, they didn't hang about, the cover-up was almost immediate."

Webber detected a note of grudging admiration. Perhaps it was plain patriotism or simply that he wanted to show Smith that for once he had inside knowledge of his own.

"It was one word," he said. "An Englishman said it to the French police that morning on the beach. He was a photographer and worked for the local paper. He had been in Vietnam among many other places. The bodies reminded him of one thing and he said so."

"Napalm."

"Yes, later on he came to dismiss the idea as preposterous. Someone in their police organization didn't think so though, did they?"

Smith said: "No. So that's how they were able to move so quickly. We wondered. It's quite an interesting jigsaw isn't it? Some of the pieces are yours and some ours. Would you care to say where you got that particular piece from?"

Webber thought of his interview with Snow's pet informer in the Foreign Office, the shy young man with the frightened eyes who was living happily and respectably with two dogs and a bearded vet and didn't want to lose his job. Consenting adults in the privacy of a Battersea flat may well have been legal but it wouldn't, Webber thought, have endeared him to his superiors in the Foreign Office. He liked Rudyard Smith but had no intention of revealing his source of information. There were limits.

Smith nodded understandably at Webber's silence. "It doesn't matter, it fills a gap, that's all I really care about. Yes, napalm, that was the dirty word that put the fear of God into the French and, when it reached us later, into us too. Le Bosquet is a depressed area, when Elberg's consortium offered to build a factory making fertilizers there the French Government was delighted. They offered cheap land and put considerable money in it themselves."

227

"Fertilizers sounds harmless enough," Webber said.

"It does, doesn't it? Unfortunately Elberg's friends didn't stop there. Legal, as I said, but highly embarrassing, the French didn't much care for their money being used for that sort of product and were in the process of trying to stop it." Smith's eyes twinkled maliciously. "Presumably it's all right to shoot people but not to burn them. They were very keen indeed to keep it quiet. I have to admit I see their point, the factory after all had largely solved their local unemployment problem. What they didn't want was publicity. It is not a popular view I'm afraid, but that is one of the awkward perils of having a free Press. When their official pathologist's report confirmed that the Waltons had been killed with napalm they jumped on it like the slam of a door, the bodies were back on this side of the Channel very quickly indeed with a neat verdict of Accidental Death." Smith sighed wearily. "And so it would have remained," he said, "if it hadn't been for you."

"The Foreign Office knew it was murder and they knew it was napalm, they had a confidential report from the French, I knew that," Webber said stubbornly. "So why was it hushed up over here as well?"

"Yes, they knew," Smith said sadly. "It would have been nice to play holier than thou wouldn't it? Unfortunately we couldn't do that, as the French well knew. You see they weren't the only ones who had given Elberg's lot money. They knew that Her Majesty's Government had helped to finance him too. Not holier at all you see. Just a very nasty mess, which as usual the Department was expected to clear up. A great deal of overtime I assure you, no union would stand for it. It has been, although I say it myself, well worth it. We moved in and took Elberg apart."

"He's a cold-blooded murderer," Webber said. "You can't hush it up."

"We come to it from different angles," Smith said smoothly. "A most interesting case by any standards. Some pieces as I said are yours, and some are mine. Now I think that in fairness it's your turn. I do like a nice clear picture. Like you I know what killed the Waltons. What I do not know is how."

❧ THIRTY-FOUR ☙

"YES, DIFFERENT ANGLES," Webber said. "You people were concerned with his involvement with the arms business. I was concerned with his involvement with murder. You'll forgive me for pointing out that you only had to satisfy your Department. I was looking for evidence that would convince a judge and jury and be strong enough to resist the attacks of a defending counsel. Even before I was able to find that evidence my common sense told me that Elberg was the man."

"Common sense of course is a poor card in a court of law," Smith said.

"Exactly, I needed more than that."

"Mercifully you are under no such constraints here," Smith murmured, and leaned his chin attentively on his joined hands. "I like common sense very much. Tell me."

Webber agreed. "There were other possibilities. Swan, Walton's partner, and the art expert, Spavin. I even considered Walton's wife. You could say that they all had a good reason for killing David Walton. You could even accept the death of the Frenchwoman, Julie Pichon, as an accident – a coincidence – and Donald Walton too. He could have been the victim of a vicious robbery. God knows there are enough of those."

"One coincidence, but not all of them together?"

"No, not all of them together. Elberg's empire was slipping away. He could see a time when he might be forced to start all over again, and for that he would need money. He played the old card. He transferred the house, and I don't doubt as much legitimate money as he could, into his wife's name, but above all there was his collection, he made sure she owned that too."

"With all my worldly goods I thee endow. The collection is very impressive I'm told."

"There seems no doubt that it is the largest and technically the finest in the world."

"Technically?"

"A lot of it is fake. Brilliant fake, but once that was shown to be true then the whole collection would be tarred with the same brush, and Elberg got to know that David Walton was not only the forger but longed for recognition and had written a book about it. Not only that, he was prepared to publish it. From that moment David Walton was as good as dead."

"When the Waltons died on that beach," Smith said almost apologetically, "Elberg and his wife were in South America."

"Rich men employ people. Elberg killed for money and he killed with money. That Walton happened to be his wife's father meant nothing to him."

"It didn't strike you as a curious thing that he was paying you to find out who did it?"

Webber shook his head. "Challenging me, would be better. No, I think he enjoyed that. Conceit; they all have it, especially the clever ones, and Elberg, you would agree, is certainly that? He didn't reckon on his wife not accepting the French verdict but once she took matters into her own hands and employed me he couldn't resist it. He was quite sure that his involvement could never be discovered. No he enjoyed it, it gave him pleasure."

"She was never involved in any way?" Smith asked.

"Only that she happened to set the ball rolling. When I met him I felt strongly that Elberg genuinely loved her, I still think he does although of course it was something I had to check. She had been very ill in Uruguay, I took the trouble to send for the hospital reports, for all I knew at that time he might have been poisoning her. That was another blind alley but it had to be eliminated. She was suffering from malaria."

"You didn't leave much to chance."

"Snow organized a friend in Interpol. A long-winded exercise but I had drawn a blank with her doctor."

"Humper? Yes we know him too. Not an easy man I agree. I've had to lean quite hard on him, successfully thank goodness. I'm sorry, I'm interrupting." Smith's face lifted into a gentle smile.

They could easily, Webber thought, have been swapping gardening hints over a pint of bitter. The thought of beer and a comfortable evening in The Bull gave him a pang of regret, as though he had opened a door and found himself inexplicably in another world.

Smith looked at this overweight policeman with the startling blue eyes and sensed his air of remoteness. He hadn't been wrong in his assessment of him he felt sure. The man was a professional. There was more to him than that though, he was, Smith thought, an interesting creature. Although he had not embarrassed Webber by mentioning some of his outstandingly successful cases he had nevertheless read about them in the official files before him on the desk and had been impressed. Reading them he had formed a different physical image of the man, leaner and more energetic. It showed how wrong you could be. This man was a cut above the policemen he had known; gentle and given to introspection. Not too introspective he hoped. It would be a pity if he developed scruples. He needed Webber very much. He looked at the shrewd blue eyes again and relaxed. It would be all right, it would depend on the way he approached him.

"Tell me about Le Bosquet," he said.

"The Waltons spent their honeymoon there, they often went back for their anniversary. He may have been a philanderer but there was another side to his life. He was fond of his wife, grateful perhaps, after all she'd had faith in him and he needed that." Webber paused, a thought occurring to him for the first time. "Elberg and Walton: both of them happily married in their own way. At least it's not your usual domestic murder. Remarkable men. If things had been different they both might well have been knighted." He fell silent.

Smith said quietly: "Easter-time wasn't it?"

"Yes and Elberg knew they'd be there. You say you recognized some of the names in Elberg's concerns. Did you know the name Koenig?"

"Johann Koenig? Yes we know him." Smith reeled off facts as though he was reading from one of his files. "German, Hitler Youth but no criminal record, too young perhaps. Yes we know him, he's been deep in the arms game for some time, an old crony of Elberg's. Talented, needs to be, he has an ambitious wife, houses in Frankfurt and St Moritz and I believe a flat in Paris. A hard worker, again he has to be with those commitments."

Webber nodded. "He was managing director of the factory outside Le Bosquet. Elberg paid him to get rid of the Waltons. I don't know how much, a great deal I imagine. Elberg never does

231

things by halves. He may have been slipping but he spent it while he still had some control left. I had hoped," he said apologetically, "to have found out the exact amount. I arranged to meet a useful informant but it's gone wrong I'm afraid. She hasn't turned up."

"How, Mr Webber? How was it done?"

Webber produced his set of photographs from his briefcase, spread them on top of the papers on Smith's desk and resumed his seat without comment.

"Are they in any kind of order?" Smith asked.

"No, they'll explain themselves in a minute. I take it you have a report on Mrs Thomas? I mean I don't have to fill her in for you?"

"No, I told you. She's obviously a remarkable woman."

"And a very brave one. She's a great believer in local gossip and to get it she didn't hesitate to let it be known why she was in Le Bosquet. She was damn nearly killed for it too."

Smith saw the change in Webber's eyes. It was hard to tell whether it was recollected fear or anger. He said nothing and waited quietly for Webber to start again.

"Elberg chose his man well. I suppose a successful tycoon learns to delegate, to trust, and I suppose too that if the fee is high enough you can buy trust."

Smith said: "Half a million, pounds not francs. He got half a million pounds. Not Elberg's personal money of course, but he saw that Koenig got it."

It was the wrong time to ask how Smith knew.

"Thank you, I wondered," Webber said. "Like so many of his countrymen Koenig was thorough. As you said, a worker. He was well in with the local business community. He hoped that Walton's death would be accepted as a bizarre accident. He was also astute enough to realize that even if napalm was implicated the chances were very high that the authorities would hush it up. Quite a few people knew what was going on in that factory, a factory which had transformed the local economy. He knew the locals, tight and secretive. It wasn't just the few people in the factory itself, the prosperity touched the economy of the whole area and everybody's pockets. Money from a brief tourist season is one thing, money all the year round is something very different."

Smith allowed his eyes to drop to the photographs but said

232

nothing. His instinct told him that for all Webber's careful reticence he was recounting facts. This wasn't guesswork, he was listening to facts and he knew that however horrible this was how it happened.

"I don't know exactly when Koenig first met Paul Colbert," Webber said. "He may have been there that day when the boy was presented with that cup you can see him holding. Perhaps he even saw him win it. Koenig, as I said, was well known in the community, certainly the factory gave funds and supported local charities and youth clubs. Colbert was a bright boy, not very good at school but clever with his hands, he fitted well into the taxi business, it was a broken home but he and his mother managed well enough with one battered second-hand car. Koenig befriended both Paul and his mother. Paul was a romantic, he was fascinated by uniforms and the two world wars which had been fought around his home. He would have been flattered by the interest of this older man, a man who was more than old enough to be his father and who could tell him about the war he never knew himself. The kid thought it was like a story coming to life and Koenig used him."

Rudyard Smith picked up the photograph and looked at it. Father Bernard had got it from the newspaper files with the help of Micky Marks before he succumbed to the cancer which killed him. It showed a proud Paul Colbert holding a silver cup, and on the judges' table in front of him, the beautiful thing he had made which had won first prize for him.

"And they killed the Waltons with this?"

"Paul did, or something like it. Koenig told him they were English busybodies, industrial spies come to steal the secrets of the formula for a new fertilizer. He was the managing director remember."

"And the boy would kill them for that!"

"Koenig said it would only make a loud noise and frighten them. He said they had been warned already to keep away and that this would frighten them enough to leave, when it killed them it was too late. The boy was terrified, too terrified to talk."

"Even to his mother?"

"Yes, it was a secret. Besides she had already accepted a new car for the taxi business. Koenig had told her that the factory needed a good local taxi service – a gesture of good will. Paul didn't want to implicate her in a mess like that – and he didn't."

233

Webber got up from his chair and walked round behind the desk. He pointed over Smith's shoulder with the stem of his pipe.

"This is a general view of the beach, Mrs Thomas took these. Miles of firm sand, and just these sand dunes here to break it up. A man could hide there and that's what Paul Colbert did that morning. Every year on those sands in August when the weather is good the town plays host to a competition. It's quite famous locally, the cup is much sought after. It goes to the man or boy who gives the best and most accurate performance with his own design of a model aeroplane. Paul won that cup the previous August and that's what gave Koenig his idea."

Smith looked at the photograph of the boy and his silver cup and his sleek machine.

"And a model like that could carry a lethal load of napalm?"

"A more powerful one could easily. Twin diesel engines, perhaps three, and radio-controlled. Some competitions have them dropping parachute flares and God knows what. This one carried a large capsule of the filthy stuff designed to explode on impact. No problem for Koenig's backroom boys, most napalm bombs contain up to four hundred of the capsules, they're meant to scatter over a large area indiscriminately. Deliver it accurately and one would be more than enough. It was, as you know." He moved his pipe and pointed to the photograph of the murder scene that Snow's film laboratory had enlarged. "These bits of charred metal are what was left of the plane before the French police tidied up. A piece of undercarriage and bits of at least two engines. Snow has a young son, he knew exactly what they were."

"But not the Scotland Yard lab men?"

"I expect it's a long time since they played with model aeroplanes," Webber said.

Smith let his eyes move to the rest of the photographs that Micky Marks had taken of the Waltons' black and twisted bodies. The flesh burnt off the faces, leaving only the teeth, white in a silent scream. He shuddered.

Webber returned to his chair.

"That's why poor Julie Pichon died. She heard it, she probably didn't see it but she heard it, and then she saw the flames. It was a frelon, she said, a hornet. She didn't mean Paul Colbert's old taxi that ran her down on that dark road. She meant the noise of the thing that killed David Walton and his

234

wife. She made a nuisance of herself and talked. If you're going to invent an accidental death and not napalm you've got to come up with something pretty damn quick. The local people did their best with blazing pipe ash and a high wind. Julie Pichon knew it was dead calm and said so. No one was sure how much she'd seen and might say, so she died. You need a nice calm day to fly a model aeroplane but it didn't fit in with the pipe-ash theory. Paul Colbert was desperate. He killed her and repaired the car in his own workshop. He nearly killed Mrs Thomas too but he couldn't face it. I think he knew the story had broken, perhaps he thought they had already told his mother. He couldn't face that and he shot himself. He was a fool, it wasn't really him, he was as unthinking as his model aeroplane and his old taxi. It was Elberg and his money and it was Koenig. With the money Elberg had given him he had more than enough to persuade people not to repeat Julie Pichon's gossip. The Bouviers got a new kitchen for the hotel. Brieux, the newspaper editor, was paid to keep quiet too. Remember it was something the French authorities were just as anxious to suppress as Koenig was. They didn't want anyone exposed to the awkward questions of the Press if they could avoid it. The juge d'instruction was conveniently promoted and soon the pathologist was furthering his medical knowledge of napalm in Afghanistan. Koenig is safely in South America and I suppose Elberg is too. So all you have to do is get them back, if you can extradite them, which I doubt. Then you can have a lovely long Old Bailey trial and try and prove it and the murder of David Walton's son too. We might charge him with paying someone to take a few shots at me while we're at it. I'm sure he's got enough money left for a really good counsel." Webber heaved himself to his feet and walked to the window and the view of the trees waving with spring leaves in St James's Park.

"Elberg isn't in South America," Smith said. "He's back in England with his wife. They're at the house in Holland Crescent. That's why I sent for you."

235

ঌ THIRTY-FIVE ও

ONE PRESENT MRS Thomas had chosen with care, she had taken the trouble to check the size with Father Bernard: she bought Father Girard a pair of very expensive football boots. The sort of boots a professional footballer could be proud of. She had been unable to resist buying something for herself. Inspired by the gaily clad joggers she had seen in the park she treated herself to a blue and white striped tracksuit. She had no intention of jogging, it would, she knew, be perfect for lounging about the house, warm, loose and comfortable and it had a pixie hood, it was ideal protection against the blasts of the East Anglian winter. In the hotel room she tried it on and was well pleased, simple and practical, she wondered why the fashion hadn't caught on before. Mr Churchill, she remembered with affection, had worn something like it during the war, not quite so brightly coloured perhaps. She had an eye, she told herself, some people had it and some didn't, smart, unusual. She was not however without self-criticism. She surveyed herself in the wardrobe mirror. The worst you can say of it, she thought, peering through her round spectacles, is that it makes me look like a cross between a garden gnome and a very cold wasp. On the other hand my love, she told herself brightening, it's bound to cause comment in the High Street. But above all it would please John. Her John. He liked her clothes. At least he always told her he did.

There was a telephone message from him at the desk. He would be busy until at least mid-afternoon. He hoped to be back to pick her up at the Glockemara by four o'clock.

"He don't want you hanging about the hotel," the old man on the desk told her conspiratorially, "says to finish your shopping or go for a walk."

That meant he thought there was still some danger. There was nothing she could do. To be honest, she told herself, that was the way she wanted it. If there was danger he would cope with it, after all he had done it many times before he ever met her. It was nearly over, he'd said so. If there was to be any glory she wanted it to be his.

In Kensington Gardens she sat on the same bench she had shared with him, how long ago was it? So much had happened. A boy no older than Alan sat at the other end with his radio transmitter on his knees, earnestly controlling a miniature battleship far out on the Round Pond. Radio control, computers, so different from the cotton reels of her youth. She remembered Paul's face too, the same look of earnest, puzzled concentration, and the horror of the bunker. So clear was the memory that she shivered and for a moment her head was filled with the smell of vomit, mint humbugs and blood. Poor Paul, wicked, terrified Paul, no wonder he'd turned to the only source of comfort he knew. He couldn't talk to his mother but he'd talked to Father Girard, scarcely more than a boy himself, and he'd told him everything in the safety and secrecy of the confessional. She remembered Father Girard's face when she'd asked him if he had connected Julie Pichon's death with the bodies on the beach.

"No madame, truthfully no, I didn't."

But he couldn't control the blush which had covered his young face. How can you accuse a priest of lying? She had left it to Father Bernard to pursue in his own way. You delegated. Webber had taught her that.

In the basement of the house in Queen Anne's Gate there was a canteen. You could hardly dignify it by calling it a restaurant although it had a respectable wine list. Rudyard Smith, like others in the Department, used it when he judged it unwise to display his visitors in public.

"Fish fingers and Vouvray, I suggest," he advised Webber. "I confess I've quite grown to like them, perhaps it's the television advertisements." He sighed. "We are all so open to suggestion aren't we? So you broke the secrets of the confessional. Golly! I congratulate you, I really do. It's something I wouldn't even attempt."

"Mrs Thomas, not me," Webber said. "She has her own contacts, she got another priest to speak to him, a much older man, I've met him too, a good man, reliable. He was able to

237

convince the boy that he had chosen the wrong calling. Father Girard left the priesthood shortly after Paul Colbert's body was found in the bunker. It had been a terrible burden for a young man, at one time Koenig tried to bribe him too you know. He was glad to talk. It was Mrs Thomas who suggested that he should embrace his true calling. Footballers can talk more freely than priests."

"I see, how very interesting, a most remarkable woman indeed. You must both come down and see my roses in Barnes — in June perhaps?"

"Thank you, I'll tell her. It depends, she does tire easily."

"Ah yes, you said. How do you find the wine?"

"Very good."

"Not too bad is it? I don't pretend to be a connoisseur but I know what to avoid here. What do you feel about capital punishment by the way?"

"When we had it," Webber said, "I hated it. Now — now I'm not so sure."

Smith smiled and refilled their glasses. "It was a clever idea of yours to contact Miss Evans, Elberg's computer lady. You took a risk of course but I imagine you hoped that the private tapes might contain records of some of his financial transactions? After all he had bribed Koenig and paid some professional hit men to kill Donald Walton too. Names even, yes indeed, you could have hoped for that. Your French evidence, even if you could have got all your witnesses into an English court, was quite vulnerable, wasn't it?"

Webber thought of long days in the witness box beleaguered by a clever and relentless counsel and nodded.

"Confirmation of some sort would have been nice," he said. "I wasn't far out either. I told her that it would have been in her best interests to tell us what she knew before the case broke. Her help at this early stage would put her on the right side. My guess was that she didn't know what had been going on, Elberg was too clever for that. She was a brilliant computer expert and that's what he wanted her for, not as an accomplice in crime. He bought brains, the best he could get, always. She agreed to come down to Flaxfield and tell us what she could. Unfortunately she must have changed her mind. She never turned up — unless . . ."

"No, she's quite safe," Smith said, "at least I hope so, certainly she was when she reported early this morning."

"She's with you, the Department?"

"We moved her in some time ago when he was expanding his underground computers. Her qualifications are impeccable of course. She's been with us ever since she left university. We got the computer firm to recommend her. She's been very useful, almost one of the Elberg family you might say. Oh, and you are quite right about Mrs Elberg, she knew nothing of her husband's affairs. Luckily Miss Evans has been able to establish quite a friendship with her."

"You didn't leave much to chance either did you?"

"We covered the chauffeur too. It meant getting rid of his girl-friend I'm afraid and putting one of our younger ladies in her place but it was useful to follow his movements, to the Continent and so on. Scheduled airlines are easy enough to keep tabs on. Elberg used company jets quite a bit. The chauffeur wasn't involved criminally, I'm pleased to say, but I had to cover him. The Filipino couple are a different kettle of fish, smelly fish too. Not privy to his affairs, I dare say, but he used them as his bodyguards and they were useful when he needed them. He has interests in Manila and picked them up there. Nasty violent things, I should think he used the man to shoot at you. Not for Walton's poor son though, too risky in the Midlands, and Miss Evans has some names that I think might interest the police up there rather more, local thugs. You're quite right, you can buy anything if you can pay for it. I'm sorry if we've spoiled Miss Evans' co-operation for you. She told us about your request of course. That's why I felt it was time we had a chat." Smith smiled mildly at Webber, "no point in us doubling up was there? Different angles as I say, and now we come together. Do smoke your pipe if you want to, no ceremony with us I promise you."

Webber felt his anal muscles contract. It happened when he was afraid.

"What do you want me to do?"

"You can say no, and if you do then I shall understand and we can pursue our separate aims. Our meeting will have been a pleasant chat. About roses perhaps, nothing more."

Webber listened and stayed silent.

"In a way I suppose you have to admire Elberg," Smith continued. "He deals big, if one financial empire collapses he comes back. Plenty of contacts, I don't mind admitting that we've had a devil of a job keeping him in our sights."

"Tell me."

"Perhaps the biggest deal he's ever done – or thinks he has. He is a tidy man, he has come back to London to clear up his affairs, the sale of his house and his collection."

"Thinks he has?"

"We have," Smith said modestly, "been able to keep our involvement in the deal secret. He has, he believes, arranged for the sale of Exocet missiles to South America, a very delicate area of interest for Her Majesty's Government as I'm sure you'll agree, you will recall the Falklands fuss? He may have failed this time but you can't keep a good man down, if that is the phrase I'm looking for."

"And he has failed?"

"He hasn't been dealing with genuine suppliers in Europe but with our people. Miss Evans has delivered messages to him which have convinced him that he has succeeded, messages from his European suppliers and from the South American government concerned. They have already partially financed his efforts on their behalf. When they discover that he can't deliver they will be very cross indeed. They have little faith in the courts you know. I forget offhand just how many people have disappeared in recent years but it's an awful lot – 'the disappeared ones' I believe they're called." If Rudyard Smith saw any contradiction in his reference to courts of law he didn't appear to. "Elberg is, as I said, a tidy man," he continued. "His house, his collection – and you. I think he would like to leave to collect his new fortune with a clear conscience. No point in keeping him in doubt. We would like you to pop in and see him. You would report that regretfully, in spite of your best efforts on his behalf, you have to admit failure."

"And if he doesn't believe me? He has already tried to kill me."

"I'm not saying it isn't a risk. I don't think there was anything personal, he just wanted you out of the way. A very tidy man. He probably wouldn't leave unless he could be quite certain that your inquiries were over. And we really would like him to leave."

"You think he will accept it?"

"I think you should charge him £10,000. It's the sort of language he understands. Miss Evans assures me that he still has petty cash available. He may think it's hush money or he may believe you. It doesn't matter, he'll leave. The Filipinos too, they are to travel with him."

"And Mrs Elberg?"

"At the moment her plans are to join him later. Sir Michael Humper is concerned for her health, he wants her to go into a private clinic for further tests. He is quite adamant that it's necessary. Hans Elberg has agreed. I think you're right, she means a lot to him."

The room was empty now, a radio played pop music in the kitchen behind the bar and a tired-looking woman cleared dirty plates from the tables. It must have been all of ten minutes before Webber spoke.

"I'll go," he said.

❧ THIRTY-SIX ❧

IT TOOK WEBBER a long time to get over that visit to Elberg at the house in Holland Crescent. It stayed in his mind, a memory as sharp as a photograph. The face of the Filipino who opened the door to him, bland and expressionless, and the pause for a blank fraction of a second before he was admitted and conducted to the underground office. Elberg himself natural and courteous, a polite businessman finding time to deal with yet another minor irritation in his affairs as he listened attentively to Webber's carefully rehearsed admission of failure and received his final account. Webber was frightened but forced himself to be a businessman himself; only then, he knew, would Elberg believe him. Not the £10,000 that Smith had told him to ask, that was too much, but £6000, including all expenses. A sane financial discussion with his employer. If he could convince Elberg that he was telling the truth then he remained safe, talking to a shrewd, busy man with a penetrating eye and a pleasant Scottish accent. If not, he was alone in a windowless room with a man who had used his money and power to kill without compunction or pity.

It was the polite interest in his face that chilled Webber in the silence that fell between them. There was no hostility. Something had gone wrong and the man was simply curious to know why. It wasn't difficult to follow Elberg's silent reasoning. Perhaps the Filipino had shot at the wrong man? Or perhaps he had identified Webber correctly and missed, and if that had happened then why was Webber standing here quietly before him, and who else knew that he was here? Webber was gambling like a fox who knows his own territory better than the hunt. Money had always been Elberg's choice of weapon, the man could believe him and pay him his fee, or he could pretend to believe him and consider it a bribe. Or he could kill him. He wouldn't do it himself but he might give the Filipino another chance.

242

After what seemed to Webber one of the longest silences of his life, Elberg reached for a pen and began to write the cheque. With relief? If he felt it then Webber could see no sign in his face. It was impossible to tell what he was thinking.

"Everything included Mr Webber?" he asked pleasantly.

Everything was indeed included, and if Rudyard Smith was right, that meant Elberg's own death warrant.

"Yes, everything."

Webber forced himself to remember the black, smoking bodies in the photographs, the maggots alive and moving on the stinking face of David Walton's son, Julie Pichon who gave sweets to children and the horror of the sad deluded Paul Colbert in the concrete bunker. How many others? He could easily have been one of them, and the man who had tried to shoot him was here too, somewhere in the house. Outside the door? Waiting for Elberg to call him in?

Webber made himself believe that soon he would be free to rise casually and walk out into the daylight. He didn't show it, he talked to Elberg as he had talked when they first met, only now he saw him through different eyes. Webber had spoken to murderers before but this man was different, the conceit was there but it was the conceit of a businessman protecting his interests, nothing else meant anything to him. Death was an entry on a balance sheet.

"A sensible man moves with events Mr Webber." When Elberg smiled it was with genuine enjoyment, as if he was taking the trouble to explain things to Webber because he liked him. "You must have read some of the financial stories in the papers? Editors are sad wee things, they like to assume a great deal of knowledge—and they don't know a bloody thing. By the way your cheque is quite safe. I'm glad you came to see me, I wanted to get everything settled."

Webber glanced at the walls and the empty display cases which had held the pottery collection.

"I hadn't realized you were selling up."

"I'm moving my base to South America for a while, Buenos Aires probably." He rose to his feet glancing at his watch. "Time waits for no man Mr Webber," he said, walking with him to the door. "We move, as I say, with events. I'm grateful to you, I can leave with a clear conscience, like you I don't approve of loose ends. Yes, I'm selling the house and the collection. It's already been taken by the saleroom, they seem very excited about it, they are working on the catalogue I believe. You have the cheque safe Mr Webber?"

"Thank you, yes."

"Good, well then you have one more task. A labourer is worthy of his hire eh? Unfortunately Mrs Elberg is incarcerated in one of Humper's clinics for a wee bit. I've written the address on this card for you."

"I'm sorry."

"It's nothing serious, Humper seems to think she needs some more tests. She can follow me out when they're finished. In a way it works out quite well, everything is in her name and she will be able to keep an eye on things for me. Miss Evans can stay behind to help her. I want you to go and see my wife. She has a great deal of faith in you, she told me so. If you have been unable to find any proof of foul play then she will accept what you say. Humper thinks her delusions are really a hangover from that wretched malaria. Between the two of you I hope you can set her mind at rest. It's what we have always prayed for."

Webber was glad to find himself at the front door and not facing the Filipino alone.

"Goodbye Mr Webber."

"Bon voyage Mr Elberg."

When the door slammed behind him it sounded like the trap door of a scaffold. He collected Mrs Thomas and allowed her to drive him home.

Slowly the village returned to normal or as near normal as any village where Mrs Thomas chose to live. Her tracksuit was an undoubted success and she bathed in its glory in every shop in the High Street.

Ted Snow went home to Finchley with Betty and the children. Rudyard Smith more than kept his promise. It was the Commissioner of Scotland Yard in person who explained to Detective Inspector Snow that the Elberg case was unlikely ever to come before an English court and that all future inquiries about that gentleman were to be handled by a quite separate department of Her Majesty's Government. Loyalty to old friends, the Commissioner informed him urbanely, was an admirable trait, but if he did it again he would be sacked.

Rudyard Smith believed in the virtue of loyalty too, and shortly afterwards Snow became a Detective Superintendent, moving to a real office with the luxury of a carpet and an armchair.

In his own armchair, in his own home, Webber took stock and let himself wonder. He was not a religious man but a man of considerable moral probity. All his working life he had in his own way pursued criminals and justice. You did your best to catch a villain. If you succeeded then the law of England tried them and your job was over. This was different and it disturbed him. Mrs Thomas had no such scruples, she was a maverick. All her life she had regarded the law of the land as a useful rule of thumb to be respected only as expediency ordained; it was a philosophy that she shared with her cat, Bunter. She thanked God, for whom she had a more healthy respect, that she understood John Webber's doubts and was confident of resolving them in her own way and in her own time. Whatever his doubts she considered that he had behaved superbly, justifying her highest hopes of his abilities. Now having saved him from what she considered a ridiculously early retirement she had no intention of allowing him to wallow in introspection. Together they found comfort in each other's company, sometimes in her home, sometimes in his. It helped him to talk and he withheld no secrets from her. He liked to recall the case from the beginning, step by step, and each time the pattern grew clearer in her mind until her instinct told her that she had found the key. Unlike him, she held her peace until she should judge that the time was right.

Smaller problems they dealt with together. Like the saleroom catalogue of the Elberg collection and Molly Motherwell's announcement that David Walton's book had been accepted for publication. There was no real difficulty, Mrs Thomas told Webber. It was a simple question of right and wrong, a question of sorting out priorities. She did it one day while she allowed him to make the mint sauce for their evening meal. She did it moving unhurriedly from her saucepans to the kitchen table where he was chopping the mint.

"It is quite wrong," she said firmly, "to let Jessica Elberg sell a collection full of her father's fakes."

"You could say it was wrong of me to let her husband go to South America."

"Good riddance to bad rubbish! Nothing to do with you and you know it. Thank God you won't have to sit in a courtroom for

245

months on end and perhaps watch the evil bastard acquitted, don't put vinegar on that mint yet, was Ted pleased with his share of the money? You never said."

"Yes, he's pleased. Three thousand pounds cash and tax free, why shouldn't he be?"

She basted the leg of lamb carefully, her face flushed and shining from the heat from the oven.

"I see, so we shall pay income tax on a cheque for the full six thousand?"

"It doesn't matter. Everyone has to pay a tax of one kind or another. What's wrong with vinegar?"

"Too fierce on its own, you want the juice of a fresh orange with it, and a zest of the peel chopped fine too. Simple."

She made everything sound simple.

"You needn't worry about Elberg's collection," he said. "The saleroom has withdrawn it. Molly went to them and told them about the book. It's not out yet of course but the publishers have produced a very enthusiastic synopsis."

Webber smiled as he remembered the face of the saleroom expert, supercilious and arrogant. He very much wished that he could have seen that face again when Molly had offered her expert services.

"It's not all fake, why do they have to withdraw all of it?" she asked.

"Jimmy says it's more or less standard practice for an auction house with their reputation. It's easier for them to wash their hands of the whole thing. None of the other salerooms would want that kind of publicity either."

"But she offered to sort it all out?"

"Yes, she guaranteed to separate the sheep from the goats, after all she is, as she told them, the only person in the world who can positively identify David Walton's fingerprints. She could have taken out every piece that he ever made, fakes, forgeries, or modern masterpieces, call them what you like. There would still be plenty of pieces of original antique pottery left in Elberg's collection."

"The saleroom wouldn't do that?"

"Apart from anything else, the man there can't stand the sight of poor Molly. 'Not the sort of person we like to do business with', he once told me. Pity, I like her, she deserves some luck, they should have swallowed hard and paid her a good fee."

"Yes, pity."

Mrs Thomas didn't totally dislike Molly Motherwell but she preferred to think of her being a busy expert in London than an attractive footloose woman in Flaxfield. She had a way of walking her dog on a lead and posing against the wind in an attitude that Mrs Thomas considered provocative. Like a glossy calendar for dog biscuits. She selected a sharp knife and ran it deep into the meat to test it.

"Where is the collection now?"

"Back at Holland Crescent with Jessica Elberg."

"She's out of the clinic then?"

"I'm going up to see her, I'm not looking forward to it. What can I tell her? That she was wrong about her mother and father and her brother's death was just a bloody awful coincidence? Lovely! I can have a nice cup of tea and we can sit among all those packing-cases that the salerooms won't touch with a bargepole."

"Does she know her father made some of it himself?"

"God knows – I doubt it, an auction house doesn't have to give a reason. They wouldn't commit themselves, too scared of libel. They'll wait until the book is published and let her find out for herself. Bugger Smith," he said fiercely. "Bugger Smith and his bloody Secret Service."

During the meal he was gloomy and silent. Mrs Thomas was silent too, silent because she was thinking. Afterwards, drinking the tea which she always served instead of coffee, he looked at her glumly and she did not fail him.

"I know exactly what you can tell her," she said. "Simple."

"It can't have been easy," Smith said after Webber had seen Jessica Elberg. "I'm afraid I've rather tied your hands. Did she accept what you told her?"

"What else could she do? A failure is a failure. I told her I felt I had let her down."

"I'm sorry."

"So am I, a rotten business. She's always been left out of everything. Elberg kept her as an attractive toy, just another asset, like something in his collection. That at least was something I could help her with."

"I hope," Smith said, "that it's something that will keep her very busy, something to occupy her mind in the next few weeks. She's going to need that."

"Mrs Motherwell will go and stay with her, so she won't be alone. She has agreed to sort out the collection for her. The genuine antique pottery she will sell in her shop on a generous commission basis. Once the book is published there should be no lack of buyers, she will be, after all, an irrefutable expert. She had the bright idea of writing the preface with a photograph of her shop for good measure."

"Very neat," Smith murmured appreciatively. "I like it. And the rest? David Walton's fakes?"

"David Walton's modern masterpieces, it sounds better. The book will help there too I think. Jessica Elberg is mounting a special exhibition of his work to coincide with the publication of the book. 'David Walton. A master potter of Staffordshire.' He would have liked that. A memorial."

"I congratulate you. Yes, that should certainly keep her mind occupied, poor thing. I'm glad she will not be alone, sadly I cannot afford to use Miss Evans as a lady's companion. She is too valuable for that, her work at Holland Crescent is over."

"She will have plenty of company. Mrs Thomas has insisted on moving in with them too, as a temporary housekeeper. I envy them," Webber said ruefully.

"You'll manage, we all have to make sacrifices."

Webber kept his temper but something of it must have shown in his eyes.

"I didn't enjoy seeing her," he said. "Not as a failure."

Smith nodded sympathetically.

"At least," he said, "I shan't ask you to tell her that her husband is dead."

❧ THIRTY-SEVEN ☙

HANS ELBERG'S BODY lying in a remote South American ditch was never reported in the newspapers, unlike the retrospective exhibition of David Walton's brilliant work which was reported at great length. Betsey Trottwood had surpassed himself and the rooms in Bond Street were presented as a fitting tribute to a master Staffordshire potter. Every piece was for sale. James Spavin considered his reputation very carefully and wrote a rave notice in *Dilettante*. The prices were indeed high, he said, but then what price could you put on genius?

Webber was pleased to see Mrs Thomas back after the long separation, but grateful that she had been with Jessica Elberg through the shock of her husband's tragic death. Lizzie had a great gift for comfort and understanding. No one could get closer than she could when she really tried.

"Poor Jessica," Webber said, "I still think I let her down. It's a small comfort I suppose but at least she'll never know who killed them."

Mrs Thomas closed her oven door gently.

"You're the best," she said. "That's what I've always told you and it's the truth. You didn't let her down John, she knew it was Elberg, she's always known, she told me."